THE
TAINTED
SNUFF BOX

The
TAINTED
SNUFF BOX

ROSEMARY STEVENS

BERKLEY PRIME CRIME, NEW YORK

THE TAINTED SNUFF BOX

A Berkley Prime Crime Book
Published by The Berkley Publishing Group,
a division of Penguin Putnam Inc.,
375 Hudson Street, New York, New York 10014.

ISBN 0-425-17948-6

PRINTED IN THE UNITED STATES OF AMERICA

This book is dedicated to Sally Osbon. Thank you, Sally, for helping make one of my dreams come true.

ACKNOWLEDGMENTS

I must once again thank my friend Melissa Lynn Jones, for sharing her knowledge and insight into Regency-era social customs, language, and history with me. Research can sometimes be a tiring, frustrating, and expensive undertaking. Melissa makes my job easier. I would note that any errors contained in this story are solely my own.

I wish to thank the staff at the Royal Pavilion, Brighton, for their kindness during my visit. I am particularly grateful to Minna for her patience and help in deciphering what the 1805 architecture and furnishings of the Pavilion consisted of. Alexander and Fotis deserve a special thank-you as well.

As usual, my friends gave me their precious support. Thank you, Barbara Metzger and Cynthia Holt.

Last, but far from least, I want to thank J. T., Rachel, and Tommy. You have my love.

AUTHOR'S NOTE

Besides Beau Brummell, the following characters were real people: George, Prince of Wales; Caroline, Princess of Wales; Maria Fitzherbert; Frederica, the Duchess of York; the Duke of Clarence; Prime Minister Pitt; Lady Hester Stanhope; Lord Petersham; Lord Yarmouth; Scrope Davies; Richard Sheridan; Lumley Skeffington; Lady Bessborough; Mr. and Mrs. Johnstone; Mr. and Mrs. Creevey; David Pitcairn; Jack Townsend; John Lavender; and, of course, Robinson.

Readers will note that even though this story takes place in October 1805, there is no mention of naval hero Horatio Nelson's victory at Trafalgar and his subsequent death. The reason for this is that people in London did not learn of these events until well after the fact.

Also of interest is that Prime Minister Pitt's illness resulted in his passing away in January 1806. His niece, Lady Hester Stanhope, was his nurse and housekeeper until the end.

Real places and events are sprinkled in the story and

are too numerous to list. However, the following might evoke a smile:

The prizefight outside Brighton did indeed take place, as did the dinner at the Johnstones'.

The wagers noted regarding Brummell's matrimonial prospects can be found in White's famous Betting Book.

And Beau Brummell did indeed give Frederica, the Duchess of York, a costly lace dress for Christmas.

1

"*I cannot believe* anyone in England wants to kill you, your Royal Highness," I said in a tight voice, my gaze fixed on the ceiling. "Except, perhaps, your wife."

George, Prince of Wales, had strolled into my bedchamber at the Marine Pavilion and interrupted me at a vital moment. I had almost reached that glorious moment gentlemen eagerly strive for, the pinnacle of ecstasy some only dream of, and I did not appreciate the distraction.

Fortunately, the Prince perceived the situation at once and waved away my awkward attempt to execute a bow to him. Prinny knew my mind was preoccupied with a goal much more immediate than learning the identity of the person who had sent him death threats.

What, you ask, could be more important than the safety of the Heir Apparent? At the present moment, the creation of my cravat.

Ah, you are no doubt saying, of course.

The letters Prinny had received in London, the warnings that had prompted him to flee to his Brighton sanctuary near the sea, could surely wait while I finished arranging one of the things I am best known for: a snowy show of sophisticated sartorial splendour. One has one's priorities, you know.

The Prince watched my every move, unconsciously mimicking the slow, careful way I lowered my head so that the folds of my cravat might settle themselves in exactly the way I desired. My indispensable valet, Robinson, stood nearby with another length of starched linen at the ready in case the white cloth round my neck proved uncooperative.

The valet's lips pursed, a sure sign of disapproval. Robinson is a bit extreme in what he thinks is proper. Right now, I am certain he felt it right that he assist me with my neckcloth. I, on the other hand, wished to perform the Tying Of The Knot ceremony solo.

Not content with watching, the Prince could no longer resist trying his hand at the skill. Impulsively, he divested himself of his coat, stripped off his own neckcloth and helped himself to the linen Robinson held. Robinson's blue eyes opened to their widest; his blond hair, cut in the fashionable Brutus cut, stood on end; and his lips were pressed together so tightly they threatened to split from the pressure.

"Which wife, Brummell?" Prinny asked, coming to stand next to me in front of the mirror. His fingers moved in unison with mine as I began tying the required knot. "You must be referring to that loud, unwashed, and ungraceful creature known as Caroline, Princess of Wales. Certainly you would not speak so of Maria Fitzherbert, the wife of my heart."

Yes, the Prince has *two* wives, one legal and one not.

It is a long story, and I do not wish to bore you. Suffice it to say the Prince "married" Maria Fitzherbert in 1785 in a private ceremony when the lady, a staunch Roman Catholic, refused to become his mistress. She had, in fact, been about to leave him and England itself. Desperate, the Prince enacted a sensational scene in which he stabbed himself with a sword to convince her of his love. The wound was not deep, but there was sufficient blood for the ploy to work. Subsequently the wedding ceremony took place. The Prince conveniently overlooked the Royal Marriage Act, which forbade the union.

Ten years—and a few flirts—later, a deeply in debt Prince ignored his first marriage and married his cousin, Caroline of Brunswick, to please his father, King George III. Need I mention a large sum of money came to Prinny along with the marriage?

Unfortunately, the cultured Prince disliked his coarse bride on sight. Somehow, he brought himself to get her with child, a girl christened Charlotte. Having done his duty—and paid some creditors—the Prince promptly returned to Maria Fitzherbert's willing arms.

"Yes, sir, I meant her Royal Highness, Princess Caroline," I said, inspecting the finished knot for flaws and finding none. "She might wish you six feet under."

"Zeus! Much as I'd like such an excuse as sedition to divorce her, the truth is Caroline has as little interest in me as I do her. She's busy with her own pursuits. Matter of fact, I hear she's with child again. I wonder whose it is. Not mine, I assure you. I shudder to think of the making of it." The Prince completed his cravat and turned to me for approval.

Loyally, for I am loyal to the Prince who has helped

me achieve the exalted position I hold in Society, *I* refrained from shuddering at the making of *his* cravat. He had given it a jolly good try after all, and while others might deem it competent, my meticulous eye perceived a slight flaw. "May I?" I inquired, indicating the neckcloth. One must remember to observe the proprieties with his Royal Highness. Prinny is not one to tolerate the taking of a liberty.

The Prince's royal brow creased as he nodded his permission.

I reached out and made a swift adjustment to his cravat. "There, your Royal Highness. You are the very quintessence of a gentleman."

He smiled, well pleased with the compliment, and allowed Robinson the privilege of helping him with his coat. The valet's lips relaxed at the honour. Prinny remarked idly, "They do call me The First Gentleman of Europe."

A twinge of envy ran through my lean frame. The Prince could not know how his comment vexed me, though I trust no hint of displeasure broke through my tranquil countenance. For The First Gentleman of Europe is a title which, I admit, I covet. I am only human, as you very well know, and have no title and no aristocratic lineage. My father was secretary to Prime Minister Lord North in his day. Recall I am *Mr.* George Brummell, or "Beau" Brummell, if you will.

I wager that my father, who sent me to Eton and Oxford so that I might freeze, starve, and endure beatings like the aristocratic boys, would have been pleased that at the age of seven and twenty I am known as the Arbiter of Fashion. Possibly. Father had been notoriously hard to please. Even though he has been dead more than twelve years, sometimes I feel I am still trying to please him.

With the Prince properly attired, Robinson assisted me into my Venetian-blue coat. Prinny eased his ever-increasing bulk into a chair made of beechwood carved to resemble bamboo by the fire. The second week in October, this year of 1805, had brought a chill to the air. Though my bones dislike cold weather, Prinny, having passed his fortieth year, deplores it even more. All the rooms in the Pavilion are overheated, even to my taste.

My opinion had not been consulted in any matter regarding the Pavilion, I might add. The former farmhouse had been transformed into a fanciful palace with its Chinese decor becoming Prinny's passion, a passion that shows no signs of abating. Even now, the Prince meets daily with his architects on the expansion of the house and the construction of the Royal Stables.

"Brummell, I need your help," his Royal Highness said, interrupting my thoughts.

I signalled to Robinson that he might take himself off, no doubt disappointing the gossip-loving valet and heralding a return of the pursed lips. Retaliation, perhaps in the form of the overly aggressive usage of a pair of silver tweezers on my vulnerable brow, surely lay in store for me.

I poured a glass of Prinny's favourite cherry brandy—awful stuff!—and handed it to him before settling myself in a matching chair. The Prince took a swallow of the liquid and looked gloomy. "Someone is threatening to kill me, I tell you. And it isn't Caroline."

His Royal Highness did appear worried. True, his personality normally runs to the dramatic, but this intrigue did not seem like one of his bids for attention. For the first time, I began to take his concern seriously. "Sir, you know you have only to give the command, and I am at your service. Do you have the letters you received in London?"

The Prince shook his head. "I threw the dirty things on the fire."

"Unfortunate," I murmured. *Unwise,* I thought.

"One of the letters had a spot of blood on it," the Prince remembered.

"Abominable." A spot of spilled wine, hopefully.

"In essence, they said that London would be the *death* of me. Can you imagine?" The Prince looked incredulous. "I've thought it over. The culprit could be Napoleon, Brummell. The monster has assembled his army and a vast fleet at Boulogne, preparing to invade England."

I frowned. "I know it is a constant worry that the French Emperor plans an imminent invasion of English soil. But, sir, why would Napoleon warn you to leave the capital? I should think he would want you to remain so he might take you prisoner."

The Prince gasped at the thought, his eyes bulging in his cherubic face.

"Not that the fiend would ever accomplish such an atrocious act," I added hastily. I reached for the decanter and refilled the Prince's glass. After seeing him take a large, comforting swallow, I waited for him to tell me more.

"The Irish Catholics have been threatening rebellion," his Royal Highness said in some agitation. "It could be a group from that lot."

"Conceivably. Sir, tell me more about the letters.

What kind of paper were they written on? Was the writing neat, or difficult to read? Did the writer appear to be educated?"

The Prince sighed impatiently. "Don't ask me for petty details, Brummell. My life has been threatened!"

Why had I not poured myself a hefty glass of wine? "What precautions are being taken for your safety?"

"Several. Armed guards are posted about the Pavilion. I go nowhere in Brighton without six footmen, armed and ready to defend me, and I am carrying one of Manton's finest pistols," he said, patting a pocket.

I gauged the angle of the pocket to my person. Prinny is an excellent shot, but in his present state of agitation, an accident detrimental to my health—or his—could occur. "What about at night?"

"Two guards are stationed outside the door of my bedchamber, one at each of the chamber windows, and my personal valet sleeps a few feet away from me with a pistol tucked under his pillow."

I hoped the valet did not shoot himself in the head in his sleep. Can you imagine what Robinson's reaction would be if I asked him to sleep on a cot in my bedchamber, a piece of cold steel under his pillow? My priggish manservant would be incurably disgusted.

"I have not done listing my safeguards, Brummell. I don't know if you are acquainted with Sir Simon, a local baronet, but he was a guest of mine at Carlton House. Though he has a large house nearby in Hove, he has been good enough to take up residence here at the Pavilion."

My mind went through a mental list of the Nobility. "Was not Sir Simon raised to the rank of baronet after accumulating vast wealth through some disreputable means?"

The Prince pierced me with an aggravated glare. "What can that have to do with anything? The gentleman put forth a plan to me that can only show his allegiance and fidelity. He has volunteered to sample dishes from my kitchen before I partake of them in case of attempted poisoning."

"A food taster?" I blurted, astonished at the Prince's use of the ancient custom.

"Yes, by God!" the Prince exclaimed righteously. "Damned courageous of Sir Simon to put himself in danger like this. Honourable. You might take a page from his book, Brummell. I'm not sure you're regarding any of this seriously enough. Come to think of it, you failed to visit me at Carlton House before I left London."

"You wrong me," I stated with dignity. "I could not come to you last week, as I was indisposed, and would never expose you to illness."

No, that statement was not precisely accurate, but it was sure to appease the Prince. He is very careful of his health at all times, you know. The smallest sniffle propels him to bed.

In my opinion he did not need to know that my indisposition stemmed from my involvement in a murder investigation, rather than a disorder of the respiratory system. Perhaps you remember me telling you about the sordid situation with the poisoned milk? Ah, good, then I need not recount it again. As you know, everything had turned out all right in the end, but I cannot like the idea of Society finding out I had worked with the Bow Street Police Office.

"You are healthy now, I presume," the Prince inquired.

"Yes. And I am indeed anxious for your safety and will do what I can to help you."

After the Prince nodded regally, indicating his acceptance of my loyalty, I went on. "As to the author of these nasty letters, I acknowledge the existence of foreign threats. But, with your present popularity, it is difficult for me to believe any English person would want to kill you. Are there other suspects? Someone angry with you personally?"

A discarded mistress or two?

The Prince looked like a sulky child. "Might be."

"You must tell me about it," I urged, leaning forward in my chair. Now we were getting to the heart of the matter. "I cannot help protect you if I do not know of every possible assassin."

"Oh, very well, then. Arthur Ainsley, one of my younger guests, has crossed my mind. Or, I should say, he thinks I've crossed him." Prinny looked uncomfortable under my steady gaze. "Seems that Ainsley believes I promised to make him a peer so that he might be called to the House of Lords. Ainsley desires a Parliament seat."

"What? Until you gain control of the government via a regency, sir, I do not see how you can name anyone a peer—"

"Yes, yes," he interrupted peevishly. "You know what it's like, though. Champagne flowed, Ainsley was being very agreeable. I might have made a remark or two about making him a peer . . ." The Prince scowled, then brightened a bit. "Ainsley is enthusiastic about my renovations to the Pavilion, did I tell you? He has a great

interest in architecture himself. Why, he even contributed money for the purchase of some fine Chinese an-
tiques for the place. The English government is miserly
when it comes to me, Brummell. It's nothing short of
cruel. A man of my sensibilities needs to be surrounded
with beauty."

I could understand that, I decided, thinking of my
Sèvres porcelain pieces, my own art collection, and the
elegant furnishings of my residence in London. "So Mr.
Ainsley contributed money, er, in exchange for your
supporting his bid for a seat in Parliament?"

The Prince shot me a withering look, one only a
member of Royalty could achieve. It is calculated to
make one feel lower than a hedgehog's dinner. "Don't
be ridiculous. Haven't you been listening? Ainsley gave
me the gift of money because he appreciates what I am
trying to achieve at the Pavilion. *Coincidentally*, he misunderstood a discussion we had about his desire for a
place in the government."

"Did you tell him he misunderstood?"

"I had one of my aides inform him he had been mistaken in his assumptions." The Prince's expression grew
morose. "Evidently, Ainsley became irate."

"Is Mr. Ainsley that eager for a seat in Parliament?"

"I suppose. Ainsley is the younger son of an earl and
is jealous of his older brother, the heir, who will take
his father's seat in the House of Lords when the earl
dies. Something about how his older brother is only in-
terested in farming and estate management. Ainsley feels
he deserves, and is better suited for, a voice in government. A permanent voice rather than one he would have
to be elected to."

"Even so, your Royal Highness, would this be motive

enough for Mr. Ainsley to try to *kill* you?" I asked doubtfully.

The Prince swallowed the rest of his brandy and turned a tortured face on me. "How should I know? All that is clear is that someone wants me dead! Think of it. My father is mad as a March hare. A regency will be established at some point in time, mark my words. If I die, my daughter, Princess Charlotte, will be next in line to rule. She's only nine years old, Brummell. And speaking of youth, I'm too young to shuffle off to the grave!"

"Calm yourself, sir," I said soothingly. "Nothing of the sort will happen, I assure you. I shall look into this Ainsley fellow. Have you thought of sending him away?"

"No," the Prince said in some surprise. "I told you he's helping me with plans for the renovation of the Pavilion."

Now, pray, do not think from this last statement that the Prince is dull-witted. Remember I told you he is passionate, and I expect I must also say single-minded when it comes to the Pavilion. He is dramatic and self-indulgent, but not a stupid man. Granted, I draw back at some of his wilder amusements, but overall he is a good fellow and my friend. Indeed, where would I be now without his friendship?

Those nasty letters had wounded his pride and made him irritable in addition to frightening him. "Are there many other guests, sir? I only arrived this afternoon and have not had a chance to look about." My thoughts strayed to one person, a certain Royal Duchess I particularly hoped might have arrived.

"I don't know," the Prince said miserably. "The usual crowd of my court, I suppose. We are to go to the Johnstones' house for dinner tonight. You'll have a chance to meet Ainsley there. Not that I am saying he is the scoundrel, Brummell."

"I understand, sir."

"A masked villain could jump out at me at any moment," the Prince said, rising.

Immediately a hellish shriek rent the air.

I vaulted to my feet, only to encounter two large footmen as they burst through the chamber door, brandishing their guns directly at my person.

2

Confusion reigned. The Prince looked wildly about for the source of the cry. He fumbled for the gun in his pocket. More armed guards crowded into the room, looking fierce and aiming their weapons at random.

Only I knew what masked villain had jumped out at the Prince.

"Sir," I said, "I forgot to tell you I brought my cat with me. He has been sleeping under your chair, and you must have inadvertently stepped on his tail when you rose."

All eyes turned downward to where I gestured. Chakkri stood regally by the Prince's chair, disapproval at this interruption of his slumber bristling in every whisker.

Remember I told you there was a certain withering look only royalty could achieve? Evidently, Chakkri's ancestral origins in the palaces of Siam enabled him to accomplish the expression quite well. He directed his displeasure at the Prince, who put his gun away and stared back at the animal in surprise.

"What a fellow he is! That cry sounded human," the Prince exclaimed. He raised his quizzing glass to better examine the feline.

Chakkri holds the distinction of being the only Siamese cat in England. His face, ears, paws, and long slim tail are of the deepest velvety brown. His lean, muscular, fawn-coloured body is more compact and limber than any other cat I have seen. But the feature that intrigues me the most is Chakkri's expressive deep blue eyes that hold the secrets to the mysteries of the East. Or perhaps just the clues to what he wants for dinner.

I suppose it would be remiss of me not to mention he possesses the palate of a gourmet and a rather loud, demanding voice. But he has a sensitivity to beauty and a fastidiousness in regards to the grooming of his person I can only approve.

A snicker at the source of the commotion, quickly stifled, escaped one of the men. I noticed with some relief that the guards had lowered their weapons.

One of them, whom I presumed to be the leader, shot a stern glare toward his troops lest one of the others dare find amusement at the Prince's panic. He then turned to stand at attention in front of his Royal Highness. "How may I serve you, sir?"

"Return to your stations," the Prince ordered gruffly, allowing his quizzing glass to fall to his chest. When the command was obeyed, and we were alone once more, he succumbed to a fit of trembling.

I had not realized until that moment just how frightened he really was. "Sir, please sit down. Shall I ring for your valet?"

THE TAINTED SNUFF BOX   15

"No, no," Prinny said, his pale face as white as his cravat. "Perhaps another glass of brandy, then I'll make my way to my chamber to rest."

I hurried to get the drink for him, alarmed at his genuine distress. He seemed to recover presently, though, and gazed again at Chakkri, who had strolled to a place by the fire, a position outside the range of the Prince's polished boots. The cat began licking his aggrieved tail.

"Brummell, when did you obtain a cat? And such an unusual one. I've never seen the like."

I felt a different anxiety grow within me. A nagging worry that the Prince, who collected beautiful objects, would take a liking to Chakkri caused my cravat to suddenly feel constricted. "I have had him some weeks now, sir. He was, er, left in London by a Siamese man who returned to his country."

Actually, the cat was a gift from one Mr. Kiang, who thought he had outwitted me in regard to a painting featuring a cat, but that is another story. Mr. Kiang claimed that Chakkri, named after one of Siam's great generals, exhibited a character similar to yours truly. My dear friend Frederica, the Duchess of York, agrees, but I feel the notion is ridiculous. I shall leave you to form your own opinions on the matter if you feel so inclined.

"Odd-looking creature, what?" the Prince said. "Rather like drawings I've seen of the raccoons that live in America."

Chakkri abruptly paused in the act of washing his long tail to look at the Prince. However, when he did so, he failed to retract all of his pink tongue into his mouth, leaving about half an inch sticking out. At the Prince.

I turned a chuckle into a cough.

"You are coughing, Brummell. Are you quite sure you have recovered from your recent indisposition?" the Prince asked warily.

"Yes, your Royal Highness."

He rose, saying, "I think I shall retire to my bed for a bit before dinner. My guests are aware of those loathsome threats against me, but I don't want to appear anxious in front of them tonight at the Johnstones'."

"Wise of you, I am sure." Relieved that the topic of Chakkri had been forgotten, I bowed low while the Prince exited the room.

Then I poured myself a glass of burgundy, regained my seat and addressed the cat. "Are you proud of yourself, you rogue? Sticking your tongue out at a member of royalty, and, I might add, the gentleman whose kitchens are generously providing you with buttered crab and soufflés of partridge."

Chakkri licked a brown paw and used it to wash around his left eye. His demeanor was one of complete indifference.

"You have made it clear since we arrived here this morning that you do not care for being away from home—pacing, sniffing every piece of furniture, and muttering under your breath while shaking your paw in repugnance—but strive for a little decorum. You are at a royal residence. Have some consideration for your host, whose very life may be in danger."

"Reeooow!" Chakkri cried out suddenly, raising his wedge-shaped head so that his deep blue gaze met my grey one. I felt a tremor of unease. Call me a Bedlamite, but his tone was like an omen of impending evil.

Devil if he did not have the right of it.

· · ·

Whenever he visited Brighton, Prinny could always depend on a loyal and hearty welcome. All the town bells
pealed at the moment his carriage arrived. You see, his
love of Brighton had brought the town from a quiet,
sleepy hamlet into a fashionable resort. Hostesses vied
for the privilege of having the Prince as a guest at their
tables.

Mrs. Johnstone was no exception to this rule. Ex-
pense had not been a consideration in the lavish evening
prepared for his Royal Highness and a few dozen exalted
guests. A quartet of musicians soothed aristocratic
senses, and every available variety of flower perfumed
the air. Wax candles illuminated the rich scene in the
Johnstones' ornately furnished drawing room where the
ladies glowed in gowns of silk, satin, and velvet, and
sparkled with emeralds, sapphires, and diamonds. The
gentlemen present had, for the most part, adopted the
fashion I have brought into style of dark coat, crisply
starched linen neckcloth, and evening breeches.

"Brummell! You have arrived in Brighton at last."

Turning at the sound of my name, I saw my friend
Lord Perry, accompanied by his charming wife. Lady
Perry had recently discovered she was expecting their
first child.

Perry clapped me on the back. A wealthy earl, he is
a dark-haired, well-favoured man, known among the ladies before his marriage as "The Greek God." He em-
ulates my simple style of dressing to a nicety. As he is
a gentleman of sense in every respect, I often seek his
opinions.

Lady Perry, a petite brunette, wore a malachite-green

gauze gown with a front panel of matching velvet. The waist was high, and the sleeves long and tight. She also wore a brave smile, but I detected an absence of the colour that normally graced her pretty cheekbones. Devoted to his wife, Perry had brought her to Brighton from London, hoping the relative calm of the seaside town would ease what was proving to be a discomfiting, though welcome, pregnancy.

"Just toddled in today, Perry." I smiled and bowed over his wife's hand. "Lady Perry, your beauty overwhelms my senses. If you were not in a delicate condition, I would beg you to abandon this brute and flee with me to foreign shores. I would have a boat ready at the Brighton docks in the morning."

She chuckled, sneaking a look under her lashes to see the effect this banter had on her husband. Not quite satisfied with the depth of his frown, she said, "I daresay he would not notice my absence for hours, so engrossed is he in examining the particular method the cellist has in plying his bow."

Perry, whose affinity for all things musical was the only rival for his wife's attention, took these taunts in good humour. "My love, although the wisdom of leaving me for Brummell could be a topic for debate, a more pressing question might be how comfortable you would be on a sailing craft of any kind. No less in the morning."

She heaved a poignant sigh. "I suspect you are right, Anthony. Mr. Brummell, we must postpone our plans once more," Lady Perry said, continuing the jest.

"Alas, 'tis a bitter disappointment," I teased theatrically.

"You are the second gentleman disappointed in his

attempt to abscond with my wife, Brummell," Perry said, a look of annoyance crossing his face. "My cousin, Victor Tallarico, arrived in Brighton yesterday and has not ceased his attentions."

"Your cousin?" I queried, vaguely recalling Perry mentioning the fellow a few times during our friendship. "I thought he lived in Italy."

"He does. My aunt married an Italian count in the diplomatic corps. Over the years, the family has divided their time between England and Italy. Why Victor has chosen to visit England at this particular moment, I cannot say. He arrived at my Town house in London and was told we were here in Brighton."

Perry nodded in the direction of a lively gentleman, dressed fashionably, but sporting a—Good God, a *pink* waistcoat—and whispering in the ear of a giggling blond-haired female. "He is staying with us until some angry husband, father, or brother challenges him to a duel."

"Oh, Anthony, Victor means no harm in his attentions to the ladies," Lady Perry protested. "He merely enjoys flirting, and the objects of his attention seem to like it just as much as he does."

"Victor has been my friend since childhood, but that does not prevent my speaking the truth. The man is a debaucher of women," Perry said, gazing with disapproval at his cousin's conduct. "No female is safe in his presence."

I raised an eyebrow. "Strong words."

Lady Perry waved her fan to cool her cheeks. "Mr. Brummell, have you ever noticed that a reformed ladies' man is the first to accuse and condemn others of his very own past behaviour?"

Smiling, I looked to see Perry's reaction to his wife's words, but he had been distracted by the musicians. "Er, excuse us, will you, Brummell?" Perry said, taking his wife's hand. "I want to speak to that cellist before they begin the next set. His talent is quite remarkable." The two walked away in the direction of the musicians. Lady Perry glanced back at me over her shoulder with an amused expression at her husband's fervour for music.

I stood alone. I turned my attention from Signor Tallarico and scanned the crowd looking for one particularly dear face. Alas, the Duchess of York was not amongst the company. I had hoped Freddie would decide to leave the comfort of her country estate, Oatlands, for a lungful of sea air. I supposed she had found she could not leave her loyal companions: upwards of one hundred dogs. I seized a crystal glass full of wine from a footman to drown my disappointment. My motto is, "When your spirits are low, get another bottle."

There was one more familiar face missing from the company. Maria Fitzherbert, Prinny's "wife," was ill and had taken to her bed. The Prince, longing for feminine companionship, had encountered Lady Bessborough at the Castle Inn earlier and brought her along to the Johnstones'.

I did my best to circulate among the guests, greeting Lady Bessborough, exchanging a social word or two with the Creeveys, talking about the theater with Sheridan, and speaking to a number of other guests known to me. All the while, I consumed a healthy quantity of Mr. Johnstone's undoubtedly smuggled French wine, and managed to determine which gentleman was Arthur Ainsley, the one to whom Prinny may or may not have promised a Parliament seat.

Mr. Ainsley, an intense-looking man with the blackest hair and palest complexion I had ever seen, unconsciously thwarted my attempts to speak to him. He spent the time before dinner in earnest conversation with a mousy young lady in a severely plain gown. Overseeing the conversation was a gentleman I thought I recognized as Lord St. Clair. Charles James Fox had introduced us some time ago, Lord St. Clair being greatly respected in Parliament and a renowned orator. St. Clair was known to have two daughters, and I thought the young lady Mr. Ainsley was speaking to must be one of them.

Seeing no way to graciously intrude on them, I had to content myself with studying the man from afar. I had plenty of time to do so, as dinner had been put back while we awaited the arrival of the Prince's brother, the Duke of Clarence, who was unpardonably late.

Prinny, cranky when kept from his food, finally suggested to Mrs. Johnstone that she should serve without the Royal Duke, a recommendation swiftly taken because of the advanced hour.

The Royal Duke arrived in due course, actually during the second course, and everyone, with the possible exception of Lady Perry, poor thing, enjoyed the delicacies provided.

However, this did not prevent the two royal brothers from bickering when we gathered in the drawing room again around one in the morning when the meal finally ended. I was chatting with Lord and Lady Perry when the quarrel began.

"A delicious repast, everything quite in order despite the unnecessary delay," the Prince said in a loud voice, firing the first volley. Everyone quieted.

William, the Duke of Clarence, or Silly Billy as the

Navy man is called behind his back, is not someone I especially admire. Uncivilized and fond of cursing as if he were still walking the decks of a ship, he rounded on his brother. "Damn me, it's not my fault the blasted magistrates interfered and the fight had to be held a goodly distance from Brighton."

Prinny's lip curled. "You insulted our hostess by delaying dinner over a pugilistic contest?"

Everyone stood riveted at the sound of raised royal voices. "I completely understand, your Royal Highness," Mrs. Johnstone said, hoping to divert the two. Her hands fluttered nervously about her diamond-clad bosom. "Would anyone care for tea?"

The Duke of Clarence was not to be distracted. "Pearce beat Gulley. It was a contest not to be missed," he said with a look that plainly said his brother should be aware of the importance of such an event.

Scrope Davies, a young fellow of my acquaintance who is mad for horseracing when he is not languishing in the arms of one of his many lady friends, piped up, "That's so, isn't it, Yarmouth? No one thought Gulley could be bested."

Lord Yarmouth, who fancied himself an amateur pugilist, nodded. "Earlier, Tom Cribb, the Black Diamond, beat William Richmond, the American Black, but it wasn't much to see. Neither one of them barely touched the other."

"I find prizefights deplorable," the Prince said with heat. "What kind of sport is it when men go into the ring, putting their lives at stake? Their very lives, do you hear?"

Everyone did, and to a man knew the reason why Prinny felt as strongly as he did. No one dared voice the words. No one except his brother, undeterred by the fact the company had formed an audience to the siblings' exhibition of animosity.

"What bloody nonsense!" the Royal Duke expostulated. "Someone should have kept you in the nursery where you belonged that day back in '88 when Tyne gave Earl that fatal blow. Might not have even been the damn punch that killed him, eh? The blighter struck his head on the rails of the stage when he went down."

Mrs. Johnstone flapped her hands in her anxiety.

The Prince, his face flushed, looked about to cry. "Don't remind me of it," he moaned in an anguished voice. "I haven't attended a pugilistic contest since that day, and I never shall! Barbaric competitions, every one of them."

The Duke of Clarence looked at his brother in disgust. "You're all sensibilities, aren't you? Paying Earl's widow and her brats an annuity, and look at you now. Hiding like an overgrown baby here in Brighton over some blasted letters from someone too cowardly to sign his name. Bloody hell! Who the devil would go to the trouble of killing you, anyway?"

3

No one dared breathe.

The Duke of Clarence had gone too far. The brothers must be distracted before a royal scandal ensued. I put down my glass and made as if to move toward the Prince, hoping a witty remark would spring to my lips and break the tension. But little Lady Perry placed a restraining hand on my arm and stepped ahead of me toward the combatants.

"Your Royal Highness," she addressed the Prince in a strong, dignified voice, "Mrs. Johnstone has told me she will not allow her dinner party to end before you favour us with a song. Please say you will. Your voice is most pleasing, and we do not get to hear you sing often enough. I know we would all enjoy hearing you now."

She turned toward the company in general for approval to this scheme. A smattering of reluctant applause compelled the Prince to remove himself from his brother's company without a backward glance. I suspect some of the present guests were disappointed at the abrupt end of the royal squabble, but I was not. Bravo, Lady Perry!

Presently, Yarmouth and Scrope engaged the Duke of Clarence in conversation. No doubt they were going over every nuance and detail of the fight they had observed.

Near where I stood with Lord Perry, the Creeveys breathed a sigh of relief. Mrs. Creevey, a friend of Mrs. Fitzherbert and a woman who loved a good piece of gossip, resumed her scrutiny of the Prince and Lady Bessborough in order to report back any flirtation.

On my other side stood a short gentleman unknown to me. He was shovelling a piece of cake into his mouth. I had observed him earlier at dinner, but averted my eyes lest I be put off my food. Now he came to my notice once again.

Perry saw the direction of my gaze. "Brummell, pray look away lest your stomach become as delicate as my wife's."

However, it was useless. Like someone enthralled by a public hanging, I had to get a better look at the stranger's manner of dress. Without my permission, my right hand raised my quizzing glass.

The round magnifier that I wear suspended from my neck by a thin black velvet ribbon told me what I had already deduced. Here was a man of late middle years, clinging to the fashions of his youth.

His satin coat was of the old-fashioned cut that flared at the knees, and sported heavy silver braid trim and silver buttons. A garishly bright sea-green in colour, guaranteed to make one sea-*sick*, it hung open, revealing a long waistcoat in a lighter shade. Froths of lace poured from his neckcloth. His wrists were also covered with lace extending from under his cuffs. Matching breeches ended in clocked stockings, and his feet were squeezed into red-heeled pumps. Hideous!

This sartorial orgy surpassed even the numerous fashion tragedies of my nemesis, Sylvester Fairingdale, whom you may recall me telling you about in a previous adventure.

But there was worse. Atop the man's head, which was just about level with my shoulder, a towering white wig, complete with curls at the temples, sat over a highly painted and powdered face. Next to bright red lips, a black patch in the shape of an animal's head—I could not tell what kind—had been affixed.

My valet, Robinson, would have fainted straightaway at the sight.

I struggled to remain expressionless. The man's overuse of a jasmine scent, a practice invariably intended to compensate for infrequent bathing, assaulted my nostrils.

He grabbed a glass of wine from a tray carried by a passing footman. Guzzling the drink down greedily, he noticed my attention and addressed me in a condescending tone. "You're new to Brighton, aren't you? I'm Sir Simon, close personal friend and intimate confidant to the Prince of Wales. I make it my business to know who associates with his Royal Highness. You'll do me the honour of introducing yourself."

Ah, Prinny's food taster! My right eyebrow shot to my hairline at the man's presumption. Lord Perry threw me a warning look. "I am George Brummell," I said in a quiet voice. There was not a trace of smugness in my voice, I assure you. But before you go admiring my self-control, permit me to tell you it was impossible to be smug in the face of all that powder, that paint, and those red lips.

Sir Simon's expression grew cold. "Faugh!" he cried, as if he were the one smelling something gone bad. "You're the upstart trying to make gentlemen believe there's something wrong with the way we've been dressing for a good many years. You want us to dress like dullards!"

"Dullards?" I replied, one hand across my heart. "Never say you think me dull. My life would be shattered." A few titters came from nearby guests. Mrs. Creevey looked our way.

Sir Simon knitted his brows, but my mockery went over his wigged head. "Well, I do say it, and damn the consequences! A man's clothing bespeaks his station in life. Your costume tells me you are common. Indeed, who was your father?" Sir Simon demanded. "I've never heard of a *Lord* Brummell."

Perry chose this moment to interrupt, devil take him. I had been about to initiate a discussion of Sir Simon's parentage. He looked like the offspring of an overbred poodle and the dustman's dog.

"Brummell, did you see where my wife went? Did she leave the room?" Perry worried. "I hope the sickness has not overtaken her again."

"Lady Perry is by the musicians, helping the Prince select a song," I said, indicating her whereabouts with a wave of my hand. I did not misunderstand Perry's goal in distracting me from the odious Sir Simon. "She seems fine, my friend. Cease your fretting. Ever since you found out she is with child, you have behaved like a domineering governess."

"Your wife is with child?" Sir Simon asked Perry in

a voice filled with disgust. "Why is she out in company if she's increasing? We should not have to view a misshapen female."

What an ill-bred man! Dear Lady Perry's figure was still slim, not that it would make the slightest difference if her condition had shown. Those people who think a lady with child should not be seen in public show a lack of sensitivity to natural beauty.

Lord Perry turned a look of frozen hauteur on the baronet. "I beg your pardon? I could not have understood you correctly."

"You may be an earl, Lord Perry, but you must be a want-wit if you'd bring a wife who's breeding along with you to Brighton's entertainments. She can only prove a burden and keep you from a man's amusements," Sir Simon pronounced.

Dash it! Now Perry's and my roles would be reversed. It would be my job to turn his attention away from Sir Simon. "Speaking of amusements, have you seen the Green Man of Brighton? He is known to only eat green food, dress only in green—"

But I got no further. Perry's face had become a marble mask of contempt. "Explain yourself at once," he commanded Sir Simon.

"There's nothing to explain, my young buck," Sir Simon replied, waving a hand dripping in lace. "Every man knows that a woman is good for only two things: pleasuring him in bed and bearing his sons. Since your wife is busy with one, she's useless for the other. She should be shut away in the country somewhere until the babe is born and she can be ready to lie on her back for you again," Sir Simon answered, his red lips spread in a lewd grin. "Apparently, she's done well at that in the past."

"Why, you blackguard," Lord Perry said a low voice, barely containing his fury. "I shall meet you at dawn for speaking of my wife in such vulgar terms."

A shiver of alarm raced through me at these deadly words. I turned to look at Perry, but he would not meet my eye. His gaze was riveted on Sir Simon. The late-night party had suddenly taken on a very dark atmosphere. "Perry, no. You ought not have said that. Come away now," I said in a voice for his ears alone. I kept my tone light and casual. "This man is beneath your notice after all. Let us cross the room to where the air is not so foul."

But my words fell unattended. "You young fool," Sir Simon growled at Lord Perry, the smile fading rapidly from his painted face. He signalled a footman to take away his empty glass. "You're challenging me? What the hell for?"

"You have insulted *my wife*, Sir Simon. Will it be pistols or swords?" Perry's hands clenched at his sides.

I feared the argument would quickly result in fisti-cuffs. Perry is protective when it comes to Lady Perry. He was serious about his challenge. "Good God, Perry, dueling is against the law—" I tried, but he ignored me.

"Insulted your wife? I merely spoke the truth," Sir Simon responded. I thought him genuinely puzzled as to why Lord Perry was angry.

"Perry, this popinjay is hardly worth your blade," I said, growing desperate. I scanned the room and saw that Lady Perry was still safely at the Prince's side. She had no notion of her husband's confrontation. But the angry tones had drawn the interest of several other guests, including the gossipy Lady Creevey, who stared at us curiously.

Perry finally looked at me. "Will you not stand as my second, Brummell?" Second is the term used for the duelist's supporters. Sometimes the support involves carrying one's bloodied friend off the field to the surgeon's care.

Before I could answer, Lord Perry's cousin, Signor Tallarico, strolled our way. Could a man in a pink waistcoat play the rescuer? I hoped so.

"Did I hear someone mention swords?" Tallarico queried, his deep, husky voice with its Italian accent making his words flow in a way I am certain makes female hearts flutter. "I'm a master at swordplay, but am always looking to increase my skills. Is there anyone here in Brighton I could test my technique against? Or must I venture to London to find an expert?" He looked from Sir Simon to his cousin expectantly.

"Angelo, the fencing master in London, is the man you want. You are Victor Tallarico, are you not?" I said quickly, seizing the opportunity to gain an ally. "By the way, I am George Brummell, Perry's friend for the remainder of time he is in England. He may have to flee to the continent in the next few days unless we can talk sense into him. If we cannot, perhaps your home in Italy will be open to him."

Tallarico seemed to become aware of his cousin's anger. "Flee the continent? *Dio mio*, what for? And look at you, Anthony." The Italian gestured with his hand toward his cousin. "The expression on your face is the very same one you had the time I pushed you in the lake when you wouldn't leave me and that young girl alone—oh, what was her name? Jenny! Jenny from the neighboring estate. What's happened to anger you?"

Before Lord Perry could answer, Sir Simon addressed Signor Tallarico. "Hope you got what you wanted from Jenny," he said with lascivious interest.

Tallarico smiled. "You doubt it?" His gaze narrowed at his cousin, and he seemed to perceive there was trouble brewing. "Her governess had the odious habit of making Jenny wear her hair in a tight braid, remember, Anthony? I requested that she uncoil it so that I could see the dark locks gleam in the sunshine. Jenny had refused the request for weeks, the little vixen, but I found her weak spot. I traded her a box of confections for the honour of seeing her hair undone. How old were we, Anthony? Thirteen, fourteen?"

"Thirteen. You were a flirt even then," Perry said, relaxing the slightest bit. "And I have done nothing but defend my wife's honour and challenge Sir Simon to a duel."

Tallarico looked at Sir Simon. My hopes that the Italian would defuse the situation vanished when I saw the glint in his brown eyes. His tone rapidly changed to one of menace. "You insulted *la bella* Lady Perry?"

Sir Simon was all annoyance. "Not intentionally, but Lord Perry here has taken it wrong—"

"*Diavolo!* You will apologize at once," demanded Signor Tallarico with heat. Then, to my acute astonishment, he reached into the pocket of his coat and withdrew a slim dagger. The tip gleamed in the candlelight.

Sir Simon's eyes popped in his head.

Swiftly, I stepped between the other guests and the sight of the knife, though I feared we might still be observed. "Gentlemen—"

"Damn you, Victor," Perry said, "I shall defend my own wife. Put that thing away on the instant."

Signor Tallarico's gaze focussed on Sir Simon's throat, as if he were gauging the exact spot to employ his knife.

"How dare you!" Sir Simon hissed, drawing back his head.

I leaned slightly toward Tallarico and spoke in the tone of a well-meaning advisor. "I am unaware of proper drawing room behavior in Italy, but here in England, it is considered the very height of incivility to threaten someone with a knife while at a dinner party. Do you see those rather enormous men who are guarding the Prince?"

Signor Tallarico briefly shifted his gaze to the other side of the room. "*Sì.*"

I nodded. "They might very well think you a threat to his Royal Highness and lock you away in some unpleasant sort of place full of rodents and minus pretty girls with gleaming hair."

A minute passed, a rather long minute, but Tallarico finally looked at his cousin and gave an exaggerated shrug. He pocketed the knife. "England has outlawed duelling, more's the pity. I was only thinking of Lady Perry and the baby should you be wounded, even killed, by this perfumed prancer, Anthony. I would be willing to deliver him to the devil myself."

Lord Perry appeared to have calmed down. Hopefully he realized that Sir Simon's opinions were beneath notice. Anyone who dressed as garishly as Sir Simon could have no more sense than a cabbage.

I raised a warning hand at Sir Simon, who I could see was ready to heat things up again. "There must not be a duel. You, Sir Simon, will apologize to Lord Perry for your ill-considered words."

Sir Simon looked at the three of us glaring at him. "This all grows tiresome. Besides, I have the Prince of Wales to protect. I cannot waste my time with trivial matters. Lord Perry, it was not my intention to insult your wife. I was speaking of women in general."

Perry seemed to weigh the words, and from his expression, I feared he found them insufficient, since Sir Simon had not technically apologized. But at that moment, the opening strains of music could be heard. Out of the corner of my eye, I saw Lady Perry scanning the crowd for her husband.

"Here comes Lady Perry. Let it go, my friend. Think of her and how upset she would be if she learned of this challenge. And she is sure to learn of it, Perry," I said in an urgent voice. I willed Signor Tallarico to help me convince him.

"It may not be worth soiling your blade with an old man's blood," the Italian said, smoothing his coat sleeve. I noticed he wore lace instead of the more fashionable pleated cuff. Mentally, I kicked myself. Had I seen the lace before, I might have foreseen that a romantic like Tallarico would be of little help.

"Very well, I shall withdraw my challenge," Perry finally said, to my great relief. It was a relief destined to be short-lived, for I could not like his next statement.

"Mark me though, Sir Simon," Lord Perry stated coldly. "Should my wife's name so much as cross your lips again, I shall not even trouble to challenge you to a duel. I shall simply kill you."

4

I spent the next quarter of an hour willing every tense muscle in my body to relax. My friend Lord Perry is normally a man of such sense that his behaviour tonight troubled me. But, after a few more glasses of Mr. Johnstone's wine, my equanimity was somewhat restored.

Later, at the Pavilion, Prinny seemed reluctant for the evening to end. Three comfortable rooms were lit with hundreds of candles. Whist, backgammon, and chess had been set out in two of the rooms. In the third, a young man played music on a beautiful rosewood pianoforte.

I gravitated toward the latter chamber, hoping the melodies of Haydn would further relax me, and praying I would find a glass of potent liquid refreshment. Do not judge my drinking habits too harshly, I beg you. Would you not view a quantity of wine a necessity had you just been subjected to a quarrel between two royal brothers, an outraged husband's challenge to a duel, a knife-wielding, hot-tempered Italian, and a greedy cad? I thought so.

Every night at midnight, champagne, punch, lemonade, and sandwiches are served at the Pavilion. Though it was long past that hour, footmen carrying trays of food and drink circulated about the room. I accepted only a glass of champagne, fearing for the buttons of my waistcoat should I try to eat anything else after our extravagant dinner, and spied my friend Viscount Petersham standing by a window. I began making my way to speak to him. Abruptly, the last sound I wanted to hear at the moment assaulted my ears over the Haydn.

"Your Royal Highness, allow me to try a piece of that sandwich before you eat it," Sir Simon's voice rang out across the room. "One cannot be too careful, especially when foreigners are in our midst."

"Foreigners? Here at the Pavilion?" The Prince's voice showed his distress, and Sir Simon leaned close to speak confidentially. No doubt the loathsome baronet was relating his meeting with Perry's cousin, Victor Tallarico. I did not see Lord and Lady Perry nor his cousin about. Perry must have insisted his wife retire. As to Signor Tallarico, he could only have sought feminine companionship.

About to continue on my way, I paused, noting the presence of two footmen standing close to Sir Simon. I surely would have remarked on them had I seen them before. They were tall, thickly built men, with muscles practically popping out of their coat sleeves, and scars marring their faces. You know the type of rough fellow of whom I speak.

What was curious was the impression I received that the burly pair appeared to be in Sir Simon's employ rather than that of the royal household. Why would two of Sir Simon's footmen be present in this chamber instead of waiting in the entrance hall for their master? Had Sir Simon volunteered their services to the Heir Apparent? Or had he commanded them to stay near after Lord Perry's threat and the appearance of Signor Tallarico's shiny knife?

When I reached the window, I saw too late that Viscount Petersham was in conversation with the Duke of Clarence. Fortunately, the Royal Duke chose that moment to end the exchange. I escaped with merely a bow. Had he remained, I might have been tempted to ask him if his sister-in-law, the Duchess of York, was in town.

"Brummell, I didn't know you'd arrived in Brighton," Petersham said, favouring me with his winning smile. Petersham had departed London for Brighton a few days earlier with his constant companion, Lord Munro, in attendance. Although we frequently debate his decision to sport side-whiskers, we have been friends since we both served the Prince of Wales in the Tenth Light Dragoons back in the 1790s.

"I arrived earlier today. I must say that never before have I felt such tension in Brighton," I replied, finishing my champagne and placing the empty glass on a nearby table.

"Robinson throwing a fit over the pebbles on the beach scratching your boots?"

I chuckled. "Matters have not sunk so low. Yet. But he does not want to be in Brighton. Robinson says London is the only place for civilized people. Actually, I think he misses his league of gossiping butlers, under-butlers, footmen, maids, and other valets. So, Petersham, I see you were speaking to Prinny's favourite brother."

"Favourite, you say? That's a good one. Prinny likes him as well as he likes a good draft of cold air. Which reminds me of why I'm standing by the window. I'll soon have a fit of my asthma if I don't get a breath of fresh air." Looking around to be certain no one was watching, he unlatched the window and eased it open a bit, letting a welcome breeze into the stuffy room. "Ah, that's the ticket."

"You were not at the Johnstones' and missed an altercation between the two royal brothers." I briefly described how they had argued over the pugilistic fight the Duke had attended.

Petersham listened, then said, "So that's what got the Duke all wound up. He was just ranting to me about how he couldn't understand why Mrs. Fitzherbert put up with the Prince, what with him being married to Princess Caroline and rumoured to be having a go with Mrs. Davies."

I raised my right eyebrow halfway up my forehead.

"Mrs. Davies?" I queried, "Surely not a relation of Scrope Davies?"

Petersham shook his head. "I don't think she is. But the Duke says the lady in question is—" the viscount broke off and looked around furtively before finishing, "—with child."

"Good God," I muttered. I remembered the Prince telling me that Princess Caroline was with child and he was not the father. It seemed both partners in that marriage were intent on having children. Just not with one another. "I wonder if Prinny is providing for her and the babe."

"I couldn't say with any certainty, but I would expect so."

"Probably. And, as you say, it is all but a rumour anyway. Did the Duke speak of his own mistress, Mrs.

Jordan? He certainly prefers to keep her in the family way."

"No," Petersham replied vaguely. His attention had been caught elsewhere. "I say, Brummell, have you met Prinny's food-taster, Sir Simon?"

"I have had the honour," I said wryly.

"Egad, I'll wager not even you, who invariably has someone trying to gain your stamp of approval, have seen anyone toady to the extent Sir Simon does with the Prince. And his clothes . . ." Petersham pulled a face.

"The perfection of studied simplicity of dress is not a doctrine Sir Simon embraces. By the way, are those two brutish-looking footmen his?"

"Yes. I think they're ex-pugilists. The baronet probably thinks being accompanied by them adds to his consequence."

Ah, then it was Sir Simon's custom to have his footmen about and not a tactic employed since Perry's challenge at the Johnstones'. Good. That scene was best kept private. One had to wonder, though, where the two had been while their master was threatened.

I kept these thoughts to myself, however, and replied, "Bathing and leaving off his powder and paint might be more to Sir Simon's credit than going about with two rough fellows. Did you attend the boxing match tonight? You were not at the dinner party."

"No, I woke late. Anyway, I cannot like the energy required in fights. So much effort is expended even just watching the contestants," Petersham drawled. "It's all too fatiguing."

You might call Viscount Petersham a trifle lazy. When in London, he never leaves his house before six in the evening. Billiards is a game whose exertions are above his level of comfort.

From across the room, the Prince's voice sounded. "I feel a draft coming from somewhere. Is there, mayhaps, a window open?"

Silence reigned as the guests looked around for the culprit.

Sir Simon raised his voice importantly. "Shall I have my men examine all doors and windows, your Royal Highness?"

Petersham quickly closed and locked the window beside us and spoke up. "I beg your pardon, your Royal Highness. I was enjoying the sea air."

"Petersham?" the Prince inquired. "It's not like you to expose yourself to a chill. What of your asthma? Surely you must always want a warm room."

All eyes turned to us.

Petersham bowed low. Not about to insult the Prince's choice in keeping the room over-warm, Petersham said, "Your Royal Highness is kind to be concerned. I am well. It is just that, as you are aware, I like to mix snuff, sir, and have found the sea air inspiring."

"Oh? Tell us about your new mixture," the Prince commanded. "I'm sure we are all eager to hear what you've come up with."

"Sir, I cannot," Petersham said in a solemn tone. "I brought several jars of snuff with me from London and am mixing a secret, unique new blend. You shall be the first to try it though, you have my word."

The Prince nodded his acceptance of this plan, and conversation in the room resumed. Petersham's lapse with the window was apparently forgiven with the promise of a new blend of snuff.

Sir Simon motioned to his footmen to build up the
fire to increase the warmth in the room. I wondered
briefly if the bacon-faced Sir Simon in all his awful
grandeur did not offer to oversee the emptying of the
royal chamber pot.

"You won't be vexed with me, will you, Brummell,
for letting the Prince try my new snuff first?" Petersham
asked me. "My motives are selfish, I admit. There is talk
the government may reinstate the tax on tea. And you
know I love to mix teas as well as snuff. I'm trying to
get on Prinny's good side so he'll use his influence to
persuade Pitt not to levy that horrid excise on tea again."

"Where did you hear that about the tax? I cannot
imagine Prime Minister Pitt reinstating it. He is the one
who cut it back in 1784."

Petersham's brows came together. "You don't expect
me to remember, do you? Remembering things makes
my brain hurt."

"Well, if you wish to remain in Prinny's favour, you
have done the right thing by not attending the pugilistic
fight."

"Munro wanted to go," Petersham confided. "He enjoys the sight of men stripped to the waist. But I persuaded him we would be better for a quiet evening at
home. He's rented a house across the Steine."

"Do not forget you promised to show me the new
snuff box Munro gave you," I reminded him, having a
collection of snuff boxes myself.

Petersham's face brightened. He is a lad with a different snuff box for every day of the year. "You'll be
overcome, I daresay, so great is the artistry. I have another with me tonight," he said, pulling a pale blue box
from his coat pocket and extending it to me.

"Lovely," I pronounced, examining the fine workmanship carefully before handing it back to him.

Petersham shrugged. "It's a good box for summer, but a trifle light for winter use."

At that moment, Lord Munro himself sauntered up to us. He is of average height and wears his pale hair in a wispy style. Oftentimes I have felt he is jealous of the friendship I have with Petersham. "Charles, it's late. Shouldn't we be going home? You cannot be much amused here." He looked at me pointedly.

Having had enough of unpleasant encounters for one evening, I exchanged a polite remark or two before wandering away with Petersham's promise to bring the new snuff box to dinner the following evening so I could view it.

I had not taken two steps when I observed Arthur Ainsley across the room with Lord and Lady St. Clair and two young ladies. I quickly decided that my slight acquaintance with Lord St. Clair would serve me well enough to gain an introduction to Mr. Ainsley.

Accordingly, I crossed the room and bowed in front of him. "Good evening, my lord."

Lord St. Clair is a tall, angular man with features that manage to look stern and kind at the same time. His hair is a dark blond with a slight wave, cut short over a wide forehead. Tonight, his clothes were unexceptional, and he wore a single ring on his right hand. A spark of recognition lit his brown eyes. "Brummell, I thought the Prince said you had arrived. Good to see you again. Allow me to introduce my wife," he said in his precise way of speaking.

"I am pleased to meet you, my lady." As the introductions were performed, I bowed low over Lady St. Clair's hand. A woman of middle years, she wore a quietly expensive gown of nutmeg-brown silk. Her jew-ellry, consisting of a golden topaz set, was also reserved in taste, but of the best quality, and her dark hair had been arranged in a classic style. All in all, the impression I received was of a woman beyond reproach in her man-ner and appearance.

"Thank you, Mr. Brummell," she responded in a for-mal tone. "May I present my daughters, Lady Prudence and Lady Chastity?"

Lady Chastity favored me with a blinding smile. Here was the girl Signor Tallarico had been flirting with ear-lier at the Johnstones'. Indeed, she is a striking female, with golden curls and merry green eyes. She had been one of the Toasts of the last Season in London, I sud-denly recalled, and had turned down numerous offers of marriage, earning her the title of Flirt. I imagined she and her mother engaged in frequent arguments over the low cut of Lady Chastity's gowns.

In sharp contrast, her sister, Lady Prudence, is very prim. Her face is the sort that rarely reveals a smile. A watercolor to Lady Chastity's oil, her nondescript, sandy-coloured hair was pulled back into a severe knot on the top of her head. Her gown was a high-necked greyish muslin.

I said everything polite, noting that it was Lady Pru-dence with whom Arthur Ainsley had been so deep in conversation earlier. Now I looked at him expectantly. "George Brummell," I said by way of introduction.

"Arthur Ainsley," he replied. He has a deep, serious voice and manner. Not a man to sit around White's Club exchanging *bon mots*. His manner was somber.

Defying the normal behaviour of mothers with daughters to marry off, Lady St. Clair did not linger to secure my approval. She quietly moved away after a murmured excuse, her husband and Lady Chastity behind her. Lady Prudence remained at Mr. Ainsley's side, gazing at him with a reverent expression.

Unwilling to give up this opportunity to speak to Ainsley, I detained him by saying, "Is this your first visit to the Pavilion, Mr. Ainsley?"

The man hesitated a moment. I thought he wanted to follow the St. Clairs. "No, I have been here a few times before."

"Ah, then you are familiar with the renovations the Prince has undertaken. Some say he has been overly ambitious in the architectural designs of his palace by the sea," I said casually, letting the words drop and waiting patiently.

The transformation my words caused was notable. Without any dramatic change in his expression, his pale face began to take on a glow of intensity. His black eyes met my gaze, and I found I could not look away.

"His detractors are fools. The Prince's ambition where the Pavilion is concerned should be honoured. He will create a lasting monument to the artistry of this age."

"Indeed," I murmured, temporarily at a loss as to how to respond to this passionate statement. "I had been admiring—"

But Mr. Ainsley did not hear me. He turned his head and fixed his gaze across the room where the Prince held court. His expression hardened. In an acid voice he said, "One could only wish his Royal Highness's aspirations for his own projects extended to compassion for the ambitions of others."

And with that, the young man abruptly strode away, Lady Prudence trailing behind.

Though the room was now almost suffocatingly hot, I experienced a chill at the bitterness Arthur Ainsley held toward the Prince of Wales.

Where would he allow his resentment to lead?

5

The next day I awoke around ten. I like to have the morning well aired before I open my eyes.

My first thought was of the Prince and his safety. Was he all right? Surely an alarm would have been raised during the night had any attempts been made to harm him. He was probably still abed, or consuming vast quantities of food. Or both.

"Reow," Chakkri said enthusiastically, as if he knew I was thinking of food. He stared at me with deep blue eyes from his position in the exact centre of the bed. That is where the feline insists on sleeping.

Before you let out a hearty guffaw, and perhaps even think me mad for allowing him to take up this prime spot, let me hasten to assure you it was not my decision. Far from it. Shortly after coming to live in my household, the cat waged a war with me when I tried to put him out of my bedchamber at night. Yes, I said a war. The prize to the victor: the centre of the bed. His weapons? A will of iron and a voice like a screaming baby.

There is absolutely nothing wrong with sleeping diagonally.

Robinson entered the room balancing a tray with a pot of coffee. Three liveried footmen followed him, carrying a large tub filled with hot water for my daily bath.

Robinson is almost my height. I often give him coats I have grown bored with, which he then has altered to his smaller frame. I cannot say whether it is the wearing of my fine cast-offs or just a natural ability, but Robinson has a general air of loftiness. "Good morning, sir. Would you care for coffee before you bathe? A roll?"

"Yes, thank you," I responded, sitting up and arranging the silk coverlet around me.

"Reow," Chakkri stood, stretched, then raised his dark nose toward the tray Robinson held. He sniffed the air. "Reeoow!"

"The cat wants his breakfast, Robinson. I daresay a roll will not do," I chided. "You know he likes André's scrambled eggs with cheese sauce."

The valet heaved a long-suffering sigh.

Oh, God. I prayed I would not be treated to Robinson's Martyr Act this early in the day. Robinson and Chakkri are hardly the best of friends. In fact, the meticulous valet had threatened to leave my employ when the cat first came to live with us. A valet's reputation is made by the appearance of the gentleman he serves. The thought of cat hair on my clothes put Robinson in high dudgeon. A devilish bad business.

A large increase in pay brought us over the first hurdle. Later, my permission for the valet to use a special cloth to remove any cat hair that dared to attach itself to my coat resulted in an uneasy truce. Still, Robinson has never quite resigned himself to living with the animal. He counts cat hairs on the furniture, and continually tries to find ways to persuade me to crate the cat up and send him back to Siam from whence he came.

I raised a brow pointedly at the valet's lack of attention to the matter of the cat's breakfast.

Robinson's lips pursed. He poured my coffee, dismissed the footmen, and with a muttered, "André has spoiled him at home with his cooking," left the room to get some eggs.

A short time later Chakkri's stomach was full, and so was mine. Using a well-licked paw, he washed around his whisker pad. Then, he leaped back onto the bed from the floor where he had been dining off the royal dishes, turned round once, lay down, and fell asleep.

I frowned.

Usually after breakfast the cat was ready for an official room inspection, the purpose of which was to determine that everything was in its place and had not been moved during the night. He normally followed this with a monitoring of outside activities from the window, and an inventory of my Sèvres collection, muttering about his findings along the way. He is a very vocal animal.

Since we had arrived at the Pavilion, however, Chakkri had chosen to sleep most of the time. Seagulls flying past the window caused him to raise his head briefly, but that was the extent of his activities. He was becoming the Viscount Petersham of cats. A lazy specimen of Siamese fur.

I mulled the matter over while bathing, but had to put the problem from my mind when it was time to begin what Robinson and I have dubbed The Dressing Hour. This is that crucial part of the day when I don simple, yet perfectly fitting and elegant clothing, and tie my famous neckcloth. Once the process is complete— and yes, you are correct, it takes longer than an hour—I never so much as glance in a mirror to check my appearance during the day. Until it is time to change clothes for the evening.

Roughly two hours later, while fashioning the final adjustments to my cravat, my mind drifted to the previous day. "Robinson, have you perchance taken note of a guest by the name of Arthur Ainsley?"

Making certain not a single wrinkle marred the way my mazarine-blue long-tailed coat set across my shoulders, the valet's expression brightened. Nothing was better than good gossip in Robinson's opinion. "Yes, sir, I have. A quiet young gentleman, but one whose emotions run deep."

"Hmmm, yes, I agree. I wonder what his feelings are toward the Prince," I said, turning to face the mirror.

Robinson paused in the act of gathering my nightlinen for the laundress. "The Prince, sir?"

"Precisely," I replied, unwilling to tell Robinson about the peerage Mr. Ainsley felt the Prince had promised him and then reneged on. I had said enough to whet Robinson's appetite and wanted to see what he could find out on his own. A seed planted and all that. You understand.

"Hand me my black velvet greatcoat, will you, Robinson? I have a mind to take a walk on the beach."

"On the beach, sir?" Robinson said, his voice rising in alarm. "Are you quite certain? The pebbles will ruin your perfectly polished Hessian boots!"

"It will not signify. I trust you to take care of the boots," I told him while putting on the greatcoat and reaching for my hat. "While I am out, perhaps you might see to obtaining some sand. For Chakkri, you know," I said, indicating the corner of the room where Chakkri's private container stood.

The valet's gaze met mine.

In a fit of pique over the cat taking up residence with us, Robinson had selected a particular container for Chakkri to use for his personal needs. The porcelain tray had been a gift specially made for me and presented by a merchant hoping to advance his daughter's chances in Society. The place where Chakkri often covered a damp spot was directly over the artist's rendition of yours truly, complete with perfectly tied cravat, tall hat, and raised quizzing glass.

Robinson's lips tightened.

"Yes," I said, snatching up the last roll from the breakfast tray and making my way to the door, "we have to fill the tray with . . . something, eh?"

I left Robinson with a moue of distaste on his face.

In the hallway, I allowed myself a smile.

Outside the Pavilion, a breeze carried the sea air to my nostrils, and I inhaled deeply, enjoying the scent. Although the autumn air chilled my face, I was warm enough in my greatcoat, despite the grey day.

Striding along the building with my gaze trained on the upper floor windows, I counted aloud. ". . . Two, three, four—aha! That should be my window right there," I said to no one. Moving several yards away from the structure, I removed the breakfast roll from my pocket and crumbled it into bits with my gloved fingers.

Busy tossing the crumbs about on the ground, I did not hear anyone approach.

"George," a sweet, light voice called from behind me.

I swung around, dropping the rest of the roll. "Freddie!"

Her Royal Highness, Frederica, the Duchess of York, stood a short distance away smiling at me. The daughter of a Prussian king and married to King George III's second son, the Duke of York, Freddie is a small, dignified lady with brown curly hair.

Today she wore a rich forest-brown pelisse over a cinnamon-coloured walking gown and matching bonnet. Her charming countenance is the dearest female face known to me. Especially when it holds such an expression of delight as it did now.

"Dear, whatever are you doing, breaking that roll and throwing it about the ground like that?" she asked.

"I thought to attract birds for Chakkri to watch from our window," I explained. I covered the few steps between us, swept off my hat, and bowed low to her. Then I brushed a last crumb from my hand, reached out and clasped her gloved hand in mine.

One of her hands. The other hand held a leash, which was attached to a dog. Freddie has what you might call a fondness for the creatures and lives with upwards of one hundred of them. This one I had not seen before. He is a sad-looking hound with big, people-like eyes, his colouring running to black and brown with a white chest flecked with black. His snout is white, and he has enormous brown eyebrows, which—I give you my word—he wiggled at me.

"Never mind that now," I said, keeping Freddie's hand in a tight grasp and looking down into her precious china-blue eyes. "You have come to Brighton at last. When did you arrive?"

She smiled up at me. "Last night, while everyone was at the Johnstones'. I had to come. I had to give you your present and could not count on your coming soon to Oatlands."

I gave her my best look of reproach. "Present? I do not need any gift other than your company. But you wound me. Almost nothing could keep me from your weekend house parties, as you well know. Now that you are here, there will be no need for me to travel to see you. You will be staying through the weekend, will you not?"

Freddie cast a look behind her where her maid, Ulga, stood at a respectful distance watching us. Gently, she tugged her hand from mine. "Oh, I cannot say, George," she said. "We will see how the Brighton air agrees with me."

What she meant was that she would have to see if her blackguard of a husband, the Duke of York, found out she had ventured away from the country estate he rarely visited, Oatlands, to travel to the Pavilion. If he did, he might decide to join her, with mistress in tow.

Yes, yes, I know the Duke is highly regarded in some circles, being the Commander in Chief of England's land forces, but he is not highly regarded in the circle of my brain. Gentlemen should be true to their marriage vows, and if they cannot be, they should at least be discreet. The Duke of York is neither.

"Will you not introduce me to your escort?" I bantered, wishing to see the smile return to Freddie's face.

"His name is Humphrey, but wait a moment before shaking his paw. Let me give you your present first,

George, before someone wanders along and finds it." Freddie walked over to a nearby tree. The dog and I followed.

With the flourish of a conjurer at Southwark Fair, Freddie reached behind the tree and produced a walking stick. She smiled and handed it to me. "I had this made up especially for you, dear, to thank you for your help with that recent nerve-rattling incident regarding Miss Ashton."

I stared down at the ebony cane in surprise and pleasure. Beautifully carved, it is topped by an elegant silver dog's head. The canine's eyes are sapphires. Such a gift would remind me of the Royal Duchess every time I carried it. "Freddie, it is handsome to be sure, but you need not have given me anything."

"Nonsense, George," she proclaimed roundly. "If not for you, Miss Ashton would be in Newgate, my reputation would have suffered, and God only knows what else. I simply desired to show my appreciation for all you did in recent weeks."

I wanted to tell her that I would do anything for her, cross raging rivers, slay dragons, rescue wounded puppies, whatever was required, but she is a married woman and I am an honourable gentleman. Dash it!

"Thank you, Freddie," I replied gravely. "This shall be the only stick I carry from now on."

"George, do not say so! I know you have a marvelous collection of canes. You must not limit yourself to just this one," she insisted. But I thought there was a spark of pleasure in the depths of her eyes even as she denounced my plan.

"Freddie, I choose to carry only this walking stick," I said in a tone that stated the subject was closed.

A hint of colour on her cheeks, she took the cane back from me. "Well, if you do carry it, it will afford you a measure of protection. Here, if you twist the silver dog's head like this," she said, suiting her actions to her words, "you have a remarkably sharp swordstick." A gleaming blade snapped out of the bottom of the cane. Freddie handed the cane back to me.

"Excellent," I said, turning the head back, causing the mechanism to retract the blade, leaving me with an innocent-looking walking stick.

"Now let me tell you about Humphrey, George. I received a petition from him—well, actually his master— who was forced to leave England. Not being able to take the dog along, he feared for Humphrey's future."

I looked down at the animal and he gazed back with the most melancholy grimace I have ever seen. He is a short-legged creature, and his long droopy ears and wrinkled jowls almost touched the ground.

"His master begged that I might give Humphrey a home, stating that with sufficient carrots and grated parmesan cheese, the poor darling would be quite content."

"Carrots?" I asked, casting a disbelieving eye at the animal's stocky body.

"Indeed," Freddie confirmed, nodding her head. "Well, George, I need hardly tell you that I offered the dog a home at once. I have not regretted the decision for a moment; Humphrey is such a loving soul. Considering that he has recently been separated from the only master he ever knew, I felt it incumbent upon me to bring him along on this trip to Brighton, so he would not feel abandoned in any way. He must know he is among friends. Will you not pet him, dear?"

With a touch of reluctance born from a mental image

of Robinson's disapproving expression when I handed him gloves covered with dog hair, I knelt down and stroked the top of Humphrey's head.

"Look, George, he likes you!" the Royal Duchess exclaimed.

Did drooling equal affection? If so, the dog was positively in love with me. I inched my buckskin-clad knee discreetly away. Robinson was skilled in his work, but I doubted he included a drool-remover in his cache of valet equipment. I looked up to reply to Freddie's statement, when, out of the corner of my eye, I caught a movement at the window of my bedchamber. Focussing my gaze, I perceived a startling sight.

Two eyes blazed at me, the orbs glinting red. A tail snapped repeatedly against the pane of glass.

Chakkri saw me petting Humphrey. Chakkri was angry.

Rescue came from an unexpected source. At that moment, Lady St. Clair, accompanied by her daughters and their maid, headed our way. I could cease my attentions to the dog without offending Freddie.

I rose, then bowed as the ladies joined us. They sank into deep curtseys for Freddie.

"Good morning, Lady St. Clair," Freddie said regally. "It is a fine day for a walk, is it not?"

"Quite so. We are honoured to have your Royal Highness amongst us. If it pleases your Royal Highness, may I present my daughters, Lady Chastity and Lady Prudence?"

There followed another series of curtseys and pleasant remarks.

Lady Chastity noticed Humphrey. "I've never seen a short-legged dog like that before, your Royal Highness."

"Chastity," Lady St. Clair said swiftly before Freddie could reply. "Do not be overly familiar with the Royal Duchess."

Lady Prudence shot her sister a pious look.

Lady Chastity pouted prettily, but did not defy her mother. Lady St. Clair's command had been gentle, but with a hint of steel underneath.

"It is quite all right, Lady St. Clair," Freddie said. "The dog's name is Humphrey, Lady Chastity. Would you like to pet him?"

Humphrey looked up hopefully.

Lady Chastity made a move forward, but her mother's words, soft but effective, stopped her. "You are very kind, your Royal Highness, but we would not keep you," Lady St. Clair said. I felt sure she did not approve of her daughter touching the dog, though nothing in her cordial tone indicated it. "The girls and I are taking our morning exercise and will continue to the Steine, if you will excuse us?"

Freddie nodded.

Lady St. Clair and her daughters curtseyed. "Good morning to you and Mr. Brummell, your Royal Highness. I hope you and Humpty have a nice stroll."

With that, Lady St. Clair moved stiffly away, daughters and maid in tow. I glanced at Freddie, who was gazing after them.

"Lady St. Clair did not remember Humphrey's name correctly," I remarked.

Freddie said nothing. She is the type of lady who does not like to speak ill of others. A little prompting would be necessary if I were to find out her opinion of Lady St. Clair. And I wished to learn as much as I could about all of Prinny's guests. "Shall we take Humphrey for a walk on the beach?"

"Good idea, George. He will enjoy it. And you can tell me all of what has transpired since your arrival in Brighton."

Freddie motioned for Ulga to follow. We began walking at a slow pace around the house. To get to the beach, we needed to walk past the grassy area known as the Steine. Neither of us wanted to appear as if we were following Lady St. Clair and her daughters. I said, "Though I have met Lord St. Clair before, I only met his lady and his daughters last night."

Freddie stepped onto the footpath bordering the Steine. The park-like area was crowded with people promenading. "Lord St. Clair is a respected man in Parliament. When he inherited his estate, Edenberry Grove, it had fallen into disrepair due to his father's excessive gaming."

"Horrid what gaming debts can do to a man. I vow I shall never be brought low by them."

Freddie gave a gentle tug on the leash as Humphrey had paused to sniff the ground. "See that you do not, George. As for Lord St. Clair, he eventually made the estate into one of the finest in the county. His lordship made a fortunate choice in wives. Lady St. Clair has done a great deal to help bring the estate to rights."

Translation: Lady St. Clair was the one with the money.

"The daughter of a neighbouring estate owner?" I asked casually, reaching down and moving the animal's front quarters in order to get him to move along. He finally complied.

Freddie smiled her thanks. "Prior to marriage, Lady

St. Clair was Miss Euthenia Beale, the daughter of a London silk importer."

Translation: Lady St. Clair was the daughter of a Cit, the common term used for *City Merchant*. This explained her air of being Beyond Reproach. In an effort to cover her undistinguished parentage, Lady St. Clair took pains not to make a single social misstep.

Neither Freddie nor I spoke for a few moments as we gazed out to the sea. The waves were rough, pounding against the shore with wrathful intensity. A bit farther down from where we were, the sea-bathing machines stood without customers. Only a few fishing boats braved the heaving water.

I glanced over at Freddie, thinking she might not wish to stroll the beach on such a day. Indeed, as I looked around, I observed only a scattering of people about. But Freddie loves unfettered nature and would not be deterred.

I grasped her cherished arm firmly and guided her down the steps. Ulga followed behind. Humphrey seemed excited, his snout raised in high anticipation of a good romp.

"Should I release him from his leash, George?" Freddie asked uncertainly.

"Yes, do. He seems eager for some exercise. I daresay he could use it."

Freddie bent and unhooked the length of leather from the dog's collar. He moved quickly for a fellow so close to the ground, his tail up and the tip wagging a bit as he traversed the pebbled ground.

"Perhaps I could ask your advice about Chakkri, Freddie," I said, taking her arm and placing it through mine. We began to walk down the beach, the sound of the waves crashing in the background.

"Of course you can, dear."

"Chakkri has been most unhappy since our arrival. He misses home."

"Have you brushed him lately?"

"Yes, I have an ivory-handled ladies' hairbrush I employ on him. He makes a game of it, though, walking away and then crying for me to continue."

Freddie laughed. "I should like to witness that."

"I would not say this to anyone else, but I know you will understand."

Freddie nodded her encouragement.

"I daresay it is more a sense of impending doom that is disturbing him. I know I feel it, too."

"The threats against the Prince? He wrote to me about them," Freddie's brow creased in concern.

"Yes. They are serious. And Prinny is feeling the strain. He stepped on Chakkri's tail yesterday. When the cat yelled, enough guards to repel Napoleon rushed the room, all pointing their weapons at me. It took me some minutes and a few glasses of cherry brandy to soothe Prinny."

Freddie made sympathetic noises.

"Besides foreign threats, the Prince has made a muddle of certain things here. A woman named Mrs. Davies is said to be carrying his child."

Freddie's lips were firmly closed.

"And there is one young man, Arthur Ainsley, who feels cheated out of a peerage he says Prinny promised him. Now he has revenge in his eye," I told her.

"Furthermore, the Prince argued in public with your brother-in-law, the Duke of Clarence, last night at the

Johnstones'. And Prinny has employed a food-taster."

Freddie's blue eyes widened. "A food taster? Great heavens, here in Brighton?"

"Yes, and the man is a cad. Sir Simon, a local baronet. Do you know him?"

"No."

"An ugly fellow. He made a coarse remark about Lady Perry, and Lord Perry called him out. It took Lord Perry's cousin, Signor Tallarico, and me to talk him out of it, though Tallarico had pulled a knife on Sir Simon."

Freddie gasped.

"Perry finally let Sir Simon go, but not before promising to kill him if he so much as mentioned Lady Perry again." I heaved a weary sigh. "Other than that, things have been dull. Petersham has a new blend of snuff he has promised to let the Prince try this evening, so we have that to look forward to."

"George! You are making up all these calamities!"

"Upon my honour, I am not."

"This is dreadful. What can happen next?"

Before I could answer, our attention was caught by a deep woof from Humphrey. His jowls flapped as he raced toward an object being washed up on shore by the angry waves.

Freddie gripped my arm. "Oh, dear God, George. Look! It is a body."

6

"*You must not* look," I commanded, grasping Freddie's left shoulder and turning her closely toward me, shielding her from the tragic sight.

Freddie's blue eyes were wide with shock and her body trembled. "George," she whispered in an anguished voice, "there is no hope that she might still be . . . if there is any possibility . . ." Her voice trailed off, and her gaze went past me, back to where the girl lay.

I placed a gentle finger on Freddie's soft cheek, applying pressure to turn her toward me again. "I do not think so, my princess, but if you promise not to look at her again, I shall make certain there is nothing to be done."

Freddie swallowed, then gave a shaky nod.

I turned and found Freddie's maid standing some ten feet behind us, staring at the body and clutching her shawl tightly about her shoulders. "Ulga! Come here at once and see to the Royal Duchess."

My authoritative tone snapped the maid out of her

trance. She came forward. After urging them both to keep their eyes averted, I walked over to the young woman.

Humphrey woofed at me.

"Yes, boy, you found her. Good dog. Now, let me see."

Upon closer inspection, I judged the girl to be hardly more than eighteen or nineteen years of age. She appeared to be a lady of quality, if the fineness of her dress was any measure. To add to the impression of wealth, there was a gold cross suspended from her neck. The chain was heavy, and emeralds graced the ends of the fleur-de-lys.

There was no doubt in my mind she was dead. Even so, I kneeled down and forced myself to edge away matted strands of her flaxen hair. I placed my fingers at her throat in search for a pulse. None could be found there, nor at her wrist.

Part of the skirt of her dress had crept up around her knees. I leaned over and tugged the soaked material down to modestly cover her cold limbs. Then my gaze shifted, and I noticed that the side of her head, toward the back, sported a lump about the size of my pocket-watch.

About to examine the spot, the sound of Humphrey's barking called my attention back to Freddie. The canine had responded to her call. She crouched down, hugging the excited dog close. A few people had gathered around, whispering and pointing.

Deciding there was nothing more I could do for the young girl, I walked back to Freddie. Addressing Ulga, I said, "Remain here. I shall escort the Royal Duchess back to the Pavilion and summon help."

"Yes, sir," she responded crisply, seemingly recovered from the shock. She did not look at the body again.

"Come, Freddie, there is nothing more we can do other than get Doctor Pitcairn and some men down here. The Prince's doctor is in residence, I am told. He will see to this." I knew the magistrate would also have to be informed, but I kept the thought to myself.

Freddie rose slowly, her face drained of every drop of colour. The wind blew a curl across her face. She reached up to tuck it under her hat, her hand shaking. I was sure to keep myself between her and the sight of the body. With the dog loping along beside us, we made our way back to the Pavilion.

"Freddie, have some tea," I said. "The footman just brought it, so it is nice and hot." She had not regained colour in her cheeks since we had returned to the house. Dismissing Ulga after charging her to take Humphrey upstairs, the Royal Duchess allowed me to lead her to a quiet room and ring for tea.

We sat in the circular drawing room known as the Saloon. A great round Axminster carpet, featuring a sunflower in the middle, fit the room beneath our feet. Golden rays like those from the sun spread from its center. A border of dragons chasing one another completed the design. Six wall panels in Chinese wallpaper rose to meet the ceiling, a painted summer sky. Eastern scents wafted from the magnificent perfume burner, making me feel we were thousands of miles away from the awful scene on the Brighton beach.

"Yes, tea would be just the thing," Freddie pronounced, reaching over and pouring us both a cup.

However, before we could taste the brew, the doors swung open, and the Prince of Wales entered, followed by Lord Perry with his cousin Victor Tallarico and Lord and Lady St. Clair. A half-dozen armed footmen filed in behind the Prince and arranged themselves at attention by the door.

Freddie and I rose from our chairs. I bowed to the Heir Apparent, while the Royal Duchess curtseyed to her brother-in-law.

The Prince looked nettled. "Brummell, what's this about a body on the beach? We had just sat down to a game of whist when I was informed you'd sent for Pitcairn."

"I did send for the doctor, sir. And the magistrate as well. The Royal Duchess and I were strolling the beach when we came upon the lamentable scene. I knew you would feel it proper that the young woman's body be removed and examined. I had her brought here."

"Here?" the Prince asked faintly. He is a bit on the squeamish side.

I nodded. "She appeared to be about eighteen years of age and was finely garbed. I thought it best to bring her here."

"A drowned young *lady*, then?" Lord Perry inquired.

"It would seem so," I replied grimly. "I expect Doctor Pitcairn to be with us presently. He will tell us more."

"Was she someone we know?" Lord St. Clair asked.

"Oh, pray do not say any more. I cannot bear it," Lady St. Clair moaned, raising a handkerchief to her mouth. "The very same age as my Prudence."

"Euthenia," Lord St. Clair said in a low voice. "Mayhaps you should retire to your room before the doctor gives his report. We do not need hysterics now."

Appalled at her own display of emotion, Lady St. Clair stood rooted to the spot, her countenance stricken.

Victor Tallarico stepped forward. "Would both of the ladies allow me to escort them to the Long Gallery for an examination of its treasures? I would be honoured."

Lady St. Clair took his proffered arm gratefully. At my side, Freddie hesitated. I performed the introductions.

Signor Tallarico bowed low. "Your Royal Highness, pardon my boldness in addressing you before we had been formally introduced. I thought only of your comfort, abandoning the conventions. Please say you forgive me." He followed this speech with a smile that showed brilliant white teeth.

Much to my annoyance, even Freddie was not immune to the Italian's magnetic charm. With dignified grace, she thanked him, and the trio left the room.

Still scowling after them, I saw a wiry man dressed in black enter the room accompanied by a footman. The latter announced, "Mr. Kearley," in ringing tones that made the man cringe.

Prinny raised his quizzing glass, causing Mr. Kearley to bow so low his nose almost touched one of the dragons. As it was, he jumped when he saw the creature woven into the carpet. "I'm the magistrate, your most Royal Highness," he said and gulped.

"Eh, well, I haven't met you before, have I?" the Prince asked in a tone that implied he wished he had not now.

"No, sir. You have a death to report?"

Another arrival distracted the Prince. "Ah, Pitcairn, at last, there's a good fellow. What have we on our hands? A drowned girl?" the Prince said, addressing a distinguished gentleman just entering the room.

I had met David Pitcairn before, as he is Prinny's personal physician. He is a dependable man, one who puts up with a good deal of his royal patron's fits and starts. At this moment, the doctor's usually amiable nature was absent. In its place was a professional air. "She did not drown."

"What do you mean, she didn't drown?" the Prince demanded. "Brummell said she washed up on shore."

"Killed by a sharp blow to the head," Doctor Pitcairn stated with finality.

For a tense moment, no one spoke.

"That's monstrous disagreeable, isn't it? Right here, on our Brighton shore, practically at my doorstep," the Prince complained, then his eyes widened. "*My* doorstep," he whispered. "Could it be by the hands of whoever is threatening me?" Prinny gripped the back of a chair.

Lord Perry snapped his fingers at one of the footmen. "Bring the Prince his cherry brandy!"

"A tragedy to be sure, your Royal Highness," Lord St. Clair said in a reasonable tone, "but certainly it can have no connection to you, sir."

The Prince accepted a glass of brandy, but then looked at it skeptically. He returned it to its tray without partaking of it. Where was Sir Simon when he was needed, I mused cynically. But my thoughts turned to the doctor's words.

"I noted a wound on the side of her head when I found her. I assume that was the fatal blow?" I said to him. At his nod, I went on, "But how can you be certain that is what caused her death? Could the body not have struck a rock or something beneath the surface of the sea after she had drowned?"

"Possibly. But it would have to have been an awfully sharp rock and the body tossed hard against it. Besides, if the body had been pitched about to cause a blow like that, one would think there would be other wounds, scratches even. But there are none."

"What are you telling us, Doctor?" Lord Perry asked.

"Although it is true that I cannot be absolutely certain, it is my learned opinion that the blow to the head is what killed her. The murderer likely took the corpse to the sea, thinking the body would never be recovered. Or if it was, that the cause of death would be viewed as an accidental drowning."

Lord Perry looked at the magistrate. "This will be a matter for the law then."

Mr. Kearley's mouth opened and closed. I thought him shaking in his shoes at the very thought of having a murder on his hands.

The Prince did not look much better.

"But who was the young lady?" Lord St. Clair asked. "We must contact her family. How can we notify them if we do not know who she was?"

Doctor Pitcairn looked at each of us. "That is where I hope you gentlemen can be of assistance. Though the body is somewhat bloated, the cold sea water has kept it preserved. The corpse should be recognizable to anyone who knows the girl. Mr. Brummell says he does not know who she is, but he is newly arrived in Brighton. Perhaps one of you who has been here longer could view the body for identification."

"Zounds!" the Prince cried, recoiling in revulsion. "I

am positive she is unknown to me. Absolutely positive."

"I shall do it," Lord St. Clair said quietly. "I have divided my time between Brighton, London, and my estate since June, but we have been in Brighton the majority of the time. I might have seen the young lady."

"Thank you, my lord," Doctor Pitcairn said.

"I shall be glad to help if I can," Lord Perry said. "My wife and I have only been in Brighton two weeks, but still, it is worth an attempt."

Everyone waited for Mr. Kearley's response. Finally, the magistrate cleared his throat. "There haven't been any reports of missing young ladies. I'll have a look at her as well. If none of us recognizes her, I'll put a notice in the *Brighton Advertiser* and see if anyone comes forward to claim her as kin. Otherwise . . ." The magistrate shrugged.

With the Prince's permission, Doctor Pitcairn departed the room with Lords Perry and St. Clair and Mr. Kearley. Prinny and I were alone. "Sir, I know this latest development has heightened your anxiety—"

The Prince rounded on me. "Why you felt you had to bring the dead girl here surpasses all imagination, Brummell. You know I have been treading gingerly since I received those death threats. My being subjected to this latest mess is unnecessary and it rankles."

I stared at him in surprise. "What would you have had me do? The young lady appeared to be Quality. For all I knew, she might even have been a guest in this house."

He let out a conceding sigh at this. "I expect you've the right of it. It's just that I am provoked beyond all reason. My feelings are much too lacerated by those damned threats to sustain the further strain of dealing with this unknown young lady's death."

"I understand. I am persuaded you would feel better for some of that brandy. If you wish, I should be glad to swallow some first to be certain of its purity," I told him, picking up the glass the footman had brought in earlier.

"No need for that," a voice boomed from the doorway. Sir Simon bowed, then advanced into the room and snatched the glass from my hand. He promptly inhaled a large gulp and grinned at the Prince. "I'm at your service, your Royal Highness."

Much to my disapproval, the arrival of the odious Sir Simon brought an expression of relief to the Prince's face. " 'Tis an honourable thing you're doing, Sir Simon, putting my life above yours."

Sir Simon swelled with pride. Or more likely, conceit. "My duty to England, sir. Only doing my duty. Well, Mr. Brummell, I hear you picked up something more than a shell on the Brighton beach this morning. Too bad the female was dead, eh? Not much good in that, is there?"

A fit of ribald laughter overtook the baronet. I was shocked to see an indulgent smile cross Prinny's face. He accepted the glass of brandy from Sir Simon, deeming it safe to drink now.

"Was she a pretty girl, Brummell? Damned waste if she was," Sir Simon went on. Then, not waiting for me to answer, he addressed the Prince again, lowering his voice. "That puts me in mind of something I almost forgot, your Royal Highness. I have one of those special foreign prints of nude ladies that I am occasionally able to obtain. Would you care to view it now? You won't be disappointed," he said and winked at Prinny.

I stood without speaking. As I told you, I draw back at some of the Prince's diversions. This sounded like one of them. Sir Simon's endless toadying to the Prince's every desire evidently knew no bounds.

Prinny must have perceived my disapproval. "Brummell, I'll see you later today. I want a report from you before we dine this evening regarding that matter I told you to keep an eye on."

I bowed as he and Sir Simon exited the room, Sir Simon's voice coming back to reach my ears. ". . . have a fine appetite myself. Would your Royal Highness care for a cold collation before you view . . ."

I hoped the chef was not serving frog's legs. If he was, the toadying Sir Simon's limbs were in jeopardy.

And the day was not over yet.

7

By the Dressing Hour that evening, I felt that the level of my frustration demanded a quiet evening in my room, a well-prepared dinner, a couple of bottles of Chambertin wine, and Chakkri my only company. Unless I could persuade Freddie to take her meal with me and the feline.

But it was not to be.

By dinner the Prince wanted a report on Mr. Ainsley, yet had maddeningly spent the afternoon closeted in his library with the very gentleman himself.

Upon my seemingly indifferent questioning, a chatty footman outside the door proved useful. He imparted the information that his Royal Highness did not wish to be interrupted, as he was deep in discussions of architectural designs with Mr. Ainsley. I was assured that half-a-dozen armed footmen were with them.

Though I lingered in the general vicinity of the library as long as I could, wanting to catch Mr. Ainsley, I finally had to give up and go abovestairs to my bedchamber to dress for the evening.

Along the way, I sought out Freddie, hoping for a few minutes of her company. I was anxious to be sure that her nerves had not been completely overset by the afternoon's events, and—very well I admit it—that she had not been too charmed by Signor Tallarico.

I sent word to her room, only to have Ulga inform me that the Royal Duchess was lying on her bed with a cool cloth to her forehead and could not be disturbed. There would be no opportunity before dinner for a private chat. Devil take it.

I did run into Perry and inquired about the deceased young lady on the beach. Neither he nor Lord St. Clair nor Mr. Kearley had recognized her. Mr. Kearley would do what he could as magistrate for the district, then the girl would be buried in an unmarked grave. A twinge of pain squeezed my heart when a mental image of her sprawled on the beach came into my mind. I shook my head over a life cut much too short. Opening the door to my chamber, I mused that someone, somewhere, must be frantic over the girl's disappearance. I wished her family could be located.

My thoughts were redirected when Robinson handed me a welcome glass of wine. We selected proper evening attire: fine white linen shirt, black breeches, and figured white waistcoat topped by a long-tailed, slate-blue coat. I always carry my father's Venetian gold watch but, other than that, wear no jewellry. My quizzing glass does not count as jewellry. It is a social necessity.

While I dressed, Chakkri slept like one dosed with laudanum in the center of the bed. As punishment for my petting Humphrey, the cat would no doubt ignore me entirely until he determined I had suffered enough.

"If I may ask, sir, when will we be returning to London?" Robinson inquired while laying out thin black shoes for my inspection.

"We only arrived yesterday," I said, giving a nod of approval to the shine on the shoes.

"Yes, sir," the valet replied with a wistful sigh.

"You and Chakkri share the same sentiments on being in Brighton. He does not care for it either. Have you noticed that he has been sleeping almost continuously since we got here?"

We both glanced at the cat, though I think the action was involuntary on Robinson's part. The valet gave a pleased smile. "Indeed, I have. Stray cat hairs have been confined to your bed. Fifteen of them this afternoon. That makes my job of seeing that you appear in public without the ornamentation of cat hair on your clothing much easier."

Chakkri opened one blue eye, stared at me, then snapped it shut without a murmur.

Perhaps I had been sentenced to thirty hours of feline indifference for petting Humphrey, unless Chakkri extended my term for the offense of bringing him to Brighton. In that case, it could be days before he spoke to me again.

"Sir," Robinson said, moving to the dressing table to retrieve a bottle of Eau de Melisse des Carmes lotion. "I inquired discreetly as to Mr. Arthur Ainsley's character. In particular, I tried to ascertain his sentiments regarding the Prince of Wales."

"And what did you find?" I asked, holding out my hands.

Robinson poured a bit of the lightly scented lotion onto my left hand and began vigorously massaging it in. Have I mentioned that my hands are beautifully pampered? One would not wish for them to appear anything less than their best while raising my quizzing glass or delicately taking a pinch of snuff.

Robinson examined my nails, which are neatly squared in shape. "Mr. Ainsley has frequently made cutting remarks about the Prince in the presence of his valet. He called the Prince 'double-tongued' and said he was capable of playing false with a man's dreams."

The Prince was double-wived and double-chinned, too, but that was beside the point. I thought of him and Ainsley in the library, poring over sketches of the Pavilion. "And to look at him with the Prince, one would think them boon companions."

"That may be, sir, but Mr. Ainsley does speak in an uncomplimentary way behind the royal back."

"Interesting." My mind went back to the previous evening. I recalled the way Ainsley had looked, and the bitter way he had bemoaned the Prince's lack of compassion for the "ambitions of others," I believe was how he put it.

"The younger son of an earl, Mr. Ainsley resents his brother, the heir to the title," Robinson continued. He reached for a small scissors and snipped a wayward cuticle. "Above anything, Mr. Ainsley wishes to be powerful. He fancies himself an intellectual and wants to display his knowledge in Parliament."

"Has he money?" I asked, dropping my left hand and extending my right.

Robinson briskly repeated his ministrations. "As to that, although he did recently receive an inheritance from his maternal grandmother, I fear it is not enough for one with Mr. Ainsley's goals."

"Yes, he would need a tidy sum to rise to power in the government," I reflected, wondering how Ainsley planned to increase his wealth.

Content with my grooming, and satisfied my clothes were quiet perfection, I left Robinson to tidy the chamber. I descended the stairs to find people assembled in the Long Gallery, drinking wine and exchanging gossip.

The Long Gallery is precisely that, being over one hundred fifty feet in length. Thanks to the abundance of enormous mirrors framed in beechwood carved to resemble bamboo on the walls, the area looks much wider than it is. Real and imitation bamboo furniture, including twelve black-and-gold lacquered hall chairs, reflect the Prince's preoccupation with Chinese design.

The walls are covered in a deep pink color—darker than Victor Tallarico's pink waistcoats—with painted rocks, trees, shrubs, and birds in a subdued tone of blue, everything in the Chinese style.

From where I was standing next to an eight-tiered pagoda, his Royal Highness stood only a short distance from me, Sir Simon stuck to his side like a leech. What made Sir Simon's clinging especially disturbing was that the Prince had obviously been making his way down the Long Gallery, greeting his guests. For him to allow Sir Simon to tag along like a favorite spaniel while he played the gracious host showed me the depths to which the Prince had fallen victim to Sir Simon's toadying.

"Brummell," Prinny said, approaching me. "Have you that report I asked for?"

He wanted it now, in front of Sir Simon? Not that I

had anything new to say about Ainsley, but the Prince could not know that.

Unfortunately for my fashion sensibilities, my gaze shifted to the baronet, tonight rigged out in his high, powdered white wig and a deep maroon satin coat. The skirts of that garment were boned to assure that they stood out around the wearer, the buttons ruby-encrusted. The display of wealth did not end there. A long, gold-coloured waistcoat sported row upon row of gold thread embroidery. As was his custom, Sir Simon wore enough lace to beggar a dozen ladies' lace boxes.

Tearing my gaze away from this fashion disaster, I bowed to the Prince. "Sir, I regret to say I cannot provide any new information. The subject of your inquiry proved otherwise engaged today. Indeed, he participated in activities that your Royal Highness might be better able to describe than myself."

"What? Oh, right, just so. Ainsley brought me a copy of *Views of Oriental Scenery*, a most inspiring narrative of Indian architecture. We spent the afternoon discussing how I could apply some of the designs to the Pavilion."

"How congenial," I said. "You can understand, then, why I was not able to perform the service you desired."

"Yes, yes, but I want you to keep an eye on Ainsley nevertheless, Brummell," Prinny said, glancing around to see if the man in question was within earshot. Several yards away, Ainsley stood in his perpetual state of brooding next to a niche filled with a large Chinese figure. The Prince stared at him and said, "Ainsley could be the one behind the threats against me."

Sir Simon's painted face wrinkled in surprise. "Do you think so, your Royal Highness? You should have asked me to find out what I can about the man."

I felt myself tense with indignation. Did this painted pudding-bag think to supplant my friendship with the Prince of Wales?

Sir Simon winked lewdly. "I wager that within a day I'd be able to tell you what he eats for breakfast and which female's slipper he drinks his wine out of."

Down the Long Gallery, I saw prim Lady Prudence gazing dutifully at Arthur Ainsley while he pontificated about some, I was sure, boring, topic. I could not picture Lord St. Clair's daughter offering, nor Arthur Ainsley accepting, her shoe as a substitute for fine crystal. Even so, Sir Simon's boastful declaration irked me.

"Mr. Ainsley is only one possibility. I trust you to keep this information to yourself, Sir Simon." Prinny commanded. "There are many possible corners, both at home and afar, from which the threats could have come,"

"Foreigners!" Sir Simon said in a disdainful tone. "You can't trust any of 'em." Taking a step closer, Sir Simon murmured, "Your Royal Highness, have you noticed that the foreigner I told you about last night at the Johnstones' is in our midst now? He's over there, flirting expertly, so he can get a leg over Lady Chastity. Daresay she looks like the type that will let him."

The Prince joined Sir Simon in a lascivious snicker. "Which one is he? God's truth, Sir Simon, you find a way to make me laugh in spite of my anxiety."

Sir Simon obligingly pointed at Victor Tallarico.

Down the Corridor, Tallarico, clad again in a dark coat over a pink waistcoat, bent close to whisper something in Lord St. Clair's other daughter's shell-like ear. Lady Chastity was all giggles in the Italian's presence.

His brown hair mixed with her golden curls, so close were the two.

Still, I saw no harm in Lord Perry's cousin. I did feel disappointed in the Prince and worried for our friendship. Sir Simon brought out the wilder side in him. I felt the Heir Apparent had strayed from his usual discrimination in his choice of friends when he chose to associate with the baronet. Sir Simon did not reflect well on Prinny's character.

Besides, I wanted no one to supplant my place as the Prince's favorite. Can you blame me? It was through my friendship with him that I first came to Society's notice. I have no aristocratic background nor any great fortune to recommend me. I have only my sense of style and the friendships I have formed to keep me on my invisible throne at the head of Society.

Suddenly I wished to be away from them. I could not bear to hear how the conversation might degenerate. I said, "I shall avail myself of this opportunity to speak to Mr. Ainsley, your Royal Highness. As for Victor Tallarico, he is Lord Perry's cousin. I believe that to be recommendation enough for his integrity."

"Dash my wig, Mr. Brummell!" Sir Simon expostulated, and at that moment I wished I *could* knock his wig and its wearer to the floor. "Many a man from a so-called fine family indulges in activities you've never even dreamed of. Just because a man is related to, or associates with, honourable people doesn't mean he *is* honourable."

"How very right you are, Sir Simon," I said, fixing my gaze on Prinny, then casting a speaking look at the baronet.

I looked at the Prince again. "Will you excuse me, your Royal Highness?"

He nodded his permission, and I turned on my heel and strolled in Arthur Ainsley's direction. I cooled my aggravation with a glass of wine procured from one of the many footmen in the room. Glancing at my pocket-watch, I noted only five minutes remained before six, the traditional time the Prince led his guests in to dinner.

Lady Perry smiled at me from where she stood with her husband and Lord and Lady St. Clair. I returned the gesture, though I did not stop to talk. My goal was Mr. Ainsley. I did notice that Lady St. Clair had a rather pinched expression on her face. Likely she did not approve of Lady Perry being in public in her condition, though there was nothing yet in Lady Perry's appearance to indicate she was with child.

Still, Lady St. Clair struck me as the sort who probably removed herself to her country estate the very day she learned she was in a family way and remained there until after giving birth, deeming it unseemly to do otherwise.

"Good evening, Lady Prudence, Mr. Ainsley," I said, wandering over to where the two stood by the fireplace. Neither one looked happy at the intrusion. "The Prince was just telling me of your discussion this afternoon regarding Indian architecture."

"I brought him a book he liked," Mr. Ainsley muttered shortly.

Not a friendly soul, is he.

"Mr. Ainsley is an expert planner, Mr. Brummell. The Prince is wise to accept his help in renovating the Pavilion," Lady Prudence declared.

Let us hope he was not planning the Prince's demise.

"Lady Prudence, have you an interest in architecture, as well?" I asked.

"Yes, Mr. Brummell, I have. Mr. Ainsley has been kind enough to educate me, and I find myself grateful to him for doing so." She favoured Mr. Ainsley with a serene smile.

I tilted my head and looked at the two. He needed an audience, so puffed up was he with his own real or imagined abilities. She was a dab of a girl, a reflection of her mother's training in the conventions, no doubt. Where Lady Chastity clearly rebelled against her mother's teachings, Lady Prudence embraced them and even expanded upon them. She needed someone as serious as she thought she should be.

I fixed a pleasant expression on my face and said, "There, Mr. Ainsley. Lady Prudence and I quite agree that the Prince is fortunate to have the benefit of your knowledge. He must have enjoyed the time you spent with him this afternoon making the ideas in his head become a reality, at least on paper."

Mr. Ainsley regarded me with derision. "Reality? The Prince does not know the meaning of the word. The Pavilion is becoming naught but a pleasure dome, an unreal extravaganza of excess. Witness the number of mirrors in this room, for example. His Royal Highness is the very exemplar of narcissism."

Lady Prudence drew in her breath sharply.

I struggled to keep a cool countenance at these heated words.

A tinkling of bells sounded, announcing dinner and distracting me. I saw the Prince lead the way to the dining room, Freddie on his arm. I stared in surprise, for I had not seen her arrival. Naturally, as the highest-ranking lady present, she would go into dinner on the Prince's arm. If I were lucky, I might be seated near her. First, though, I must finish my conversation with Ainsley.

But when I turned back to him, he and Lady Prudence had gone. I looked around and saw them joining Lord and Lady St. Clair, Mr. Ainsley smiling at something Lord St. Clair said.

The riddle of Mr. Ainsley would have to be dealt with later. Right now, I must content myself with studying him over dinner. There were more gentlemen than ladies present, so I did not have a lady to escort. As I was about to enter the Eating Room and find my place, Viscount Petersham and his friend Lord Munro caught up with me.

"I say, Brummell, well met," Petersham greeted me with a mischievous grin. Lord Munro gave me a brief nod.

"Petersham, what has got you in high spirits?" I asked as we crossed into the Eating Room.

"I've my new snuff box, the one Munro gave me," Petersham said, casting a fond glance at his friend. "It's beautiful and it's filled with my new special blend, the one I promised the Prince he'd be the first to try."

"Splendid," I said, peering over people's heads trying to see if the Prince was going to follow the conventions when seating the guests. If so, Freddie would be on his right. There might be casual seating, though, since there were only a few more than a dozen of us. Perhaps I could sit next to the Royal Duchess after all.

"Here it is," Petersham said, pulling the snuff box from his pocket. "Remember I said I would show it to you? Take a quick look."

Diverted, I picked the snuff box up from Petersham's outstretched hand and examined it with pleasure. An antique, the box was dated 1633. Made in the shape of a book, the box was inlaid with mother-of-pearl and engraved with a head of Charles II.

"What's going on back there?" the Prince called. "Brummell, come and sit down, will you? Gad, Petersham, does that box Brummell is holding contain your new blend? Remember, you said I should be the first to try it. I shall not stand for your breaking your word."

"Yes, sir," the viscount responded proudly. "And you shall be the first."

"Lord Petersham and Mr. Brummell, you vexing men," Lady Bessborough called from her place on the Prince's left. She acted as hostess while Mrs. Fitzherbert remained ill. "Do put that snuff box aside until after dinner. I am persuaded the Prince would not like his food to grow cold."

Petersham looked like a little boy told to put away his favourite toy.

Lord Munro grasped his arm. "Why don't you put the snuff box on the sideboard for everyone to see, Charles? Then after dinner, the Prince can sample your new blend."

"Good idea, Harold," Petersham said. He walked to the great sideboard and looked for a place to display the box. Plucking a pineapple from the top of a silver epergne, he put the snuff box in its place.

The Duchess of York smiled at me from her seat beside the Prince. The angel had reserved the place next to her for me.

I made sure all the ladies were seated, then slipped into my chair. "Freddie," I said in a low voice, "I tried to see you earlier. Are you quite recovered from this morning's shock?"

She nodded. "I suppose so, dear. Thank you for asking. Has there been any word as to the girl's identity?"

"No one recognized her. As sad as it is, there is nothing more we can do at the moment." I could not take my eyes from the Royal Duchess, and felt the day's tensions draining away now that I could gaze upon her lovely face. Tonight she wore a magnificent emerald necklace set off to perfection by a rich green velvet gown.

"George," she whispered. "We must pay attention to the company and not be rude."

As if waking from a sleep, I looked around the table to see a few curious gazes cast our way. I took a deep swallow of the wine a footman stationed behind me had just poured.

Have I mentioned to you recently how much I dislike the Duke of York?

I turned my attention to the table. The food had been laid out before the guests came into the room. There were as many as forty dishes on the table: meats, vegetables, jellies, potatoes, more than we could ever consume—although on my other side, Sir Simon made a hearty attempt to do so all on his own. Naturally, he took it upon himself to admonish the Prince not to try a single dish until he had partaken of it first.

To be fair, I must say I contributed to the demise of the fine dinner as well. I enjoy a zestful appetite, one that has yet to display itself on my still lean person, thank heavens.

Once the first course was complete, an army of footmen came in and brought in another round. We dined on these sumptuous dishes, then finished with a dessert course and the table was cleared.

Around ten o'clock, Lady Bessborough signaled for the ladies to follow her to the Saloon, leaving us gentlemen to our fruit, walnuts, and port. There was a general shuffling about as gentlemen got up, walked around, and stretched their legs. With the ladies gone, we could all sit together, arranging ourselves down the table from the Prince.

I took Freddie's chair next to the Prince just in time. Sir Simon made a move for it too late and had to settle for sitting next to me, with Petersham and Munro on his right. Directly across from me was Lord St. Clair, engaged in conversation with Mr. Ainsley on his left, followed by Lord Perry, Victor Tallarico, and Doctor Pitcairn.

A trio of footmen came in carrying an unexpected treat. For our amusement, the Prince's pastry chef, obviously not a Frenchman, had made a delightful confection. On each plate stood a spun-sugar frog, coloured green, complete with raisins for eyes, looking ready to leap from our plates. Frenchmen are commonly called Frogs, you know.

The Prince laughed uproariously at the chef's sense of humour. "We must have no fear of the Frogs, gentlemen. Instead we shall eat Napoleon and all the Frenchies alive if they come to invade us."

Everyone joined in the laughter as port was poured into glasses.

Petersham had no sooner sat down than he sprang back up. "My snuff box!" He retrieved it from the sideboard and took his seat. "Before we devour these Frogs, your Royal Highness, you must try my new snuff."

"Pass it this way at once," Prinny commanded jovially.

With great ceremony, Petersham passed the box to Sir Simon, who passed it to me. I was about to hand it to the Prince, when suddenly, Sir Simon reached across and snatched the box out of my hand. Everyone looked at the baronet expectantly.

Sir Simon bounced in his chair—rather like the toad he was—hopping up and down. "You cannot be too careful, your Royal Highness. For your safety, I insist on trying it first."

"Egad," Petersham protested to the Prince. "I wanted you to be the first to try my new blend, sir."

Sir Simon clutched the snuff box. "Your Royal Highness, you must allow me to take a pinch of the snuff first. After all, we cannot have you succumb in front of the Frogs."

Good God, frogs on our plates and a toadeater at our table. I half expected to wake up and find myself on the banks of a stream, watching Sir Simon on his lily pad.

Did he really think Viscount Petersham would poison the Prince? No, he just wanted another opportunity to fawn over Prinny.

However, I seemed to be the only one with uncharitable thoughts toward the baronet. Except Petersham and Munro, everyone else, including the Prince, was chuckling at Sir Simon's jest.

"Go on then, Sir Simon," Prinny said. "Take a pinch, then pass the box along to me."

On center stage now, the baronet placed a line of snuff on the back of his hand, raised it to his nose, and inhaled deeply.

He turned a triumphant face to us, red lips grinning.

Then his eyes bulged. The snuff box slipped from his fingers, bouncing from the table down to the carpet, particles of snuff flying.

Sir Simon's breath came in rapid gasps, an ugly sound.

The laughter around the table died.

Abruptly, Sir Simon's hand went to his throat. He made a final choking sound, then keeled over, his head crushing the frog confection on his plate with a loud clatter.

8

"*Oh, dear God,*" the Prince uttered.

Sir Simon's two brutish footmen rushed to their master.

The baronet's eyes stared sightlessly at me. I quickly reached over, thinking to untie his lace cravat, but Doctor Pitcairn was around the table in a flash. "Good thinking, Mr. Brummell, but I shall see to him." He waved the footmen away and examined Sir Simon.

The stunned silence that had prevailed until now broke.

"Is he dead?" Lord Perry asked.

"What a shame," Signor Tallarico said without a hint of sorrow.

"Must be dead," Lord St. Clair concluded precisely.

"If he is dead, he has died a hero," observed Mr. Ainsley with a piercing glance at the Prince. "He saved the Heir Apparent."

The Prince's eyes rounded, and his mouth opened and closed, little moans escaping him.

"Let us not jump to conclusions," I said with as much composure as I could muster. "Sir Simon is of a certain age, and, not to put too fine a point on it, has just consumed a large amount of food and drink. Perhaps he has suffered a heart seizure."

"Too bad, though it would be dishonest for me to say I liked the fellow. All that jasmine scent he wore, you know. Likely to bring on one of my sneezing fits," Lord Petersham commented.

"Petersham," I said rather sharply, "let us be quiet now and let the doctor do his job." Dash it all, did the lazy viscount not realize the implications of this event? Sir Simon's attack had come upon partaking of *Petersham's* snuff.

Apparently, though, the viscount was oblivious. "Well, I don't mean to sound unfeeling, but you didn't like him either, did you, Brummell?"

I experienced a sudden urge to whip my neckcloth from around my throat and stuff it in Petersham's mouth to silence him.

"I say, where is my snuff box?" Petersham went on blithely. "Pitcairn has things in control here. I've a mind to join the ladies. Get away from this unpleasantness, if his Royal Highness agrees."

But Prinny's eyes were fixed on Sir Simon as if envisioning that the baronet's condition might well have been his own fate. His shock could not have been greater if someone had slapped him.

"I see the snuff box on the floor under Sir Simon's chair," Lord Munro said. "I'll get it for you, Charles."

"I am afraid you must not, my lord," Doctor Pitcairn said, his examination of the baronet complete. "The magistrate will want nothing moved. Sir Simon is dead. It was not a heart seizure. He was the victim of a strong poison."

Several people glanced in Petersham's direction. I felt a surge of outrage that a life had been taken right in front of me.

The Prince of Wales began to sob into his hands. "Someone tried to kill me. God help us. Maria, Maria, I need Maria. Oh, God, I could be the one dead."

I rose and helped him to his feet. "Come, sir, I shall see you to your chamber. Word will be sent to Mrs. Fitzherbert. Her current illness is not contagious, is it?" I inquired more to take his mind away from Sir Simon than anything.

"No, no, a mere disorder of the stomach. Send for her, Brummell, do. Oh, how my pulse gallops," the Prince moaned.

I had never seen him so agitated.

I looked toward Doctor Pitcairn. "Perhaps it would be best for you to see to the Prince. I shall send for Mrs. Fitzherbert and the magistrate, as well, and then join you."

Doctor Pitcairn nodded his agreement to the plan.

"Not that fool Kearley," the Prince protested weakly. He leaned against me, and I supported his weight. "Jack Townsend. I want Jack Townsend here. He's the principal officer in the Bow Street Police Office in London and handles all matters relating to the royal family. Send for him. And no one is to leave Brighton," he ended, his gaze resting for the briefest of moments on Lord Petersham.

"You may rely upon me, sir," I assured him.

"Can I?" the Prince regarded me dubiously. He waved a plump hand to encompass the room, complete with dead body. He cut me a desperate look before Doctor Pitcairn led him away, followed by a retinue of footmen.

I felt the sinking sensation of despair. Did the Prince of Wales think I could have prevented what happened here tonight? Worse, did he think Petersham responsible?

Despite the Prince's request for Jack Townsend, Mr. Kearley had to be informed of the assassination attempt. After all, it was a six- or seven-hour ride to London. Mr. Townsend could not be expected to arrive until one or two the following afternoon. We could not wait that long for an official to take a report on Sir Simon's death.

I gave orders for one footman to run to Mrs. Fitzherbert's and another to Mr. Kearley's. This done, I turned to the gentlemen. "We should join the ladies and break the news."

Everyone rose stiffly, averting their eyes from where Sir Simon lay slumped over the table. The baronet's two burly footmen were standing over his body, grim-faced. Not even the odious Sir Simon deserved to be murdered.

"You must watch over your master until the magistrate arrives. Do not move him," I told them. Then, motioning to one of the Prince's footmen, I said, "Remain here. See that nothing in this room is touched, especially that snuff box," I directed, pointing at the box, open and lying on its side on the Persian carpet.

"What about my snuff box, Brummell? You can't expect me to leave it abandoned on the floor," Petersham complained.

I took him by the arm and spoke in a low voice. "You had best not say another word about that snuff box. Do you not see that people will think it was the snuff that was poisoned?"

Petersham looked at me as if I had sprouted another head. "Fiddle-faddle! Why would they think that?"

Making sure to keep my voice as soft as possible I said, "Because it is the most plausible explanation. The snuff is the only thing that Sir Simon was alone in consuming. All the food and drink was shared amongst us."

"But I mixed the snuff myself," Petersham said, obviously bewildered.

Struggling for composure I said; "I know. So does everyone else, for you said it was a new, special blend the Prince must be the first to try."

A sudden thought occurred to me. Could Petersham have unknowingly mixed a poisonous blend? I needed to speak with Doctor Pitcairn to find out if that was possible.

"If there was poison in that snuff, someone else put it in there. At any rate, who would want to poison my snuff?" Petersham said incredulously. "I don't have any enemies. Takes too much effort to make people angry."

"The poison was meant for the Prince, not you, my friend."

"Oh," Petersham replied. "That makes more sense."

I heaved a sigh. It was clear the viscount felt no responsibility for the tainted snuff and could not see how others might think differently.

Before I could say more, Lord Munro placed a possessive hand on Petersham's sleeve. "Charles, let us go

into the Saloon and have another drink. We can collect
the snuff box later." He shot an accusatory glare in my
direction before leaving the room, Petersham in tow, as
if I were somehow at fault for the evening's events.
Sometimes I cannot help but associate the phrase "devil's spawn" with Lord Munro.

On my way down the Long Gallery to find Freddie
and tell her what had happened, my pace suddenly
slowed. Petersham's denial that anyone would want to
poison him rang in my head. Could it be that the poisoned snuff was indeed intended for Petersham? I discarded the idea almost instantly. The viscount was
correct in that he possessed not a single enemy.

I recalled that the snuff box had remained unattended
on the sideboard, prominently displayed on top of the
epergne. Assuming Petersham had tried the snuff before
putting the box into his pocket and coming to the dining
room—and I would have to ask him if he had done so—
then the killer would have had to have added the poison
sometime afterward.

I thought back over the evening. Petersham had
placed the box on the sideboard while everyone was already seated at the table. Everyone had remained seated
while the ladies were present, but once the ladies had
withdrawn to the Saloon, the gentlemen had moved
freely about the room. Any of them could have slipped
a poison into the snuff box at that time.

Including Arthur Ainsley.

I remembered how last night Petersham had declared
that the Prince would be the first to try his new snuff.
Several people heard him say so, including the resentful
Arthur Ainsley.

Then, just before we ate, Petersham had again announced that his new blend was ready for the Prince to try. If the killer had been biding his time, carrying a snug little vial of a poisonous powder, waiting for an opportunity to poison the Prince, what better chance would he have than to place the poison in the snuff?

Questions swirled in my head as I entered the circular Saloon. One thing was certain: Whoever had caused Sir Simon's death must be held accountable for their actions.

Victor Tallarico sat on a small settee with a distraught Lady Bessborough. The Italian held a vinaigrette in one hand, offering it to the lady. She nodded gratefully, and he waved the tiny silver box under her nose, then handed her a glass of wine. Obviously, it did not matter that Lady Bessborough possessed a daughter, Caroline Lamb, not much younger than Signor Tallarico. He could charm a lady of any age.

Across the room, Petersham and Munro huddled together downing a bottle of Madeira and admiring an ormolu-and-porcelain clock.

Arthur Ainsley stood alone brooding by the fireplace. This presented me with a good opportunity to question him, but the sight of Freddie, ashen-faced and surrounded by Lord and Lady Perry and Lord St. Clair, caused me to temporarily abandon any thoughts of speaking with Mr. Ainsley. I surmised Lady St. Clair had taken her daughters to their rooms.

"Two deaths in one day. If this continues, Brighton shall have only seagulls for visitors," I said wryly. Managing to position myself next to Freddie, I gazed reassuringly at her. She favoured me with a warm look, but I could tell she was concerned for her brother-in-law.

"Unrelated though the deaths were, they are both

tragic," Lady Perry said. Lord Perry had a supportive arm about her waist. I would wager he did not share his wife's view where Sir Simon's death was concerned. But then, she did not know of the baronet's ugly remarks about her nor about her husband's subsequent challenge.

Lord St. Clair looked skeptical. "With all due respect for Doctor Pitcairn, I wonder if he is mistaken about this being a case of poisoning. Sir Simon was a fine fellow, doing his best to serve his country and such, but he did have a great fondness for rich food. Mr. Brummell, I cannot help but think your initial assessment of a heart seizure might be accurate."

"If it was Sir Simon's heart, the Prince would certainly be easier in his mind," I said. "Rest assured, my lord, I intend to question Doctor Pitcairn and find out how he knows it was poison." Privately, though, I did not doubt Pitcairn's conclusion.

"Speaking of rest, I am taking Lady Perry home," Lord Perry announced.

"Anthony, I am quite well. If I might just sit down," she said, brushing a curl from her eye. Her hand lingered at her temple to rub it lightly.

"We shall see you in the morning. If Mr. Kearley wants to question anyone tonight, give him my direction, Brummell." Perry firmly led his wife away amongst murmured wishes for a good night.

"If you will excuse us, Lord St. Clair," I said. "I must go to the Prince. I am persuaded the Duchess of York would like to accompany me."

Lord St. Clair bowed to Freddie. "Of course." He turned and went to join Arthur Ainsley.

I looked at Freddie. "Have I done right? You do wish to see the Prince?"

"Exactly so, dear," Freddie replied. "I do not know how it is sometimes that you are able to see the thoughts in my mind. Let us go to his chamber at once."

She took my arm, and I led the way, feeling an absurd sense of satisfaction at Freddie's words. But now was not the time to indulge in such thoughts.

Double the previous number of guards stood outside the Prince's bedchamber. Inside, more armed guards were ready to defend the Heir Apparent.

We found the Prince, attended by Doctor Pitcairn, propped up in bed on half-a-dozen pillows and clad in a paisley dressing gown. The bed, which one could only reach by climbing a few steps, was hung with green silk, with a green-and-white checked silk lining.

Mrs. Fitzherbert, a beautiful woman with brown eyes and a rose complexion, sat in a chair by the side of the bed, holding the royal hand. Doctor Pitcairn had the other, taking the Prince's pulse. At our entrance, Mrs. Fitzherbert stood and dropped a deep curtsey for Freddie.

"Good evening, Mrs. Fitzherbert. How kind of you to leave your own sickbed to give the Prince comfort," I said and bowed, observing out of the corner of my eye that Freddie gave Mrs. Fitzherbert a curt nod. The Prince's "marriage" to Mrs. Fitzherbert is not acknowledged by the royal family, of which Freddie is a member. Freddie is too kind a person to cut Mrs. Fitzherbert, as some other members of the royal family do. Personally, while I cannot condone the Prince having two "wives," I believe Mrs. Fitzherbert has a good influence on Prinny, reining in some of his wilder impulses. God knows, someone must.

Mrs. Fitzherbert gazed fondly at the Prince. "I came at once, of course."

Freddie addressed the Prince. "I am told you have sent for Jack Townsend. He will help, I am sure."

"Thank you, Frederica. I only hope you are right," Prinny said.

"This has been a terrible night. To think someone here at the Pavilion would wish the Prince of Wales harm. It is beyond all reason," Mrs. Fitzherbert said, indignation in every word.

"If it were not for Sir Simon, I would be the one dead," the Prince reiterated, groaning. Mrs. Fitzherbert glanced at him sympathetically and patted his hand.

Here was my cue. "Doctor Pitcairn, I cannot help but admire the rapid way you concluded Sir Simon had been poisoned. How did you do it?"

Doctor Pitcairn released the Prince's hand. "Your pulse is returning to normal, your Royal Highness." The respected doctor looked at me, then gathered instruments into his bag. "As to the poison, in my opinion, it was Prussic acid. A distinct odour of bitter almonds, combined with the blueness of Sir Simon's mouth and the speed with which the death occurred, leaves me in no doubt."

So much for a heart seizure. Or an accident.

"Oh, do stop speaking of it," the Prince cried. "What shall I do now that there is a killer at the Pavilion? How can I leave my room? How shall I eat without Sir Simon testing my food?"

Mrs. Fitzherbert dipped a lace handkerchief in a bowl of water and tenderly stroked Prinny's brow.

Freddie looked at me. In a low voice, she said,

"George, what can be done? Will the Prince be safe here?"

"He has enough guards. He can appoint one of them to be food taster," I responded. "I barely know Jack Townsend, but—"

"What are you saying, Brummell?" the Prince demanded. "Do you know something? After all, it was your friend Petersham's snuff which caused all this."

Everyone in the room was suddenly very still.

Suspicion fell on Petersham, just as I had feared it would.

"Sir," I said earnestly, "I know for a certainty that Lord Petersham could have had nothing to do with this. He and I have been friends for years. He is simply not capable, nor would he have reason to harm you. He is your friend as well as mine."

The Prince sat in his bed, looking as miserable as a child with a putrid throat kept indoors on a fine day. "Friend or no, it was his snuff box and his snuff. I don't know whom to trust. These past days have made me doubt my own judgement. I don't know if even Jack Townsend's skills will be enough to get to the bottom of this." Prinny began to cry.

Mrs. Fitzherbert soothed him.

Freddie stood beside me, looking up at me with her china-blue eyes. You may call me silly, but I believed she was waiting for me to offer my help. Indeed, I felt she expected it of me.

And I confess, I was feeling a bit puffed up with my own consequence after having recently solved another case of murder. The process had not been easy, but perhaps I could do it again.

And there was Petersham to think of.

I cleared my throat. "Sir, I give you my word of honour as a gentleman that I shall find out what is going on. I shall do everything in my power to uncover the killer."

Freddie gazed at me approvingly.

The Prince's tears ceased, and he fixed me with an unwavering glare. "No matter who he is?"

"No matter who he is," I promised.

Considering what happened in the ensuing days, I have to wonder if standing in front of a fire-eating dragon might not have been a better course of action.

9

Despite the fact that it was nearly three in the morning before I retired, I did not sleep well. At one point, I pulled out the portable writing desk I always have nearby and made a list of everyone present at the Johnstones' when Petersham first spoke about his new blend of snuff. Then I made another list, this one of the people present at dinner last night.

Satisfied, I returned to bed only to toss the covers aside once more. Pulling out another sheet of paper, I made a diagram of the seating arrangements both before and after dinner.

Chakkri slept through all my tossing, turning, and getting in and out of bed. I vow the cat is determined to snub me for bringing him to Brighton, not to mention my petting Humphrey.

I slumbered until nine. Pulling the bed hangings aside, I was about to summon Robinson, when I spotted him sitting in a chair by the fire.

He sprang to attention. "Good morning, sir. Er, well,

that is not quite accurate, is it, with the tragedy of last night casting a shadow over the Pavilion?" The valet's eyes were bright with curiosity. No doubt the servants' hall had been abuzz with gossip.

"A devilish bad business," I said noncommittally, wondering what he knew.

"They all think Viscount Petersham tried to poison his Royal Highness, but I told them they had windmills in their heads. My lord would have no reason to wish the Prince harm."

"That was good of you. I am sure Diggie would appreciate your defense of his employer."

Robinson stiffened at the mention of Diggie. "Mr. Digwood was not my concern. Although I did hear that he is guarding Viscount Petersham's house like a watchdog. He resembles a bulldog, come to think of it."

You may know that Petersham's valet, Mr. Digwood, or Diggie as he is called, and Robinson have a long-held rivalry. The enmity is made worse by the fact that Diggie tends to lord it over—if I may use that expression—Robinson's head that Petersham is a viscount while I am a plain mister.

On the other hand, Diggie knows that Petersham would replace him with Robinson if he could, a fact Robinson invariably uses to try to win the occasional disagreement with me. Most recently, he utilized it when trying to persuade me to return Chakkri to Siam.

I ignored Robinson's pique. "Such devotion can only be to Diggie's credit. Will you bring me some tea? Perhaps a few rolls to go along with it. And ask the footmen to hurry with my bath. I wish to bathe without delay."

"Very good, sir," Robinson said. He bowed, and with a back so rigid you could have bounced a ball off it, exited the room, disappointed. I was sorry for him, but had no time to gratify his need for scandalous details.

I had decided to begin my investigation that very morning.

While it might risk our friendship, the first thing to do was speak to Petersham as soon as possible. Even if it meant storming Diggie's defenses.

The viscount never leaves his house before six in the evening, and seldom rises from bed earlier than three in the afternoon. But this day would have to be an exception, no matter what.

I needed to try to impress upon Petersham the gravity of the situation he was in, and also try to find out if he had tested the snuff before bringing it to the dining room last evening. This would help narrow the period of time in which someone could have added the poison to the box.

I deemed it imperative to review the events with Petersham before Jack Townsend began questioning him. The lazy viscount might end up incriminating himself by failing to defend his snuff.

Robinson returned with the tea. I had only consumed one cup when the footmen brought in my bath. Nevertheless, I put aside my breakfast and bathed while the water was hot. As you know, I am a strong believer in daily baths, a conviction not shared by all my fellow members of Society, much to my dismay.

Afterwards, I had just donned my Florentine dressing gown and seated myself at the dressing table when Chakkri woke. The cat stretched his long, fawn-coloured body and greeted me with a faint "Reow."

"Joined the land of the living, have you, Chakkri?" I said. Then, to Robinson, "Bring me another cup of tea, will you? I am always thirsty after consuming as much wine as I did last night."

"Yes, sir. As to last night—"

He got no further. As Robinson reached for the tea-pot, Chakkri bounded from his spot on the bed, leaped across the table containing the teacup and my rolls, and sent the cup flying to the floor, where it shattered on the carpet. Robinson held the teapot high out of reach.

The cat never acknowledged the destruction he had caused. Instead, he walked calmly to the window to say good morning to his seagull friends.

Robinson *tsk*ed, glared at the cat, and began cleaning up the mess.

I sat in open-mouthed astonishment. The feline was not in charity with me, true. But Chakkri was a graceful creature if there ever was one. It was not like him to be clumsy. Why had he knocked the teacup over?

Just before one o'clock, I made my way across the grassy Steine to the house Petersham and Munro were leasing. On the way, I bowed to Lady Kincade, a young matron in Society, and to the Creeveys, who were accompanied by Lady Bessborough. The latter was no doubt sharing every salacious component of the previous evening.

Smelling the sea air, my thoughts turned to the young girl found dead on the beach yesterday. Now everyone's efforts would be concentrated on finding the attempted assassin of the Prince of Wales. Her death would fade into obscurity.

Or so I thought.

The breeze picked up the folds of my black velvet

greatcoat. The weather had grown colder today and no sun shone.

I rapped on Petersham's door with the handle of my new dog's head cane, the one Freddie had given me.

Mr. Digwood answered my knock. He is a portly fellow with brown eyes that tend to bulge. I fashioned my expression into one of apologetic chagrin. "Now, Diggie, I know precisely what you are going to say. Lord Petersham is still abed at this early hour."

"Indeed, sir. My lord is not receiving—"

I crossed the threshold and handed Diggie my things. He looked aghast. "I am afraid I cannot announce you," he said.

I held up a forestalling hand. "You are simply going to have to look the other way while I make my way upstairs."

Diggie's eyes popped. "It could mean my position, sir."

"Nothing of the sort, I assure you. I will tell Petersham that you had no choice in the matter, which you do not. It is for his own good."

Diggie spluttered, but I ascended the stairs, hoping I would not run across Lord Munro. Why had I not asked which room belonged to Petersham?

Sighing, I slowly eased open the door at the top of the stairs, muttering a prayer that it was Petersham's and that he was alone. A quick glance inside told me I had the room I wanted.

Snoring at the top of his lungs, Petersham lay sprawled on his back in a four-poster bed. Thankfully, I had not had to peer behind bedcurtains to ascertain if the body sleeping in the bed was his.

I approached the bed, stopped about a foot away and said, "Petersham, wake up."

Snore.

"Petersham!"

Snore.

Fortunately I had retained my dog's head cane. I used it to tap Petersham on the arm. "Wake up, old friend!"

An assortment of snorts and sniffles later, the viscount opened his eyes, shielding them from the light with a linen-clad arm. "Egad, Brummell, is that you? Where's Diggie? Is the house on fire? Tell him to put it out."

"No, the house is not on fire. Try as he might, Diggie could not stop me from coming up. I need to speak to you."

"Oh," Petersham said. He turned on his side and shut his eyes.

"Petersham!" I employed the cane again.

"What the devil is it?" he asked, running a hand through his hair. "Is it the Frenchies? Are we invaded?"

"No. I want to talk to you about the snuff box."

"Love it dearly," he mumbled sleepily. "Munro gave it to me. Go away now, Brummell. I'm trying to sleep."

"You cannot sleep now. We have to talk."

Petersham opened an eye and glanced at the bedside clock. The eye opened a fraction wider. "Is that one in the afternoon? You're mad. Come back in about four hours."

"We dare not wait that long. Jack Townsend will be in Brighton before then and ready to question you. We need to discuss the new blend of snuff you mixed and then placed in the new box. Did you try it before you brought it down to dinner?"

Snore.

My patience tried, I tossed my cane on a nearby chair, sat on the edge of the bed, leaned over, and grasped Petersham by the shoulders. I pulled him to an upright position and glared into his startled face. "You nodcock, I am trying to help you! Sir Simon is *dead*. Had he not been first to try the snuff *you* mixed, the *Prince of Wales* would be dead. The most renowned of the Bow Street Police officers is on his way to the Pavilion to investigate. Do you understand? Your snuff has *killed* someone. *Will* you talk to me?"

A trifle more conscious, Petersham said, "Very well, Brummell, I shall do as you ask."

At that moment, the door to the adjoining room crashed open and Lord Munro stood framed in the portal. His gaze swept over me as I sat on Petersham's bed, holding the viscount about the shoulders.

"And what exactly has Mr. Brummell asked you to do, Charles?" Lord Munro inquired in a dangerous voice.

I rose with dignity and faced Lord Munro. Clad only in an expensive pair of breeches—I recognize cashmere when I see it—he had clearly been woken from his sleep and donned the first available article of clothing. It was also clear he was furious.

I felt my own temper surge. Time was running out. Jack Townsend could arrive in Brighton at any time. "Lord Munro, I have an urgent matter to discuss with Petersham. Please excuse us."

Lord Munro glanced at Petersham. The viscount was in the process of settling himself back under the bedclothes, his eyes closing.

"Charles doesn't converse at this hour. If you were

truly his friend, you would know that," Lord Munro said frostily.

"Dash it! Damn and blast," I said. "Do neither of you comprehend the enormity of what is happening here? Petersham, sit up at once and tell me whether you tried any of that snuff before bringing it to the Pavilion."

Petersham gave a cavernous yawn. "Brummell, I can't think properly when I haven't had enough sleep."

"Go back to sleep now, Charles," Lord Munro advised.

"Right. Eh, Brummell, you're worrying about all this too much. Sir Simon's death must have been an accident. No one will think me responsible. I'm a viscount, a peer of the realm. Don't trouble yourself with it." His eyes shut.

Lord Munro took a step toward me. "I'll thank you to leave. You have disturbed Charles enough."

"He is not as disturbed as he will be once Jack Townsend begins questioning him," I ground out.

Lord Munro's eyes narrowed. "I can't for the life of me think of why everyone admires you, Brummell. I hear you bathe in milk."

I stood with my head to one side. Milk? To bathe in? What a repugnant notion. But I am used to people making up the most ridiculous stories about me. I do not know why this latest one should surprise me. That Lord Munro believed it true told me something about his character.

I was playing with the idea of confirming the story, and confiding that the milk came from a particular cow in Green Park who was fed roses so that the milk might be perfumed, when raised voices from the hall interrupted us. I recognized Robinson's voice as one of them.

The door swung open and Robinson stepped inside. His hair, normally in strict control, stood out from his head. But this was nothing compared to Diggie, who was breathing hard and quite red about the face and neck.

"What the devil?" I exclaimed.

"My lord," Diggie said to Lord Munro, his breath coming in gasps. "I have tried to protect the peace of this house, but this person—" here he shot a look of loathing at Robinson "—pushed me, I say he *pushed* me out of the way. No *true* gentleman's gentleman would behave thus, as I am certain you would agree, my lord."

Petersham snored away.

Lord Munro's face was a study in agitation.

Robinson paid not the slightest attention. Instead, he addressed me. "Sir, I thought you would wish to be apprised of the arrival at the Pavilion of Jack Townsend. Also, the Prince is asking for you."

Without another word, I picked up my cane and walked from the room. The fat was in the fire now.

❧ 10 ❧

After passing an army of guards, I entered the
Prince of Wales's bedchamber to find a number of persons present. My jaw almost dropped when I beheld one
of them, but I shall tell you about that in a minute.

Dinner guests were to be questioned regarding the
previous evening's events. The Prince, apparently too
sick from worry to rise from his bed, but determined to
be present at the inquisition, as it were, held court in his
bedchamber.

He sat propped up in his raised bed, wrapped in a
purple robe, a starched white neckcloth cascading in
front, his cherry brandy on a table near to hand. He
clutched a Brussels lace handkerchief that I knew with
a certainty cost forty-five guineas.

Mrs. Fitzherbert sat in a chair by his side, a pretty
shawl around her shoulders, ready to support her "husband" in any way.

Jack Townsend, now well over forty years of age and
for many years with the Bow Street Police Office, stood

next to a rosewood desk with his hands clasped behind his back. "Beau Brummell!" he exclaimed in a hearty voice. "I haven't clapped eyes on you since that sunny day during the last Brighton racing season. Made a tidy sum, didn't you?"

"Mr. Townsend, good afternoon," I said by way of greeting. "As to my winnings at the race, they would hardly be enough to cover the cost of a new coat. Done in the first style, that is." I eyed his clothing, a gesture that did not escape the sharp little rotund man's notice.

"What think you of my costume?" he asked, holding his arms out to display his white coat. I raised my quizzing glass. His breeches were also white, and he sported a flaxen wig. A white hat with a broad ribbon around the huge brim sat on the edge of the desk.

"You are a pearl amongst men," I prevaricated, letting the glass fall to my chest.

He bellowed with laughter. "Ah, and you're a knowing one. I count many knowing ones among my acquaintances." He grinned, then his countenance sobered. "But we're here today on a matter that doesn't induce mirth, does it? Our Prince narrowly escaped being put to bed with a shovel—ah," he interrupted himself. "Forgive me, I slip into cant too often. I meant that but for the sacrifice of Sir Simon, an assassin would have accomplished his aim."

A moan came from the bed. Mrs. Fitzherbert patted Prinny's hand.

Mr. Townsend nodded gravely. "His Royal Highness insisted you be present during my questioning of the guests present, Mr. Brummell. I've already discussed the poisoning with the good Doctor Pitcairn and know how Sir Simon died. Now we need to find out who put the poison in the snuff box. The Prince informs me that you are to help us discover the villain."

"I shall do my best." The knowledge did not seem to affect the head of the Bow Street Police Office one way or another. But then, as he had just said, Mr. Townsend likes associating with the upper circles of Society.

His colleague, on the other hand, did not seem in the least bit pleased at my arrival. That man's complexion turned a dull red, and the freckles on his face darkened.

"I've brought along a man from my office to assist us. This is John Lavender," Mr. Townsend informed me. He gestured to the other side of the desk where the stockily built Scotsman, whose bristly red hair was going to grey, stood.

He need not have performed the introductions. I am already acquainted with Mr. Lavender. He was the Bow Street investigator assigned to the case of murder I had recently solved. My involvement in that incident had chafed the Bow Street man, to put it mildly. My acquaintance with his daughter did not sit well with the Scotsman either.

I hold a grudging respect for Mr. Lavender's dedication to his work, but he has a way of shaking his finger at me, usually during a warning to stay out of his business, that I cannot like. In addition, he always sports the same—unless he has a wardrobe full of them—salt-and-pepper game coat over worn corduroy breeches and scratched top boots. Worse, he wears bushy side whiskers and an enormous mustache. Frequently, a crumb of oatcake can be found in the latter.

"Good afternoon, Mr. Lavender," I said blandly. I could not help but hope he held his tongue as to the nature of our past dealings. I did not want it known in Society that I had worked with Bow Street. My reputation as a foolish dandy might suffer, you know.

"Mr. Brummell," the Scotsman said casually enough, but the slight burring of the *r* in my name gave away his annoyance at my presence. Still, he seemed no more eager than I to reveal our knowledge of one another.

"Now, the first thing I need to know is who exactly was present at dinner last evening," Mr. Townsend said, approaching the royal bed.

Mr. Lavender produced a tattered notebook.

The Prince took a swallow of brandy. "Hard to think clearly, Townsend. I've been in a muddle since everything happened."

Mr. Townsend nodded, the yellow curls remaining in stiff place. "Understandable, sir, understandable."

"I can tell you," I said.

Mr. Townsend swung around to face me. "By all means, do so, Mr. Brummell," he cried with a smile.

"To begin—" I started.

"We won't be needing a description of what everyone was wearing. Just their names," Mr. Lavender interrupted, a stub of a pencil poised over the notebook.

As though I would resort to such an unnecessary narrative! I took a deep breath. "Besides his Royal Highness and myself, there was the Duchess of York, Lord and Lady Perry, Lady Bessborough—I am not going too quickly for you, Mr. Lavender, am I?"

"Continue," was the terse reply.

"Lords Petersham and Munro, Signor Tallarico, Doctor Pitcairn, Arthur Ainsley, Lord and Lady St. Clair, and their two daughters. Oh, and Sir Simon, of course."

"The hero of the evening," Mr. Townsend pronounced.

"God rest his soul," the Prince murmured, then took another swallow of brandy. Mrs. Fitzherbert removed the empty glass from his hand and put it firmly on the table. Prinny might remember things a little better if sober.

"Is everyone on this list present at the Pavilion?" Mr. Lavender asked.

"No. Lord and Lady Perry have returned to their rented house in Brighton, as have Lords Petersham and Munro," I responded.

Mr. Lavender's bushy eyebrows came together. "What a pity witnesses were allowed to leave the scene of the crime."

"Everyone is still in Brighton, I assure you."

"Your assurances mean everything to me, Mr. Brummell," Mr. Lavender said. "Mr. Townsend, we'll be questioning these people now, won't we?"

"Yes, Lavender. You," he said pointing to a footman. "You will consult with my associate, request the presence of all the people on the list, and have them assembled in the Long Gallery. No sense in telling them they can't talk to one another. They've had all night."

The footman hurried to Mr. Lavender's side.

Mr. Townsend addressed the Prince. "We need not involve the local magistrate, Mr. Kearley, any further, had we?"

"No, indeed not," the Prince proclaimed. "He's a simpleton and has his hands full with a local matter. A drowned girl."

"A murdered girl," I reminded him.

Prinny looked annoyed. "Brummell, how can you pick over small points when we are discussing an attempt on my life?"

I shook my head in a manner that suggested I could not possibly be in my right mind to have thought of anything but his Royal Highness.

Mr. Townsend said, "Lord and Lady St. Clair visiting, eh? I know his lordship, a fine orator in Parliament from all accounts. I'd value his opinion on what is going on here."

He had his opportunity a few minutes later as Lord and Lady St. Clair were escorted into the room. Lady St. Clair, dressed impeccably, stood to the side as her husband greeted the men. Amidst much bowing, Mr. Townsend managed to elicit Lord St. Clair's opinions.

I took up a position next to the fireplace to listen, a short distance away from where Mr. Lavender stood with his notebook.

"I have thought this matter over carefully," Lord St. Clair said slowly. "And I find that I hesitate to point a finger at anyone without hard evidence of his or her guilt. Doing so would be irresponsible, since I saw no one put anything in the snuff box."

"Admirable sentiments, St. Clair," Prinny said, impatiently. "But give us your opinion anyway."

Lord St. Clair could do naught but answer. "Well, then, I think that though he seems the logical suspect, Lord Petersham cannot be responsible. He simply has no motive."

I gazed upon his lordship in admiration. Thank God someone else would come to Petersham's defense.

Lord St. Clair continued, "In light of the fact that Napoleon, already Emperor of France, crowned himself

King of Italy last May, I say it is deuced odd to suddenly find an Italian, namely Victor Tallarico, in our midst."

I repressed a groan.

The Prince and Mr. Townsend looked at one another. "He has an excellent point, your Royal Highness," the head of Bow Street said.

Prinny grimaced. "I knew it! Did I not tell you there were threats to me from foreign soil, Brummell?"

I struggled to maintain my famous cool countenance. "You did, indeed, sir. But in the case of Signor Tallarico, I must say that Lord St. Clair cannot be remembering that the Italian is Lord Perry's cousin."

"Unfortunately, I do remember," Lord St. Clair said regretfully. "And while I agree wholeheartedly that Tallarico is from a good family, I must point out that the two men have not seen each other for years. That fact, combined with a lack of other suspects, forces me to consider him as suspect. I grant you, though such an action might be repellent to Tallarico's good bloodlines, perhaps the new environment of Napoleon's influence may have been enough to sway a weak man to new opinions."

"A wise deduction, my lord, and one that merits our scrutiny," Mr. Townsend said approvingly. "We are in your debt."

Lord St. Clair held up a hand. "Again, I must repeat that I have no evidence on which to base my speculations, and that they are merely that: speculations."

"We are grateful, St. Clair," the Prince said, then turned to Lady St. Clair. "Do you have anything to add to what your husband has told us?"

Lady St. Clair looked surprised to have her opinion consulted. "No, your Royal Highness."

"You will ask your daughters if they saw or heard anything that may be of use to us?" Mr. Townsend asked.

"I already have," Lady St. Clair said in a tone that implied she would never do less than her duty. "Neither Lady Prudence nor Lady Chastity observed anything suspicious."

Lord and Lady Perry were brought in after the St. Clairs took their leave. Lady Perry, I noticed, seemed extraordinarily pale, and clung heavily to her husband's arm. During the introductions, Perry glanced over the assembled company, his gaze suddenly shifting from me, then back to Mr. Lavender. He probably remembered my mentioning Mr. Lavender during the previous murder investigation.

With some annoyance, Perry said, "Look here, I do not mind answering any questions, but my wife is in a delicate condition."

Lady Perry turned to him. "It is all right, Anthony. Please, Mr. Townsend, ask us what you wish to know."

"Anything you can think of, dear lady, to help us determine who put the poison in the snuff box with the intention of killing the Prince."

A choking sound came from the area of the bed.

Mrs. Fitzherbert relented and poured Prinny a small amount of brandy. He downed it in one gulp.

"I saw nothing, not even the effect the contents of the snuff box had on poor Sir Simon," Lady Perry said. "The ladies had already withdrawn to the Saloon."

"Poor Sir Simon?" her husband repeated. "The man was a blackguard."

"What do you mean by that?" Mr. Lavender broke in.

Perry paused. I think he realized that he would now have to explain how he had challenged Sir Simon to a duel after the baronet had made disparaging remarks about pregnant women. He looked at his wife in dismay. Likely, he could not bring himself to speak of something so callous in front of Lady Perry. He said, "I could not like the way the man was such a sycophant where his Royal Highness was concerned."

"He saved my life!" Prinny cried.

"Of course we must be grateful to him for that," Perry allowed.

"Lord Perry, I'd like to ask a few questions about your cousin, Victor Tallarico," Mr. Townsend said.

"Victor? Why Victor?" Lady Perry inquired, her hand going to her throat. "What about him?"

"Nothing to be alarmed about," Mr. Townsend hastened to assure her. "We just don't know much about him since he's new to England, isn't he?"

Lord Perry was not fooled. He seemed to perceive at once in what direction the Bow Street man's thoughts were going, and spoke in a manner that let Mr. Townsend know he was speaking to an earl with three income-producing estates. "Victor Tallarico is a rogue with the ladies. Nothing more. He has no political ambitions. Neither my wife nor I saw anyone put anything in that snuff box. We know of no one who would wish the Prince of Wales harm. Should you have further questions, you may contact me at my Town house in Grosvenor Square. The air in Brighton no longer seems beneficial to my wife's health."

Without another word, Perry bowed to the Prince, then took his wife's arm and led her from the room.

"Defensive, wasn't he?" Prinny asked the company in general.

"Very much so," Mr. Lavender concurred.

"He may have been insulted. Or he is hiding something about that cousin of his," Mr. Townsend mused. "You will question him further, Lavender."

"Count on it," the Scotsman replied.

"Sir," I said, addressing the Prince. "What of Arthur Ainsley?"

"Who?" Mr. Townsend asked.

"Let us first speak to Victor Tallarico, then we can deal with the others," Prinny said, dismissing Mr. Ainsley for the moment.

When Tallarico walked in the room, I could not prevent a wince when I saw he wore yet another pink waistcoat. Obviously, it was some sort of personal trademark.

I shifted my weight from one leg to the other and caught a glimpse of Mr. Lavender's mocking gaze. He must have comprehended my disapproval at the Italian's choice in waistcoats.

Mr. Townsend took the direct approach with Signor Tallarico. "State your business in England, sir."

With a twinkle in his eye, the Italian gave the Bow Street man an elaborate bow, complete with several flourishes. "I am here to enjoy the lovely seaside, the lovely countryside, and," here he gave that smile of his that shows off his white teeth, "the lovely English women."

"To what sovereign are you loyal?" Mr. Townsend demanded.

"Venus," the flamboyant Signor Tallarico responded promptly.

My God!

I meant that as an expletive, not literally.

Mr. Townsend surprised me by laughing. "If Mrs. Fitzherbert will forgive my speaking plainly in front of a lady, I'll say that sentiment is shared by me. But, you know very well I am inquiring as to your politics, sir."

My admiration for Mr. Townsend's way of handling people grew. He is a shrewd man, make no mistake.

Tallarico's countenance changed. He spoke in a low, serious voice. "We'll get our country back from that monster. With help from our English friends." He turned toward the Prince of Wales and bowed. This time, it was a respectful gesture, not like the comical demonstration he had given Mr. Townsend earlier.

"Are you planning on staying in England long?" Mr. Lavender asked.

Tallarico shrugged. "I do not know. I plan to join my cousin, Lord Perry, in London. I'll see how things go there."

"Please be my guest one evening at White's club for gentlemen," I said, wanting Prinny to know the man had my approval.

"*Gràzie*," Tallarico promptly responded.

"Be sure to let me know if you change your plans," Mr. Lavender directed.

When Signor Tallarico had departed, I rounded on the Prince. "Now, sir, may we question Arthur Ainsley?" He seemed the most likely suspect to me, and thus far Prinny had avoided questioning him. From what I could tell, he had not mentioned Mr. Ainsley to Mr. Townsend. I wondered if the Prince was embarrassed over the situation he had found himself in with Mr. Ainsley and was reluctant for the story to come out.

"Er, yes, a most disagreeable young man, though one

with a talent for architecture," the Prince said in response to Mr. Townsend's questioning look.

"That is correct," I said, deeming it best not to make matters worse for his Royal Highness. "Mr. Ainsley harbors an unmerited grudge against our Prince."

"A grudge, you say?" Mr. Lavender asked.

"Indeed. Somehow, Mr. Ainsley brought the Prince into a conversation regarding the young man's desire for a seat in the Lords side of Parliament. He is the younger son of an earl, so you can see his predicament."

"He wants a voice in the government badly, does he?" Mr. Lavender queried.

"He does," I concurred. "So badly, he, er, misunderstood, something the Prince said to him regarding the matter. He believes the Prince promised to elevate him to the peerage in the event the King is declared mentally deranged and the Prince is made Regent."

"What a pretentious young pup!" Mr. Townsend exclaimed. "We must speak to him next. Lavender, you start things off."

Mr. Lavender nodded, but said nothing. The Prince squirmed on the royal mattress.

A few minutes passed and Arthur Ainsley entered the room. He bowed low to the Prince and was introduced to the Bow Street men. His countenance was much as it always is: a paper-white complexion topped by the blackest hair and eyes.

Mr. Lavender came around the desk with his notebook in hand and fixed Mr. Ainsley with an unswerving gaze. "Are you loyal to the Prince of Wales?"

Mr. Ainsley appeared startled by the question. "Yes, of course I am."

"Have you ever had an argument with his Royal Highness?"

Mr. Ainsley's gaze swung to the bed.

Prinny met his eye.

The young man looked back to Mr. Lavender. "No."

"No?" Mr. Lavender repeated skeptically.

"No, we have never had an argument," Mr. Ainsley said firmly.

"I'll remind you, laddie, that you are dealing with Bow Street, besides being in the presence of Royalty. It won't do to lie."

Mr. Ainsley was all indignation. "Are you calling me a liar, sir? My father, the Earl of Bentley, shall hear of this!"

Mr. Townsend stepped forward, motioning Mr. Lavender behind him. "Calm yourself, Mr. Ainsley. We are all gentlemen here. With the exception of the lovely Mrs. Fitzherbert," the head of Bow Street said with an ingratiating smile.

Mr. Ainsley's angry expression relaxed one fraction of the length of a bee's stinger.

"What I think Mr. Lavender is trying to get at is, have you and the Prince ever had a disagreement of any sort?" Mr. Townsend said. "You know what I am speaking of, Mr. Ainsley, the sort of conversation that results when one person misunderstands another and the result is a touch of animosity."

"I suppose you could say that we have," Mr. Ainsley admitted grudgingly. "But I did not try to poison his Royal Highness!"

"No one claimed you did," Mr. Townsend said in an avuncular manner. "Though it would be helpful if you saw anyone tamper with the snuff box Lord Petersham brought to the dinner party."

I frowned. I could not like the way Mr. Townsend made it seem that unless Mr. Ainsley could give him another suspect, more might be made of the misunderstanding—if it was a misunderstanding, and Prinny had not made the promise in a fit of drunken boastfulness—between Mr. Ainsley and the Prince over a peerage.

Mr. Ainsley seemed to interpret the Bow Street man's words the same way. "No. I mean, no, I did not see anyone put anything in the snuff box. It puzzles me why you are questioning me, and the others, for that matter. What happened is clear. Lord Petersham mixed a fatal blend of snuff for the Prince. I confess I know not why—"

"Lord Petersham did no such thing," I said in a confident voice. "For he had no motive to do so."

Mr. Ainsley glared at me. "You cannot know that. Who can discern what is in another's mind? Who can say Lord Petersham might not have been tempted with money by the French, or another enemy? He strikes me as a man who requires a lot of funds to maintain his comforts. Simply because you do not know of his motive, Mr. Brummell, does not mean Lord Petersham did not have one."

The Prince of Wales sat forward in his bed. "Zounds! I had not thought of Petersham in that light before. But a different snuff box every day, and ones of such quality, must cost him a fortune."

"Which his family has," I swiftly reminded the Prince. I looked at the skeptical faces around me and focussed on Prinny. "Sir, you have known and trusted the viscount for years. Lord Petersham did not add poi-

son to that snuff, your Royal Highness. I am certain of
it."

"I'm not," Mr. Lavender said.

"Nor am I," Mr. Townsend said. "You may go, Mr.
Ainsley. Guard, bring in Lord Petersham."

❧ 11 ❧

Had I not heard the Prince's words with my own ears, I would not have believed him capable of voicing doubts about Lord Petersham aloud. Suspicion from Bow Street I could understand. Suspicion from a so-called friend, I could not.

Lord Munro, rather than Petersham, entered the room next.

The guard who accompanied him said, "Viscount Petersham is not downstairs. I brought Lord Munro up since he's on the Bow Street list."

Lord Munro looked haughty. "Charles will be here momentarily. Diggie was helping him dress when I obeyed the summons to the Pavilion."

"I don't believe we've met," Jack Townsend said.

"I know you by reputation," Lord Munro replied.

"Good. I understand you and Lord Petersham are sharing a house in Brighton. Is that true?" Mr. Townsend asked.

"Yes, it is."

Mr. Townsend glanced at Mr. Lavender. That man turned a page in his notebook. As if by some silent signal he took over the questioning. "Lord Munro, were you present when Lord Petersham mixed the snuff he brought here last evening?"

"Of course I was. I admire Charles's superb taste and abilities in most things, snuff included," Lord Munro stated. "I enjoy watching him mix blends."

"After he mixed the snuff to his satisfaction, he then placed it in a special snuff box, is that right?" Mr. Lavender said.

Lord Munro nodded. "The box was a gift from me. The snuff was a new blend which Charles promised his Royal Highness he might be the first to sample."

Mr. Townsend had been pacing a few feet back and forth, but came to a stop at these words. "Did he say why the Prince would be the first?"

I could remain silent no longer. Before Lord Munro could answer, I said, "Because Lord Petersham counts himself honoured to be one of the Prince of Wales's friends." I followed this statement with a penetrating gaze at Prinny.

"Well, the fact is, I encouraged Petersham to let me be the first to try the new blend he'd been working on," was the royal comment.

"So you see, Mr. Townsend," I said equably, "there was nothing ominous in Lord Petersham's mixing a new blend of snuff. Just as there was nothing ominous in his honouring the Prince with the first pinch. I was present in the room when the viscount told the Prince he was working on the snuff. Lord Petersham allowed his Royal Highness to be the first to try it in order to please the Prince."

"Nothing ominous, Mr. Brummell, except that someone dropped dead after partaking of that new snuff," Mr.
Lavender pointed out. He turned his back to me, effec-
tively giving me the message that I should keep my
thoughts to myself, and resumed his questioning. "Lord
Munro, after Lord Petersham mixed the snuff, did you
sample it?"

"Of course I did," Lord Munro replied somewhat indignantly. "Charles always asks my opinion."

"And what was your opinion?" Mr. Lavender asked.

"That it wasn't quite right yet. Something more was
needed, I'm not sure what . . ." Lord Munro trailed off.

"And did Lord Petersham take your advice? Did he
continue working on the snuff?"

"Oh, yes, why—" Lord Munro suddenly hesitated. It
seemed to me that he had thought of something, but was
reluctant to divulge it.

Mr. Lavender and Mr. Townsend perceived it too.
Both men stared at Lord Munro. Mr. Townsend said,
"You saw him mixing the snuff again?"

Lord Munro swallowed, looking uncomfortable. "I
can't remember," he finally said.

"Think hard," Mr. Lavender directed.

Lord Munro fixed him with a cold look. "I've told
you I can't remember. That is all I have to say."

A short silence followed. Then Mr. Townsend said,
"Very well, Lord Munro. I'll ask you one final question:
Have you any reason to believe that Lord Petersham
might wish the Prince of Wales ill?"

"None whatsoever," Lord Munro pronounced. "I have
cooperated with you, but I draw the line at the thought
that Charles might have had anything to do with the
attempt on the Prince's life. The very idea is insulting."

For once I found myself in agreement with his lordship.

Lord Munro bowed to the Prince and backed from the room as one does in the presence of royalty. Mr. Townsend and Mr. Lavender had their heads together while Mrs. Fitzherbert whispered to the Prince. I wished for a glass of something strong. Anything.

Petersham sauntered into the room a few tense minutes later. He was faultlessly dressed in a rich plum-coloured coat over pale buckskin breeches, but dark circles were evident under his eyes. From our long friendship, I know this to be a telltale sign that the viscount had not had enough sleep.

He bowed to the Prince, then looked through heavy-lidded eyes at the rest of us. "What's going on here?"

"Petersham, they—" I began, only to be quickly cut off by Mr. Lavender.

"That's all right, Mr. Brummell. I'll ask the questions."

I stood leaning against the fireplace, resisting the urge to drum my fingers on the mantel in irritation.

"Who'd you say you were?" Petersham asked, covering his mouth and suppressing a yawn.

"I am John Lavender from Bow Street. This is Jack Townsend."

Petersham strained to open his eyes wider. "Townsend? Devil take me if I've seen you since the races in Brighton last summer. I say, I like that hat. Rather a broad brim. Good for keeping the sun out of one's eyes. Did James Lock, the hatter, make it?"

"No, but I can give you the direction of the hatter who did." Mr. Townsend smiled. Obviously he was going to let Mr. Lavender ask the harsh questions so he could remain on good terms with the high-born Lord Petersham.

"My lord, let us change the topic, if we may—" a tinge of sarcasm touched Mr. Lavender's words—"to snuff boxes."

"Be glad to," Petersham said, looking around. Near the fireplace where I stood, not too far from the desk, was a bamboo-style chair. The viscount dropped into it, his long legs stretched out in front of him. "His Royal Highness has some of the best snuff boxes I've seen. Sorry, Brummell, but it's the truth."

"That is quite all right," I said magnanimously, pleased at the frustrated look on Mr. Lavender's face. Surely he would see there is no guile in the viscount.

"The box you brought last evening to dinner—"

"Ahh, that particular one is special, Mr. Lavender. It was a gift to me from Lord Munro. I daresay the Prince covets it, as beautiful as it is. Oh, but you never had a chance to really examine it, did you your Royal Highness? That ugly scene with Sir Simon." Petersham shook his head. Then, "That reminds me, where is my snuff box?"

The Scotsman looked hard at Petersham. "It's being held by the Bow Street Police Office as evidence in a case of attempted assassination of the Prince of Wales."

"When will I get it back?" Petersham wanted to know.

Mr. Lavender looked incredulous. "My lord, do you not realize that the snuff in that box killed a man?"

Petersham looked blank. "I know that some minor baronet who did not dress well and smelled awfully of jasmine will soon be six feet under."

Prinny said, "It was an attempt on *my* life, Petersham."

The viscount sighed deeply and pondered the statement. "You know, I've given the matter a bit of thought."

"I hope the effort was not too much for you," Mr. Lavender said.

"Not at all," Petersham waved a hand. "Brummell here told me that everyone would think the snuff was poisoned, but I thought the notion nonsensical."

Mr. Lavender pinned me with a glare I thought might blind me. Though in all fairness, I must say the Bow Street man would likely settle for turning me into a mute. That way, I could not meddle in his investigations . . . or his daughter's life.

Petersham went on: "But, you know, I trust Pitcairn as a good doctor, so I suppose I've got to accept that poison was in the snuff. I just can't figure how it got there. Or why anyone would want to besmirch snuff that way."

"The person who did so wanted to kill the Prince," I reminded him.

"That's ridiculous. Who would want to hurt his Royal Highness?" Petersham asked. "Weren't any Frenchies about."

The Prince grasped chunks of the bedclothes in his fists.

Mr. Lavender calmly lifted a slim box from his pocket. Made of ivory, with a small turquoise in the center, it contains toothpicks. I know because I gave it to him. Mr. Lavender once saved my life. The Scotsman selected a toothpick and popped it in his mouth.

I did my best not to cringe at this ungentlemanly habit.

Petersham observed the box and cried, "Say, that's a nice little box for a Bow Street man."

I tensed. Would Mr. Lavender force me to explain why I had given him the gift?

The Prince leaned forward to get a better look, but after only the briefest of glances in my direction, Mr. Lavender pocketed the box and said, "Catching criminals can be lucrative. Now, my lord, let me pose a question to you. You say you can't think of who would put poison in the snuff. How do you think it got there then?"

Petersham shrugged. "I don't know."

Mr. Lavender removed the toothpick from his mouth and pointed it at Petersham. "You are telling me, my lord, that you don't know the content of your own snuff?"

"Of course I know what's in my snuff," Petersham stated, much offended.

"Then you must have known it had poison in it," Mr. Lavender said flatly.

"Well, I didn't," Petersham said.

"Did you try the snuff before you brought it to the Pavilion, Lord Petersham?"

Here was the question I had tried to ask Petersham in his bedchamber.

"Of course I did," came the reply.

"Then the killer must have added the poison to the snuff sometime during the long dinner, or just afterward," I interjected. "What a relief. That narrows matters down considerably."

"Mr. Brummell, if you don't mind, I am conducting this questioning. I cannot bar you from this room, much as I'd like, but I must ask you to remain silent and let me ask the questions," Mr. Lavender said, his patience tried.

I told you he wanted to turn me into a mute.

I put on my best bland expression, so he turned back to the viscount. "Lord Petersham, I put this question to you: If you tried the snuff before bringing it to the Pavilion, then why are you still living while Sir Simon, the first to try your snuff, is dead?"

Petersham rose languidly to his feet. "How should I know? Someone tampered with it after dinner, I suppose. Look here, I'd stay and chat with you fellows, but unless you're ready to return my snuff box to me, I'll take myself off. I'd like to drop by the Old Ship Inn for a bottle of their French brandy. Can I bring you a bottle, your Royal Highness? I hear they just received a new shipment."

I passed a hand over my eyes. Everyone knew the Old Ship's French brandy was smuggled. Not to mention that the last time Petersham had tried to give the Prince something to ingest, someone had died.

Perhaps by Petersham's very lack of pretense, the men from Bow Street would see his innocence. Then again, perhaps not.

"Just one minute, my lord." Mr. Lavender doggedly ticked items off on his fingers. "Since you have told me that you mixed the snuff, that you sampled it before bringing it to the Pavilion—"

Jack Townsend raised a hand. "Gentlemen, I think we've questioned Lord Petersham on the matter sufficiently."

Mr. Lavender viewed his superiour with an expression of utmost frustration. Undoubtedly the Scotsman had not given any consideration to the penalty of accusing a peer of the realm of wrongdoing. Especially a seditious crime.

But Jack Townsend had thought of it. Most likely, he envisioned what the reaction of Petersham's father, the Earl of Harrington, would be to any accusations made against his son. That, I judged, was the reason why Mr. Townsend had stopped Mr. Lavender from pressing too hard, and why he was willing to let Petersham go on his way. For the moment.

The second the viscount was out of the room, Mr. Lavender rounded on Mr. Townsend. "Why didn't you let me finish?"

"Let's not rush our fences," Mr. Townsend said, stroking his chin thoughtfully. "Three suspects—Victor Tallarico, Mr. Ainsley, and Lord Petersham—have emerged as the most likely candidate for assassin, but it's early days yet."

"Early days?" Prinny expostulated. "How long are you going to take to find the villain? Long enough for me to die? What if the killer tries again?"

Mr. Townsend consulted Mr. Lavender's list. "I see we have only the Duchess of York and Lady Bessborough left to question."

"You can do that on your own, Townsend," the Prince said, exasperated.

I made up my mind instantly that Freddie would not be questioned without my attendance.

At that moment, a footman in the King's livery entered the room and bowed low. "I have a message from

His Majesty, King George the Third, for his son, the
Prince of Wales."

"Bring it forward, man," the Prince commanded.

He scanned the few lines and glanced at Mr. Townsend in a manner I could only describe as accusatory.
"My father and Mr. Pitt have learned of the attempt on
my life. Did you tell them?"

Mr. Townsend spread his hands in a depreciating
manner. "The Prime Minister would not take it well had
I not."

"Well, now my father is demanding I return to London. He says I will be safer at Carlton House. I suppose
I can only be grateful he did not command me to rus-
ticate at Windsor."

The Prince tossed the letter aside and curtly addressed
the footman. "You may tell my father he has wasted his
ink in writing me. I had already decided to return to
Town. Tomorrow. I need a meal and a good night's rest
before attempting such a journey."

The King's footman backed out of the room.

"Shall I send word to the kitchens to send something
up to you here, my dear, or will you dine with your
guests?" Mrs. Fitzherbert inquired.

"I'll dine in my room and only after a food taster has
sampled each dish," the Prince replied crossly. He
looked my way. "Brummell, remember your promise to
get to the bottom of this—no matter who is implicated.
That includes Petersham, you know."

"Sir, I am aware of the fact and confident the viscount
is completely innocent of any malice," I said.

I contemplated the expression of acute aggravation
on Mr. Lavender's face at this reminder of my involve-

ment in the matter. And on orders from no less a personage than the Prince of Wales.

The Scotsman's toothpick bobbed up and down furiously as he no doubt ground his teeth against it.

❧ 12 ❧

On Friday, the eleventh day of October, we set out for London in a sort of cavalcade of coaches. The Prince's return to Town meant a return to the metropolis of his court followers. And probably of his would-be murderer.

As the view of the sea receded, a mental image of the girl Freddie and I had found dead on the beach flashed through my mind. Who was she? Who missed her? Would I ever know?

Ahead of me, Lord and Lady Perry rode at a careful pace in their coach. They had invited me to make the journey with them, but I cannot help feeling that a married couple is most comfortable on their own. So I declined.

Nonetheless, the Perrys were not left to their privacy. Victor Tallarico accepted Lady Perry's kind invitation, kissing her hand and ignoring his cousin's muttered curse.

I travelled with only Chakkri to keep me company. I

hoped our normal fellowship would return once we arrived home. The cat had hopped into his lidded wicker basket eagerly enough, as if he knew our destination. He had promptly fallen asleep with a grin on his feline face. Yes, a grin. Would I exaggerate?

As for Robinson, he made the journey under circumstances which could only be abhorrent to him: He rode in a coach hired for the servants. These included Lady Perry's maid, Betty; Lord Perry's valet, Mr. Hearn; and most disturbing to Robinson's equilibrium, his archenemy, Mr. Digwood.

Petersham and Munro, you see, had decided to quit Brighton the evening before, leaving Mr. Digwood to close the house they had been renting. Thinking of Robinson and Diggie riding shoulder to shoulder, animosity oozing between them, I almost shuddered at the atmosphere in that conveyance. At that very moment they were probably in a heated debate as to whether cedar shavings or chippings of Russia leather were best for protecting clothes from moths.

There was one person of importance to me who would not be travelling to London.

Alone, with nothing more to do than reflect while the coach rambled along the London Road, I thought of Freddie on her way back to Oatlands. Much as I had tried to persuade her to come to Town for a bit, as usual she preferred the comfort of her country estate to the uncomfortable sight of her husband, the Duke of York, cavorting with his mistress all around London.

My thoughts turned away from the Duke—you know I try not to think of him—and I contemplated the previous evening. Dinner at the Pavilion had been a solemn affair. True to his word, the Prince had dined with Mrs.

Fitzherbert in his chamber. Doctor Pitcairn had asked for a tray to be brought to his room so that he might be close at hand in case his royal patient had need of him.

This left Freddie and me, the St. Clairs, and Mr. Ainsley the only Pavilion guests at table. By tacit agreement, the chair in which Sir Simon had partaken of his last meal remained vacant. Despite the empty place, Sir Simon was very much on everyone's mind, and conversation was sparse. I thought the St. Clairs pensive and Mr. Ainsley exceptionally nervous. He looked like a man about to burst from his skin.

I knew I should try to draw him out, but he excused himself the moment he finished his meal. You think I should have followed him from the room? Well, I suppose you are right, but I chose not to. Freddie was present, clad in a most fetching gown, gold-coloured with blond lace. I convinced myself that questioning Mr. Ainsley could wait. Mr. Townsend and Mr. Lavender might call at any time to interrogate Freddie. I needed to stay close to her. And, no, I do not think I am making excuses to justify enjoying a few moments of the Royal Duchess's company!

As soon as the empty syllabub glasses were taken away, I approached Freddie. "If you wish to take Humphrey for a walk on the Steine before retiring, I should be glad to accompany you."

Freddie quickly agreed to the plan, sending a footman upstairs for Humphrey and her cloak. I could not suppress a sigh when Ulga appeared, dressed for the outdoors, bringing the cloak and the dog to her employer.

Outside, I found the cold air refreshing for once and did not regret the lack of my greatcoat. The Pavilion had been stiflingly hot.

With Ulga several yards behind us, we walked along. I outlined for Freddie the details of the afternoon of questioning by the Bow Street men, as well as my study of Mr. Ainsley.

"What are your thoughts, dear?" she asked when I had finished. We paused so that Humphrey could sniff an irresistible tree.

"I am concerned for Petersham."

"You do not think he could have been the intended victim, do you?" Freddie asked.

"No, he is too lazy to have made any enemies."

"Quite right."

"Freddie, the entire affair makes no sense to me for one simple reason: I cannot believe anyone present at that dinner had reason to kill the Prince of Wales. Even Mr. Ainsley, who has been the subject of my own inquiry, does not appear to have enough motive."

"From what you have told me, I agree. But perhaps we do not know all there is to know about Mr. Ainsley, George," Freddie suggested. "And if by nothing else but process of elimination, he must be our chief suspect. Did you mark how his nerves were all to pieces tonight at dinner?"

"Yes. And in my mind I have replayed the minutes last night after the meal when the ladies retired to the Saloon and the gentlemen mingled. Ainsley approached the side table where the snuff box sat more than once," I told her. "But anyone in that room could have gotten to the snuff box. I do not know what to think, Freddie."

Freddie tugged on Humphrey's leash. The short-legged dog obeyed the command. "The day has been long, dear. You will pursue the matter back in London and will discover the truth. I have no doubt of it. Look at what an admirable job you did clearing Miss Ashton's name in that recent unpleasantness."

I gazed down on her upturned face. The moonlight glowed on her skin and she looked very young. I knew we would write to each other, and one weekend soon I would ride out to Oatlands for one of Freddie's weekend parties. Still, at that moment, I could not bear the thought of having to part from her.

I experienced a moment of supreme irritation when our peace was disturbed.

"Egad, Harold, take a look at the Duchess's hound. That's a new one, isn't it?" came Viscount Petersham's voice from the darkness.

"No, Charles, I've seen Brummell with the Duchess time out of number," Lord Munro quipped as the pair came into view.

"Harold," Petersham remonstrated, but then spoiled it by chuckling. Reaching us, he bent and patted Humphrey.

Over his head, I gazed at Lord Munro in silent contempt. Had Freddie not been with me, his lordship would now be tasting sea-water.

The two bowed to Freddie and she greeted them in a bright tone.

"We were just coming to say good-bye," Petersham informed us, surreptitiously wiping dog drool from his hand. "Brighton is as flat as champagne flowing from a fountain. We're for London tonight."

I stroked my jaw. "Have you told Jack Townsend your plans, Petersham?"

The viscount looked puzzled. "Why should I? If he wants to see me, he knows my direction in London. Well, we're off then. Hope to see you at Oatlands soon,

Your Highness. Brummell, I'll see you at White's."

And with a cheerful wave, Petersham turned on his heel and headed back across the Steine, Lord Munro at his side.

I stared after them. "Freddie, do you see how Petersham is so completely oblivious to the . . . awkward, shall we say, position he is in?"

"I think it is because he is innocent and finds it impossible to think anyone would judge him otherwise," Freddie observed.

"Let us hope Bow Street conforms to that view."

Strolling back in the direction whence we had come, I saw the very men of whom I spoke. Mr. Townsend and Mr. Lavender were walking through the entrance to the Pavilion.

"Freddie, have you been questioned by the Bow Street men yet?"

"Why, no. Do they intend to speak to me?"

"Yes, it was my understanding they would. I see they are at the Pavilion now. Shall we go back?"

"If we must," she answered. I could not help but be pleased that she did not seem eager to end our walk.

Presently, while rambling along in the coach, I recalled how the meeting went. I remembered Jack Townsend's respectful bearing toward Freddie, Mr. Lavender's attention to Humphrey—which afterward caused Freddie to tell me she thought Mr. Lavender a fine example for Bow Street—and Lady Bessborough's appearance on the scene. That lady had no qualms letting it be known that she viewed Lord Petersham as the obvious guilty party. Everyone knew he was, as her ladyship put it, "odd."

Upon hearing this witless remark, I had fixed my expression to one that clearly indicated Lady Bessborough could not be taken seriously, while Freddie, very much the *grande dame*, said she had known Lord Petersham for many years.

The farther we got from Brighton, the more I wondered how long it would be before questions about the death of Sir Simon, and whispers about who might be responsible it, would fly around London. Since Jack Townsend had sent word of the Prince's jeopardy to the King and Mr. Pitt, the Prime Minister, it was entirely possible we would return to gossip-loving London to find the bibble-babblers having a hey-day.

All of a sudden, my driver pulled the coach to a stop. I reached a hand over to make sure Chakkri's basket remained secure on the seat. I let down the window to see the Perrys' vehicle halted in front of me. A farmer led a herd of black-faced sheep across the road. Amongst much bleating and scrambling, the man hurried the creatures as best he could, recognizing from the crest on Lord Perry's coach that he delayed the journey of a nobleman.

The chilly air entered my coach. I went to close the window. In the process of doing so, a sad sight made me pause. A woman of middle years walked by the side of the road, looking dazed and muttering to herself. One does see such unfortunates on occasion, but what made this woman different was her bearing and dress. Instead of the rags usually to be seen on persons fallen on difficult times, this woman's dress was fine. Though dirty and torn at one shoulder, exposing a sliver of white flesh, the gown was of an expensive-looking dove-coloured silk. Her brown hair, heavily streaked with grey, had

been messily pinned to the top of her head in a disor-
dered knot.

On the seat next to me, a rustling sound came from
the wicker basket. Chakkri woke. A minute later a
brown face, followed by a fawn-coloured body, emerged
from the lidded container. The cat stretched his neck to
an almost impossible length, placed one paw on my
shoulder to brace himself, and looked out the window.
He uttered a sharp "Reow."

The farmer drove the last of his sheep across the road.
We would be on our way in a moment. My gaze swung
back to the woman. She looked the same age as my
favourite aunt.

Impulsively, I opened the door to my coach and
alighted from the vehicle. Making certain the door was
shut tightly so Chakkri could not get out, I shouted to
Perry's coachman to wait before proceeding. Then I took
a few steps toward the woman.

"Good afternoon, madam. Do you need some assistance?"

Instead of welcoming my offer, the woman shrank
from me, terror clearly written across her face.

Surprised by this response, I did not attempt to step
any closer. "Do not be alarmed. I only want to help
you."

The woman's plump form began to tremble. Her eyes
were wide with fear despite my assurance. In a heavy
French accent she whispered, "No, no, no." Then she
crossed herself as if to ward off evil.

Switching to French, I asked her again if I might help
her. Instead of the sound of her native language reassuring her, the woman remained paralyzed with fear.

Then her gaze went past me. Lady Perry had emerged

from her carriage and walked toward us, Lord Perry waiting for her at the coach door. "What is wrong, Mr. Brummell? Is the lady hurt?"

"I do not know. I think she is French, but she will not speak with me in English or French. She seems greatly afraid."

Lady Perry smiled reassuringly at the woman. "I am Lady Perry. Can we help you? Are you lost?"

The woman reached a shaking hand out to Lady Perry, but then her gaze darted back to me. She cringed, took another step backward, and resumed muttering the word *no* over and over.

"She does not seem as frightened of you, Lady Perry," I said in a low voice. "She reminds me of a rabbit, easily startled, and ready to flee at any second."

"Indeed. May I make a suggestion, Mr. Brummell?"

"By all means."

"Will you go and stand next to Anthony? Perhaps this poor creature will be more willing to tell another woman what has happened to her."

"Very well." I made a slight bow in the woman's direction as a way to reassure her I meant no harm. Then, casually, I joined Perry. Victor Tallarico had alighted from the vehicle as well.

"What is amiss with that woman? Is she mad?" Perry asked.

"She looks harmless enough, like someone's *gover-nante*," Tallarico said.

"Governess or not, who can say?" I told them. "Lady Perry is going to try to find out what happened."

Perry frowned. "I wish Bernadette would not walk in the brush like that. She could trip and fall."

I clapped a hand on his shoulder. "Relax. Lady Perry

is all that is graceful. Nothing of the sort will happen."

Lady Perry had taken a step toward the woman. Although the frightened creature did not move away, her gaze remained fixed on Perry, Tallarico, and me. She shook her head at whatever Lady Perry asked her. From where I was standing, I could hear her repeating the word *no.*

Robinson chose that moment to emerge from the servant's coach, standing behind mine. "If I might inquire as to the nature of our delay, sir?" he called.

The effect of yet another man's presence on the strange woman was startling. She shrank behind Lady Perry as if seeking to protect herself. Her entire body shook.

"Robinson, wait in the coach," I ordered. He pursed his lips and put his foot in the doorway of the vehicle.

Lady Perry said, "Robinson, if you will be so good as to ask my maid to come out."

"Here I am, my lady," announced Betty, easing her bulk out of the servant's coach and pushing past Robinson. Betty is a practical country girl. Lady Perry had first hired her as housemaid. Later, when Lady Perry could no longer tolerate the snobbish ways of her lady's maid, she had let the woman go and given a grateful Betty the position.

Betty joined her mistress and the Frenchwoman.

Above her and Lady Perry's gentle talk, I could hear the mysterious Frenchwoman saying, "No, no, ze animals, ze animals."

Could it be she had merely been afraid of the sheep? But she had cringed from me, Perry, Tallarico, and Robinson. She was afraid of men.

While Betty put a comforting arm around the Frenchwoman, Lady Perry walked over to us. "The poor thing is in a state of hysteria. We cannot make any sense out of what she says for all she will say is 'no' and 'the animals.' Anthony, I would not be able to live with myself if we simply left her here." Lady Perry looked at her husband, her velvet-brown eyes pleading.

Perry sighed. "What do you propose to do with her?"

"I have an idea," I said. "I know a woman in Town who runs a shelter for 'destitute and downtrodden' women, as she puts it. Miss Lydia Lavender is her name. The shelter is called Haven of Hope."

Lord Perry's eyes narrowed. "Would this woman be a relation of John Lavender from Bow Street?"

"Er, yes. His daughter," I replied, a bit uncomfortably.

"Oh, Mr. Brummell, do you think Miss Lavender would help? If so, it would be the very thing," Lady Perry said. "We could take this poor woman to our Town house, and you could send word to Miss Lavender."

"How are we going to get her to London?" Perry asked. "She would need to ride in the servants' coach. She does not seem inclined to let a man near her and since Robinson, Diggie, and Hearn are there . . ."

We looked toward where Betty tried to calm the Frenchwoman.

Lady Perry spoke. "Anthony, darling, I am persuaded the woman would ride in our coach with Betty and me. If Mr. Brummell would not mind, perhaps you and Victor could ride with him."

"An excellent scheme, Lady Perry," I said.

"*Va bene*," Tallarico agreed.

My gaze shifted to my vehicle. Chakkri's face was

at the window. The cat was watching the proceedings. His mouth opened and he voiced a "reow" I could not hear.

Perry did not look at all pleased at the thought of being separated from his wife, but I knew he would not deny her wishes.

As it turned out, I was right. However, the matter was not easily accomplished. Lady Perry had to explain the scheme, in French, three times before the woman agreed. Still, no explanation of what had happened to her, and no other phrases could be coaxed from her other than "no" and "ze animals."

Once Perry, Tallarico, and I were ensconced in my carriage, the woman allowed herself to be taken up with Betty and Lady Perry. Our cavalcade started out once more, with an added member to our number.

Little did I know then of the ramifications there would be from our having rescued her, and how she would hold the key to questions I had not yet even asked.

❧ 13 ❧

Once in London, I ordered Robinson to convey Chakkri to my house in Bruton Street, while I joined the Perrys in their Adam-styled drawing room in Grosvenor Square.

Setting aside my trepidation that Robinson might seize the opportunity to "accidentally" lose Chakkri in the crowded Mayfair streets, I accepted pen and paper from Lady Perry. In a few short sentences, I described the mysterious Frenchwoman's plight, and begged Miss Lavender to come to Grosvenor Square as soon as she could.

I sanded the note, and Lady Perry ordered a footman to hurry its delivery to Miss Lavender personally at the Haven of Hope. In case he should not find her there, which was entirely possible since it was nearing five o'clock, I also gave Miss Lavender's direction in Fetter Lane.

Meanwhile, Betty had bustled her charge to the kitchen, proclaiming that a hot cup of tea was just what the woman needed. Privately I thought a good deal more than tea would be required to quiet the Frenchwoman's nerves.

Lady Perry then turned her attention to directing a maid to make up a room for Victor Tallarico.

"No, you must not," the Italian protested, rising. "I'll seek a hotel for the night. In the morning I'll inquire about renting rooms."

"I shall not hear of it," Lady Perry proclaimed. "Anthony, you must convince Victor to remain with us."

Perry picked up a bottle of Madeira wine and poured out a large measure. "Why not stay here until you can make more permanent arrangements, Victor?"

Tallarico did not miss his cousin's lack of enthusiasm for the plan. "*Grazie*, but I tend to keep erratic hours, and would be more comfortable at a hotel."

"Oh, surely not—" Lady Perry said, sending her husband a speaking look.

"I insist, *mi bella*," Signor Tallarico pronounced. Kissing her hand and favouring her with a wink, the Italian gave me a nod of farewell and then exited the room.

Lady Perry retired to her chamber to change from her travelling dress, but not before letting her husband know of her displeasure at his lack of warmth where his cousin was concerned.

"It is not that I dislike Victor," Perry said, as he and I seated ourselves in rose-coloured plush chairs by the fire. "He is just not as settled as I might wish. His activies run to the racketing sort. He is better off, as he himself said, at a hotel."

"Er, Perry," I said, taking a swallow of the fine Madeira. "Have a care to whom you express that opinion of your cousin. After what happened at the Pavilion . . ."

Perry ran his hand through his dark hair. "I was referring to Victor's escapades with females, but I know what you are talking about, Brummell. Jack Townsend's brain is failing him, though. Victor would not take time away from his pursuit of the ladies to involve himself in spying or plotting with Napoleon's allies."

I studied Perry's face carefully. I found it disturbing when I saw the slight bit of doubt in his eyes—almost as if by speaking the words aloud, he was reassuring himself that they were true. "As Tallarico intends to remain in London for a time, you will have the opportunity to renew your acquaintance, perhaps be an example to him."

Perry snorted. "Victor has never listened to anyone. Certain people must find their own way in the world, eh, Brummell?" He turned to look at me. "You have not followed my lead either, have you? While I cannot think you indulge in the sort of dissolute behaviour Victor does, you are as yet unwed at the age of seven and twenty."

"Ah, Lady Perry, you have rejoined us at precisely the right moment," I said, rising and sweeping her a bow. A servant followed her into the room carrying a tray laden with tea and sandwiches. Yes, I was relieved that the conversation with Perry had been interrupted.

While we ate and exchanged small talk, a corner of my mind examined the absent Victor Tallarico. I allowed this corner free rein to consider him as a suspect in the poisoning. A mental image of the Italian standing in front of an emissary from Napoleon in Rome, accepting orders to act on the new King of Italy's behalf, formed in my mind's eye. Could it be true?

I remembered the glint of the knife he had so quickly produced when he thought his cousin might need his assistance. Signor Tallarico's chief interest in life was women and, more specifically, his conquest of them. Perhaps it had been a woman who had persuaded him to carry out the deed.

And the man did wear a pink waistcoat. Could he really be trusted?

As I said, I tried to come up with every devious political plot in which I could cast Signor Tallarico, but the fact remained that I did not believe a single one of them. The man was guilty of no more than filling a lady's ear with whispered promises of delights he claimed only he could deliver.

The entrance of the butler broke my thoughts. "Miss Lavender, my lord."

Perry and I rose to our feet as Miss Lavender advanced into the room. Her gaze found me and her lips curved into a slight smile.

That smile made me pause. Not only did it brighten an already attractive face, but it seemed to convey the spirited signal that Miss Lavender considered herself my equal.

"Good afternoon, Mr. Brummell," she said. "I came as soon as I received your letter."

I performed the introductions, all the while admiring the translucence of Miss Lavender's porcelain-like skin and the sheer richness of her auburn hair in the candlelit room. As is her custom, she wore a neat, serviceable gown, this one in a rust-coloured wool that complimented her hair. I suddenly found myself feeling rather pleased that Tallarico had taken his leave before Miss Lavender arrived.

"How good of you to come," Lady Perry said. "Will you not sit down and have a cup of tea?"

Here is an example of what a kind person Lady Perry is. Another lady of her rank may not have deigned to sit down and share refreshments with a social inferiour. The daughter of a Bow Street man moves in an entirely different world than the one Lady Perry inhabits, and their worlds meet only on limited levels. Those levels do not normally include taking tea.

Miss Lavender accepted the offer of a seat, I suspect because she did not wish Perry and me to remain standing. She gazed about her elegant surroundings with interest, but declined the tea saying in a businesslike manner, "I'd like to hear more about this woman's condition. Has she been beaten?"

Lady Perry seemed taken aback at Miss Lavender's direct approach. I could have told her that the Bow Street investigator's daughter was not one to engage in roundaboutation. No pampered Society girl, Miss Lavender seeks to ease the wrongs women endure due to the limitations imposed upon them by the law, social customs, and the ruthless treatment they often suffered at the hands of men. Or so she has told me.

Gazing into her green eyes, I suddenly wondered what actually motivated Miss Lavender. Was there something in her past that led her to be so conscientious in helping other females?

To answer her question regarding the Frenchwoman's physical condition, I replied, "No, Miss Lavender, the woman did not appear physically harmed, at least not that I know of." I raised an inquiring eyebrow at Lady Perry.

Her ladyship gave a little shake of her head. "When

Betty came up to help me change out of my travelling dress, she told me the Frenchwoman had not said a word about her situation. Betty had all she could do to get a few sips of tea past the woman's lips. The woman said nothing, would accept no food, and is still frightened to death. We do not even know her name."

I nodded. "As I told you in my letter, Miss Lavender, the woman seems terrified of men, specifically. Had not Lady Perry been present, I feel the woman would have run off rather than go anywhere with me."

"How lowering for you, Mr. Brummell," Miss Lavender said.

Before I could deliver a reply to this saucy comment, she continued speaking. "So we have no idea who she is or what happened to her. Only that she has suffered some upset which has paralyzed her with fear." Miss Lavender sighed. "Bring her to me, please."

"Of course," Perry said. Lady Perry rang for Betty. "Do you have room for her at your shelter, Miss Lavender?"

"I will not turn her away."

"Do you have many women to look after?" Lady Perry queried.

Miss Lavender thought for a moment. "We had a new arrival this morning, a fifteen-year-old girl heavy with child, who brings our number to nineteen. A chambermaid, the girl had been turned out without a reference after the master of the house—the very one responsible for her condition—learned she was pregnant. She's been living on the streets for the past four months and only learned of my shelter when she was caught stealing an apple. The grocer happens to be one I frequent. Mr. Lavell took pity on her and rather than bring charges against her, he brought her to me."

Lady Perry listened to this account with one hand placed protectively over her stomach. "How dreadful! And how good the merchant was to realize the poor child was merely hungry."

"A rare man, indeed," Perry concurred. "Many would have had the chit hauled away to the nearest round-house."

"Yes, Mr. Lavell is good," Miss Lavender said with a fond smile.

Was that smile indicative of a warmer relationship between the two? My brows drew together. Miss Lavender could do better than a grocer, surely. I reflected that one day soon I might decide to visit Miss Lavender's shelter, and the surrounding neighborhood. I am a curious fellow, you know.

At that moment, my attention was caught by the sight of Betty standing in the doorway with the Frenchwoman. Betty, bless her, had provided what I suspect was one of her own dresses to the distressed female. And distressed she most certainly remained. The Frenchwoman shrank at the sight of Perry and me, clinging to Betty and making the sign of the cross. Betty managed to inch her into the room.

Miss Lavender rose from her chair. "Good afternoon, my name is Lydia Lavender. What is yours?"

The Frenchwoman did not respond. Her rounded eyes remained focussed on Perry and me as if at any moment we might attack her.

The next few minutes were all confusion.

A voice with a Scottish lilt sounded from behind where Betty and the Frenchwoman stood.

"Lydia! What are you doing here?" Mr. Lavender demanded.

The sound of a male voice so close at hand startled the Frenchwoman into a scream, followed by a rapid repetition of the word *no*. She stood rooted to the spot, her entire body trembling.

Betty and Miss Lavender rushed to comfort the woman. Lady Perry would have joined them, but her husband placed a gentle hand on her arm in a restraining manner.

Mr. Lavender abruptly became aware of my presence and shook his finger at me, a mannerism I feel he employs to put me in my place. "What's this all about? What are you doing here, Mr. Brummell?"

I eyed the Bow Street man with mock gravity. "We are holding a tea party. May I see your invitation?"

Lord Perry took command of the situation. "Mr. Lavender, I did not hear you announced," he said in glacial tones.

"How could you with all that caterwauling going on?" Mr. Lavender said.

"Father, please! I am trying to help this woman."

"At whose request, Lydia?" A muscle in Mr. Lavender's jaw flicked angrily. "Wait, don't tell me. Mr. Brummell's, no doubt. We'll have to have another talk about your hob-a-nobbing with him."

"Now there is something for you to look forward to, Miss Lavender," I said in a perfectly pleasant voice.

"If I might ask you, Miss Lavender," Lord Perry said, "are you willing to take this lady to your shelter?"

"Yes, I am, and we'll leave at once, my lord," Miss Lavender said. "Lady Perry, may I beg the assistance of your maid? I think it will ease this woman's coming to me if Betty sees her settled in. I assure you I will return Betty to you safely this evening."

"Of course," Lady Perry agreed. "I shall walk to the door with you. Oh! I daresay we need another cloak. Betty, would you . . ." The four women exited the room, Miss Lavender informing her father he might take his evening meal at Ye Olde Cock Tavern, as she expected to be home quite late.

This news did nothing to improve the Bow Street man's temper. "I've some questions for you, Lord Perry."

"I expect you had best sit down," Perry said in a resigned tone as we resumed our seats. "I suppose this is about the attempt on Prinny's life?"

Mr. Lavender looked uneasily at the plush chair Perry indicated before seating himself. "Is your cousin here?"

Lord Perry was every inch the earl. "Victor? No, he has gone to look for a hotel. If you have come to question me about him again, you are wasting your time. I have nothing further to say."

The two men's gazes met and held.

Mr. Lavender looked away first. He pulled his tattered notebook from his pocket. "Very well, my lord," he said, burring his r. "Let us discuss Lord Petersham."

The wave of disapproval emanating from me would have cowed a lesser man.

Lord Perry snorted a laugh. "First my cousin, now Petersham? Surely you do not think the viscount capable of concocting an assassination?"

"Lord Petersham tries to give the impression of one lazy beyond comprehension, but I'm not fooled by the act. No man," Mr. Lavender said, tapping the notebook with emphasis, "can be that slothful, my lord."

I chuckled. "You obviously are not well acquainted with the viscount."

"When I said 'my lord' I was addressing Lord Perry, Mr. Brummell," Mr. Lavender barked. He rarely misses an opportunity to remind me of my rank. Or lack thereof.

"Brummell is right," Lord Perry stated. "Petersham is content with the usual gentleman's pursuits, and he enjoys mixing blends of snuff. Tea, as well, I believe. There is not an ounce of harm in him."

"There was certainly more than an ounce of harm in that snuff he mixed," Mr. Lavender said.

"But he did not intend for there to be," I said.

The Bow Street man ignored me. "Lord Perry, how long have you known Lord Petersham?"

Perry thought, then said, "As long as I can remember."

"And in that time, have you ever heard him speak ill of the Prince of Wales? Ever heard him say England would be better off without his Royal Highness?"

Perry looked at Mr. Lavender with contempt. "This is ridiculous. Of course not. You will never convince me that Petersham had any intention of poisoning the Prince. That snuff box was on the sideboard in the Eating Room for a good part of the evening. Anyone present could have added poison to the contents of that box."

"That is precisely what I tried to tell Townsend and Mr. Lavender yesterday," I said to Perry, then turned to the Bow Street man. "Petersham had a public conversation with the Prince about his new blend of snuff. A number of people knew the Prince was to be the first to try it. As Perry said, *anyone* in that room could be responsible, even the servants. Logic will tell you Petersham is not that person."

"Logic, eh?" Mr. Lavender said. "Let me tell you, laddie, logic doesn't often play a part in crimes like murder. Passion, greed, and revenge, they are the ones."

"There you are," I said triumphantly. "Even though Bow Street thinks it logical that Petersham is responsible because it was his snuff, he is not. You must look for the person with one of the motives you yourself outlined for us, Mr. Lavender."

The Bow Street man was not convinced. "You have a way of muddling things, Mr. Brummell, I'll give you that."

"I am not muddling anything! What could possibly be Petersham's motive? There is none, I tell you."

Mr. Lavender pocketed the notebook and rounded on me. "You are very protective of your friend."

"Yes, I am. I have no wish for his name to be bandied about in a such a disgraceful manner. And I don't want you going about insinuating Lord Petersham is responsible."

"And *I* don't want *you* involved in another murder case," Mr. Lavender said, his voice well above the level of normal conversation.

"*The Prince of Wales* does want me involved," I shot back.

"Madness runs in his family." With that, Mr. Lavender shoved a hat shaped like a coal-scuttle on his head and stomped from the room.

"I do not think we convinced him of my cousin's or Petersham's innocence," Perry said ruefully.

"Neither do I," I said, with growing concern. "Would you pass me the Madeira?"

14

Robinson opened the door to No. 18 Bruton Street upon my arrival home. "Good evening, sir. I trust everything worked out to your satisfaction regarding that strange woman you found on the London Road."

I crossed into the black-and-white tiled hall. "Miss Lavender is taking her in. Remember, the Bow Street man's daughter runs a shelter for women in trouble," I said, handing him my greatcoat, gloves, and hat.

I retained the dog's head walking stick Freddie had given me, reflecting that I missed the Royal Duchess already. I would write to her in the morning, telling her about the Frenchwoman.

Robinson followed up the stairs behind me. "Will you be dining at home this evening, sir?"

"No, I am not hungry at the moment. I shall be spending the evening at White's and will order something there later. You may bring me some tea, though," I said as we entered my bedchamber.

This room contains every luxury a gentleman of fashion might require. The floor is covered by a red, blue, and ivory floral-designed Persian carpet. A set of large mahogany wardrobes line one wall. A tall, mahogany-framed dressing glass, one that rests on casters and can be moved about the room at will, stands in one corner. In another corner, a black lacquered screen is set up, Chakkri's private sand-tray resting behind it. Engravings and paintings make my walls a delight to ponder, while my most prized Sèvres porcelain collection sits on a crescent-shaped side table. The room is dominated by a tented bed with ivory silk hangings.

Er, perhaps I should amend that to read as follows: The room is dominated by a compact bundle of Siamese fur named Chakkri. Asleep in the exact centre of the bed, the cat woke at my entrance, let out a low "reow," and stretched until it seemed he was a yard long. Then he stood up. Looking at Robinson, the cat made as if he would knead his sharp claws on the ivory silk coverlet.

The valet sucked in his breath on a horrified gasp.

Satisfied, Chakkri sprang from the bed without so much as a claw nicking the costly material. I am not surprised the animal did no damage. The cat has shown me from the day he arrived in my house that he holds an appreciation for the finer things in life. He slinks around fragile crystal, purrs at my delicate Sèvres, and rolls in delight on the fur rug of my sedan-chair.

"Good evening, old boy," I greeted him, placing my stick across one of the chairs. I bent and petted his incredibly soft fawn-coloured fur. "Are you happy to be home?"

But Chakkri was not inclined toward conversation at the moment. A new article had entered the house and must be inspected. He rose on his hind legs to sniff every inch of the dog's head walking stick. Despite the canine motif, the cat appeared to approve the new addition, rubbing his whisker pad against it, giving the silver dog a playful nip on the nose. Finished with his examination, Chakkri moved to a position in front of the fire and began toasting his fur.

Robinson unpursed his lips long enough to ask, "Shall I have the twins bring up a bath?"

"Absolutely. I am anxious to rid myself of the dirt from travelling."

"So am I," Robinson claimed with a pointed look at the feline; then he exited the room. The valet had ridden home from the Perrys with Chakkri in his charge. I suppose I should be grateful the cat was not halfway to the coast in a carton marked "Siam."

"Quite a bumble-broth in Brighton, eh, Chakkri?" I said, moving to the wardrobe to select my evening clothes. "Who would have thought a short jaunt to the seaside would give us two deaths? I cannot help thinking of the girl Freddie and I found on the beach."

The cat turned his head toward me. "Reow," he said urgently, his tail switching from side to side.

"A sad sight indeed," I agreed, gently lifting a gentian-blue coat from the wardrobe. "I shall keep in touch with that worthless magistrate, Mr. Kearley, and see if the girl's identity is discovered. Freddie will want to know of any news as well."

The cat turned his attention back to the fire, his tail tapping impatiently on the carpet.

I studied my selection of waistcoats. The white silk or the white jacquard? The silk. "More pressing, though, is the matter with Prinny. I have given my word as a gentleman that I shall find his would-be assassin. Even if I had not made my promise, someone needs to lift a hand to help Petersham before he finds himself mixing snuff at Newgate prison. Freddie said we cannot know everything about Arthur Ainsley's motivations and I agree. Robinson can discover the man's London residence and habits so I can discreetly inquire more fully into his life. Meanwhile, White's is sure to be rife with speculation. I want to hear what is being said."

Chakkri remained silent, his posture now one of unconcern. He stared into the fire so long, I feared his eyes would dry up and fall from his head onto the Persian carpet. Why he turned his back on my musings about Prinny's would-be assassin I cannot say. I confess to having given up trying to understand his feline brain.

At that moment, my servants Ned and Ted entered the room, carrying a large copper tub filled with hot water. Robinson followed, fussing, and directed them to place the tub close to the fire. He set a small tray with a pot of tea and a teacup on the table next to the chair.

Ned and Ted are completely identical twins, tall country boys with golden hair and muscular physiques. They have only been in my employ as chairmen a short time, having recently arrived in London from Dorset where they had lived on a pig farm with their mother. They are devoted to her, their main goal in life being to send money home to "Mum."

Though Robinson balked at their coming to live with us, claiming that between them they do not have the intelligence of a turnip, I optimistically believe he is growing accustomed to having them around. They do the heavier work about the house, in addition to carrying my sedan-chair. Previously, I had to hire men from the

Porter & Pole. Most were none too clean, nor sober for that matter.

With the tub in place, Ted adjusted the sleeves of his blue and-gold livery—garments I personally designed— and said, "Welcome home, Mr. Brummell, sir. Did you have a good time in Brighton?"

Without waiting for me to reply, Ned said, "We were supposed to take a trip to the sea once. It were a fine summer day, and Pa went to feed the pigs afore we left, while Mum loaded the farm cart. We never seed Pa alive again. Best we can tell, he slipped on somethin' greasy and fell into the pigs' swill. Miss Frances, Mum's favourite pig— and the fattest thing you ever did see—must of come chargin' over the minute she seen Pa face down in her breakfast. I reckon as how Miss Frances was only trying to get Pa out of her way when she run over and threw herself atop him in the slop, but if there's one thing I've learned in life, it's that things don't always work out the way a body plans, ain't that right, Ted?"

His brother shook his head sadly. Ned barely paused for breath before continuing. "Naw, I reckon Pa couldn't get hisself out from under almost three hundred pounds of hungry pig. Mum found him smothered in the corn gruel. To this very day, the sight of corn gives me a turn. And if I try to eat it, well I . . . ." Ned looked puzzled for a moment, then asked, "What was I sayin', Ted?"

Ted raised the sleeve of his coat to his eye and wiped a tear. "You was tellin' Mr. Brummell why we ain't been to the sea. You're finished now."

"You must make the journey another time," I said.

Robinson looked at the twins in revulsion. "I shall be certain to instruct André never again to prepare his corn soufflé."

Later, after having made short work of my bath, I donned my black breeches and a white linen shirt and began the exacting task of tying my cravat. "Robinson, what was the talk in the servants' coach of the Prince's brush with death?"

His expression scornful, the valet said, "Mr. Hearn, got into a heated exchange with Lady Perry's maid, Betty, over Signor Tallarico. Betty cannot see any harm in the Italian, while Mr. Hearn believes his lordship's cousin must be a spy for Napoleon."

Was there no female immune to Tallarico's charm? "Did Mr. Hearn give any reason for his convictions?"

"No, sir."

"Here, I have done with my cravat; my fingers are nimble today. Help me into this coat, would you, Robinson. What did Diggie have to say?"

"That fool," Robinson snapped. "Do you know Lord Munro told him some idiotic story about your having two glovemakers and Mr. Digwood believed him? One glovemaker for your thumb and one for the rest of your hand. Have you ever heard the like?"

"Great heavens, how did you respond?"

Robinson briskly smoothed the back of my coat across my shoulders. "I did not lower myself to reply to such utter twaddle."

I chuckled. "Next time, you might tell him, just between the two of you, that I use three glovemakers. Why should I be remiss when it comes to my pinkie? Surely that finger requires special care. But, tell me, did Diggie say anything about Petersham's snuff box and how the snuff came to be tainted?"

"No, sir. Mr. Digwood gave the impression Lord Petersham is not in the least concerned about the matter, which, if I may say so, sir, seems unwise."

"Hmmm. Yes, quite right," I said, putting on a pair of narrow black shoes. "What of Arthur Ainsley? Was anything said about him?"

"Indeed, sir," Robinson crooned, in the manner of one saving the best morsel of information for last. "I paid particular attention, as you had expressed an interest in Mr. Ainsley. Apparently Betty had it from Felice, who serves the St. Clairs, that Lady Prudence talks to her sister, Lady Chastity, frequently about Mr. Ainsley. Though Lady Prudence finds all that is to be admired in the gentleman, Felice found it shocking to hear that in Mr. Ainsley's opinion, England would be better served if the Duke of York were appointed Regent in the event of the King being declared incompetent to rule."

The Duke of York made Regent? I had never considered the idea. Of course, it could happen if the Prince of Wales were deceased. His daughter was only nine years old. The Duke could be made Regent until Charlotte came of age.

And what would that mean for Freddie?

I stood transfixed by the very idea. How would she be able to continue her life at Oatlands, where yours truly is so frequently to be found? Freddie might be obliged to live with her husband at Windsor Castle or Buckingham. Suddenly I had an inkling of how Ned felt when he saw corn.

"Sir, are you all right?" Robinson asked. At my nod, he continued, "Evidently, in a fit of pique, Mr. Ainsley told Lady Prudence that the Prince of Wales was a laughingstock and unable to even lead the fashions— you being the superiour to him in matters regarding elegance—so why anyone should think him capable of running the country was beyond Mr. Ainsley's imagination."

"Well, we already know Mr. Ainsley has decided opinions in matters related to the government."

"But, sir," Robinson said severely, "you have not heard everything. Only listen to this: Betty reported that Felice was positively worrying herself to flinders over Lady Prudence's relationship with Mr. Ainsley, fearful of his single-minded intensity. Her anxiety reached new heights when she overheard Lady Prudence talking to Lady Chastity. According to her, Mr. Ainsley said he wished with all his heart that you had not allowed Sir Simon to take the snuff box back from you when it was being passed to the Prince. He wished Sir Simon's fate upon the Prince."

Good God.

"Reeooow!" shrieked Chakkri, startling me out of the shocked state Robinson's words had put me into. My gaze swung in the direction of the cat, only to see him leap onto the blue chair and then pounce down on the tea tray, sending it sliding to the very edge of the table.

Robinson saw the cat's deed, too. He sprinted across the room in time to catch the tray before the teapot and its contents crashed to the floor. "That fiendish feline!"

But I thought Ainsley was the one who had earned the description of fiendish.

❧ 15 ❧

The outward preoccupation of the fashionable gentleman is his clothes and his appearance. But there are other things with which he can relieve the boredom of a life spent in leisure. Chief amongst these is gaming.

The most stylish place for a gentleman to throw the dice is White's Club in St. James's Street. With four hundred and fifty members, White's may be privileged, but there is nothing exclusive about who may lose their fortune over the turn of a card. For example, some years ago, one Sir John Bland found he was thirty-five thousand pounds down after an evening of wagering at White's. He shot himself.

White's also has a notorious Betting Book, of which yours truly has been the subject on more than one occasion. Twice in the past seven years, bets as to whether or not I shall marry have been entered. One was by my own hand: shortly after obtaining my majority and being elected to White's, I bet Mr. Osborne twenty guineas that I would be married before him. Mr. Osborne was the richer for my folly. In 1801, two friends made a bet that one of them would not be married before I was. He lost as well, sad to say.

Some whisper that I am too particular in my tastes to settle on any one companion. Is there anything wrong with wanting the very best? And if I cannot I have the best because she is already married—er, I mean for whatever reason, well . . .

Ned and Ted carried me in my sedan-chair down St. James's Street to the entrance of White's. I opened the door to my conveyance, the autumn air stinging my face and feeling more like winter this evening. It was too cold for the boys to remain outside waiting for me, since I had no idea how long I would be. If they whiled away the time in a nearby alehouse, God only knew what sort of condition they would be in by the time I was ready to go home.

Thus, I gave the twins leave to take themselves back to Bruton Street, instructing them to see if Robinson required anything of them. I hoped the valet would not order the boys to jump into the Thames.

I climbed the few steps to White's. Delbert, the club's Shakespeare-loving footman, threw open the front door for me.

"Good evening, Mr. Brummell. I am happy to see you returned from Brighton." The white-wigged footman looked around furtively before whispering, " 'I would have him poison'd with a pot of ale' may best describe the situation at the Pavilion, eh?"

"Snuff, it was snuff, not ale," I remonstrated, giving my brain a chance to work on the quotation. At last I said, *"King Henry IV, Part One*, I believe, Delbert."

Delbert looked blue-devilled. "I am fast losing hope that I'll ever catch you out, sir."

I chuckled. " 'Where most it promises, and oft it hits, where hope is coldest and despair most fits.' "

Delbert stood stricken. I handed him my greatcoat, hat, gloves, and stick, and walked toward the sounds of laughter coming from the gaming tables.

"*All's Well That Ends Well!*" Delbert called triumphantly.

I turned and favoured him with a slight bow that acknowledged his success. Privately, I thought all had not ended, and all was not well. Thus, my aim was to discover what I could from the gamblers.

Scrope Davies and Lords Yarmouth, Petersham, and Munro had just finished a round of whist.

"Brummell!" Scrope called out. "Come join us. I think we have done with play for the moment."

"All rolled up, are you?" I teased him. Barbs flew back and forth following this taunt, including a few regarding my own bad luck at the tables of late. A waiter brought bottles of wine, and glasses were filled. Lumley "Skiffy" Skeffington, Lord St. Clair, and Richard Sheridan wandered over and sat down.

Ignoring Lord Munro's dour look, I greeted Petersham and the others, then pulled up a chair between Scrope and Yarmouth.

Much to my dismay, one of the inhabitants of this earth whom I least wanted to see chose that moment to mince his way onto the scene. While he was not greeted with any warmth, my nemesis, Sylvester Fairingdale, affixed himself to our group. He and I looked at one another; then, as if by mutual consent, each of us hastily looked away.

Fairingdale is a fop of the first order. The coxcomb thinks he practices the art of dressing better than I do, and he continually searches for a way to prove himself in the eyes of the *Beau Monde*. He would like nothing better—and would stop at nothing—to topple me from the invisible throne from where I rule London Society.

Tonight he wore another ghastly ensemble which he, no doubt, considered the very glass of fashion. His cravat was wound up so high, it forced his chin up even higher than he normally holds it. His long nose stood in danger of being burnt by one of the candles in the chandelier.

His clothing was selected, I suspect, for its autumnal theme. I say "I suspect" because I do not pretend to understand such a graceless lack of taste. His clothes are well tailored and of fashionable cuts, I grant you. But the combination of colours he chooses . . . well, I shall allow you to judge for yourself. Tonight his breeches were straw yellow, his waistcoat was Indian red and brown striped, and all was topped by a coat of copperish orange.

If he rode down Hyde Park's Rotten Row in that costume, the trees would shrink in revulsion. That is, if he could find a horse to ride that would not roll its eyes and gallop away, frightened by the sight of him.

Petersham lifted his glass and caught everyone's attention. His reddened eyes, disheveled hair, and giddy grin told me he had already raised quite a few glasses. "What shall we drink to, gentlemen?"

" 'Tis obvious!" Scrope cried. "The hero of the hour, the day, the week, perhaps the century: Sir Simon." He raised his glass. "To Sir Simon, for saving our Prince!"

"Sir Simon!" Skiffy cried.

"Here! Here!" added Yarmouth.

Petersham beamed, then raised his voice to recite: "To Sir Simon, Though he didn't know how to dress, We won't wish him bad cess, As he saved Prinny from sore distress."

Everyone found Petersham's attempt at poetry very funny, which is a testimony to the state of inebriation around the table.

Amid the drinking and joviality, Lord St. Clair said, "Oho! Now you toast the departed baronet, Petersham, but at dinner that night you protested strongly against Sir Simon being the first to try your snuff."

Fairingdale's ears perked up at this tidbit of information. His ears were difficult to see behind his shirt points, true, but I am certain they stood out like an alert deer's.

Lord St. Clair's offhand remark may have put Fairingdale on alert, but the rest of the company viewed it as merely more fodder with which to tease Petersham.

"Sir Simon foiled your plan to assassinate the Prince, did he, Petersham?" Sheridan laughed.

Skiffy snickered. "Confess, Petersham, it was jealousy over the Prince's snuff box collection. Wasn't his collection of mistresses, I know that."

A loud burst of laughter greeted this remark, while glasses clinked together.

I kept an amused expression on my face, but silently worried that my friends were not helping matters by making light of the situation. Bow Street, after all, was not laughing.

Neither was Lord Munro. When the noise died down, he could be seen with a severe look on his face. "I don't think this is humourous. May I remind everyone here that Charles comes from a long, honourable line of men of military distinction."

"Harold, they are only joking," the viscount said, waving his glass at his friend's concern. "No one believes me responsible for the poisoned snuff."

"That's right, Munro," Sheridan said. "We know that if Petersham wanted Prinny dead, he would have simply executed him in a military fashion with a single shot to the chest, rather than going to all the bother of poisoning him."

This witticism set off another round of mirth.

"Did the snuff box ever come into your hands, Brummell?" Sylvester Fairingdale asked with elaborate casualness. "Mayhaps with the Prince out of the way, you would be known as The First Gentleman of Europe."

Shock held my tongue still. What made this accusation, disguised as a question, more damning was the fact that, as you know, I *do* want to be known as The First Gentleman of Europe. Call me arrogant if you will, but it is a well-known fact that Society looks to *me* rather than the Prince for standards of elegance. Why should he be the one with the debonair title? Does not Prinny have titles aplenty?

Before I could form a reply, Lord Munro tittered. "Brummell did have the snuff box, now that you mention it, Fairingdale. Why, when Charles showed Brummell the box before we all sat down to dinner, the Beau took so long a time examining it that Lady Bessborough chided him on it."

Fairingdale sat back in his chair and adopted the air of one who has clearly gained the advantage over an opponent. "Lady Bessborough, you say?"

I gazed at him with a cool expression. "Indeed, I held

the box so long that, had I thought of it, I could have pulled my own snuff box from my pocket and juggled the two for the company's entertainment."

A few sniggers erupted at my sarcasm, but a tense atmosphere had settled over the table.

"You had ample opportunity to get to that snuff box, Brummell." A silken thread of menace entered the farouche fop's voice.

"I hardly think Brummell would try to kill one of his best friends over some vague accolade," Lord St. Clair opined, in the manner of one who had been amused, but now found himself impatient.

Fairingdale barely acknowledged his lordship's words. "Before he left for his family's country estate, I heard Arthur Ainsley describe the entire incident. He says you had the box once more, Brummell, as it was being passed up the table, before it was to reach the Prince."

I paid no heed to the taunt, not really hearing anything after the information that Mr. Ainsley had already left London for the country. Had he *left* London or *fled* London? How long would he be gone? How could I question him if he were not in Town?

Lord St. Clair finished the contents of his glass. "If you have been treated to a description of that evening's events, Fairingdale, you would also know that Brummell would have to be adept at sleight of hand to have added anything to the snuff box in the short amount of time he held the box."

I gazed at his lordship in mock chagrin. "Alas, my reputation is such that I am known for the intricacies of my cravat. What is more, I have a way of taking snuff that is emulated by even his Royal Highness. One could easily say my hands are deft," I said in an attempt to restore levity.

"He's right, you know," Sheridan proclaimed. "Nobody is Brummell's equal, even in my theatrical performances."

"Gentlemen," I said in my best somber tone. "Let us drink one last bottle before I am led to Newgate." Amidst much laughter, I gauged the reaction my words had on the company. To a man, the consensus was that Fairingdale spoke nonsense. Still, I could not be easy that my enemy now possessed damning information about me which might be misconstrued by less friendly persons.

"Depend upon it," Lord St. Clair said. "The snuff box sat on the sideboard all during dinner, from what I understand. Anyone could have tampered with it."

Angry at Lord St. Clair's rationalization, Fairingdale was bold enough to say, "Including you, Lord St. Clair?"

Lord St. Clair spoke with quiet dignity. "I am no exception, though I challenge you to find a reason why I would wish the Prince of Wales dead."

Not one reason was voiced. From what Freddie had told me, I knew that Lord St. Clair had married for money. He did so to restore prosperity to the estates his father had let fall to wrack and ruin, and to return respect to the St. Clair name. The renowned Parliamentary orator had feathered his fine nest and was now content to crow from it. He had no motive to kill the Prince of Wales.

Finished with his drink, Lord St. Clair rose from his seat. Before taking his leave, he paused to speak to me. "You will soon be receiving a card of invitation for a party at my house, Brummell."

"When is it to be held? Is there a special occasion?"

"The twenty-first. My wife planned the thing on the coach ride home from Brighton. My daughter Chastity had all the young bucks at her feet last Season. I think Lady St. Clair wishes to keep up the momentum until Spring. You will come? Lady St. Clair wishes you to be present, and you know what a dust-up women can cause if they are frustrated in their multitude of schemes."

"Yes, I will be honoured," I responded, thinking as his lordship walked away that Lady St. Clair did not seem the sort to resort to strong hysterics when thwarted.

Scrope and Yarmouth were about to leave as well. I waited for an opportunity and pulled Lord Yarmouth aside. "How is your family?"

"Well, thank you. I plan to leave for Sudbourn Hall tomorrow. I miss the children."

"I have a question for you. I know you are awake on every suit when it comes to pugilism."

Yarmouth nodded. "What do you want to know?"

"Sir Simon's footmen, if one could call them that—"

"Say no more," Yarmouth said with a smile. "You noticed that, did you? I recognized them at once, of course. Been following the sport since I was in short coats and fancy I know all the participants."

"So I am correct in thinking they are both ex-fighters?"

"Oh, yes. And both were thrown out of the ranks of pugilists for the same reason—dirty fighting. One calls himself Devlin the Devil and the other is Jemmy Wheeler."

"I wonder why Sir Simon hired them?" I mused out loud.

"I questioned that myself and came to a conclusion. You know, Brummell, quite a bit of smuggling still goes on around the Brighton coast."

"So I have heard, though it does surprise me, given the respectable nature of the town."

Lord Yarmouth leaned closer and lowered his voice. "Make no mistake, Brighton is lively. I've heard tales of a secret club located somewhere on the sea coast. Their activities go beyond the pale. Far beyond. As for smuggling, it's widespread. And given Sir Simon's background . . ."

I tilted my head, remembering the talk that Sir Simon had amassed a great deal of money through unsavoury means. "What exactly is—er, was the baronet's background?"

Lord Yarmouth thought for a moment. "My father told me Sir Simon made his fortune in smuggling. The baronet was not born to the title. He got it after he'd given vast sums of money to Pitt for a favourite project of the King."

"The Crown overlooking the fact the man was a criminal."

"Oh, yes. Money, you know, erases many sins," Yarmouth said with a twisted grin. He left me and caught up to Scrope, who was almost out the door.

I looked back at the table and knew the rest of the party would continue well into the small hours of the morning.

I collected my things from Delbert and, after dropping a few coins in his hand, exited the club. As often happens, a heavy fog had descended on London. Scrope and Yarmouth had disappeared into the night. I hoped they had hailed a hackney. Nights like these are a pick-pockets' and footpads' heaven.

Standing on the curb, I had barely formed the idea of hailing a hackney myself when a shabby sedan-chair carried by two lackeys came around the corner from Jermyn Street. The link-boy running ahead of the chair to lead the way held his torch high.

Congratulating myself on my luck, I tossed the boy a coin, and the vehicle came to a halt in front of me. It was nothing like my own superiour sedan-chair, but it would get me home. I gave my direction to the lead chairman, settled myself inside—brushing the dirt from the seat first—and was on my way.

Immediately, my mind went back over the evening's events. Three things stood out among them. One: Petersham, secure in his position as a peer of the realm, continued unaffected by the shadow of suspicion on him. Two: Fairingdale would try to use the information he had gleaned about the fateful dinner to cast doubt on me. The jackanapes! And three: Sir Simon had been a smuggler. What did it all mean? My tired brain could not work it out tonight.

At length it occurred to me that we had been travelling for a longer period of time than necessary to reach my house.

About to rap on the roof and ask if the chairmen knew where they were going, I was thrown to my knees when the vehicle was dropped unceremoniously to the ground. Instantly, a beefy hand jerked open the door. One of the chairmen grabbed a fistful of my coat and dragged me outside.

My stick! The dog's head cane with the concealed swordstick Freddie had given me! If I could just reach it. I pushed my assailant with all my might.

Freed, I lunged back inside the chair. My hand closed tight around the stick, but there was no chance for me to turn the mechanism before I was dragged from the chair's interiour.

The two chairmen were on me now, pulling my protesting body down a dark alley. The link-boy was gone, and the thick fog prevented me from determining anything about my location or my attackers.

I fought them with my feet, as they each had one of my arms, and made satisfying contact more than once. Abruptly, one of the men held me in a tight grasp while the other punched me in the stomach. I doubled over in pain, the stick clattering to the cobblestones beneath me. Escape seemed impossible.

"Here, take my money," I gasped when I could, judging any sum I carried not worth the battering of my person. I hoped the thieves would not take my pocketwatch, as it had belonged to my father.

My offer was met with cruel laughter and a hard knock across my knees with some sort of club. Crumpling to the ground, I was swiftly brought upright again.

In pain, and confused as to why the men did not take my valuables and go, my head spun. I feared I would lose consciousness at any second.

One of the villains must have thought the same thing. He grabbed my shoulders and brought my head to an even level with his. His foul breath washed over my face. "Iffen ye don't want no more o' what we be givin' ye ternight, keep yer bleedin' nose out o' Bow Street work."

The other man guffawed and poked his partner in the ribs. "Ye ain't made 'is nose bleed yet."

The first man grunted, drew back his fist, and made sure the task was accomplished.

A final *thwack* on the side of my head and the sensation of falling are the last things I remember.

❧ 16 ❧

"Sir, now that you have bathed, should you not return to bed?" Robinson asked.

"No. Stop coddling me. Between you and Chakkri, one would think the Grim Reaper was at the door."

"Reow!" the cat commented from where he was winding himself around my ankles. Since I had arrived home in the early morning hours, Chakkri had not left my side. He had curled up in the crook of my arm while I slept, offering a murmured comment of concern and a sympathetic paw stretched to my chin whenever I woke in pain, which was frequently.

"I could put a drop or two of laudanum in your tea—"

"What you could do is stop fussing like a mother hen and help me dress," I snapped.

"Yes, sir," Robinson intoned with an injured air.

God, not his Martyr Act this afternoon! Did I not have enough to bear with a head that felt it contained a quantity of Vauxhall's fireworks ready to explode? Not

to mention muscles—even ones I was previously unaware of—feeling as if they had been run over by the
Royal Mail coach.

Time marched on despite the condition of my person.
I needed to find out when Arthur Ainsley was expected
to return to London and how the Frenchwoman at Miss
Lavender's shelter fared, and I wanted to visit Petersham
and try to have a rational conversation with him—one
which would bring the lazy viscount to the realization
that he might be in a spot of trouble.

Later, I planned to visit the home of one John
Lavender regarding last night's incident.

Gritting my teeth against pain as Robinson eased me
into a Saunders-blue coat, I heard the knocker sound
downstairs.

"See who that is, Robinson," I said, sitting down in
a chair by the fire to relax a moment. Dressing had
drained me of strength.

Immediately, Chakkri jumped up into my lap and
looked at me with concern. I stroked his soft fur. "Now
see what you have done. Robinson might miss cat hairs
on my light-coloured breeches, but he is sure to notice
them on this coat."

The cat purred.

Robinson opened the bedchamber door.

Chakkri turned his head and let out a guttural "reow."

The valet rushed to the dressing table and picked up
the special cloth he employs on my coats before I leave
his presence to rid the garment of cat hairs, anxious to
have it ready to use.

"Who is at the door?" I inquired, continuing to stroke
the cat's fur.

"Mr. Lavender is belowstairs requesting to see you.

I expect he must wish to see the result of his handi-work," the valet said at his most imperious. "Shall I send him away, sir?"

I heaved myself out of the chair, placing Chakkri on the floor. "No, indeed."

Robinson held the cloth up, and I stood impatiently while he briskly brushed the material clean. There fol-lowed an awkward dance when I opened the door to go downstairs and Chakkri tried to follow. "No, old boy, I shall see the Bow Street man on my own."

Chakkri grumbled a complaint and tried to dart out the door.

"Robinson, hold him while I make my escape."

The valet looked at me, plainly outraged at the sug-gestion he touch the cat. "Sir, Viscount Petersham has often expressed the wish—"

"Pray, do not start that routine about going to work for Petersham now! Go out the door, then, and leave me to deal with Chakkri." The command was hastily obeyed. I picked up the cat and told him firmly that he must remain in the room, all the while questioning the sanity of speaking with him. Alas, it is a habit I cannot seem to break since Chakkri seems to understand every word I say.

"I appreciate your desire to play nurse-cat to me, Chakkri, but I have other things to do." Placing him on the bed, I executed a mad, painful dash out of the room, slamming the door in the feline's face.

"Reeeooow!" he protested.

Ignoring repeated cries from my bedchamber, I de-scended the stairs. Robinson met me in the hall and gave my coat a final cleaning with his cloth. "Mr. Lavender awaits you in your bookroom."

I crossed into that room to find the Bow Street man, clad in his usual attire, standing by the fire. I assumed my most frigid demeanor. "Come to add a personal warning to the one given me last night?"

The Scotsman swung around to face me. "Personal warning? What does that mean? And what is that screaming coming from upstairs? Are you housing a baby?"

Closing the door to keep out the sound, I advanced into the room. I put my hand on the back of a high-backed chair near the fireplace. "Never mind the noise. Do you not think it rather bad form to have two thugs beat me senseless and tell me to stay out of Bow Street work?"

Mr. Lavender's face registered honest surprise. "Let's back up a minute, laddie. I came here out of courtesy after I read a report from one of the watchmen saying he'd found George Brummell in an alley last night, the apparent victim of footpads."

I studied him thoughtfully. When the attackers had told me to stay out of Bow Street work, my muddled brain had assumed John Lavender had stooped to this deplorable act to keep me out of his way. Now, faced with the man himself, I realised I had done him an injustice.

"Sit down," I said wearily, motioning to a chair near the desk. "Would you care for a brandy?"

Mr. Lavender checked the time on my tall-case clock and then seated himself. "Seeing as it's after noon, I'll accept that offer. Mind, just a nip of the stuff. Tell me what happened."

Handing him a glass and retaining one for my own, I eased myself into the comfortable leather chair behind my desk. "Around midnight I left White's Club and hailed a passing sedan-chair to carry me home. I specifically wanted to avoid walking the foggy streets at that hour, lest I be set upon by footpads."

Mr. Lavender took a sip of brandy, put the glass on the edge of the desk, and pulled out his notebook. "Description of the chair?"

"Oh, I do not know. Cheap. Unfashionable interior."

Mr. Lavender looked at me from under shaggy eyebrows, pencil poised over the notebook.

I shrugged and immediately regretted doing so when pain shot through my left shoulder. "What do you want? It was dark. At any rate, I noticed we had travelled farther than necessary, and was about to question the chairmen, when the chair was dropped to the ground. I was taken by force from the conveyance, and beaten."

"You don't have a scratch on you."

My lips formed a tight smile. "Efficient men. I assure you they did a thorough job despite the lack of evidence on my face."

"Paid bullies?"

"How should I know? They had a purpose, I assure you, and it was not to rob me. I still have my money, my watch, and a rather expensive walking stick. But when they were almost finished with me, one of them warned me that if I did not want more of the same, I should stay out of Bow Street's work."

"Bow Street's work? And you thought I had ordered this?" Mr. Lavender said curtly, shock yielding quickly to anger.

I took a swallow of brandy. "I apologize. I had not given the matter careful thought."

Mr. Lavender relaxed in his chair. Balancing the

notebook on one knee, he pulled the ivory toothpick box from his coat. He spit on the lid, then wiped the box clean on his sleeve.

I would have cringed, but the action would pain my sore muscles.

The investigator extracted one of the wooden sticks. He popped it into his mouth and spoke around it. "Think carefully now, and tell me who you think might be responsible."

I rubbed my forehead. "All I know is that it was impossible to make out faces. After the last blow to the head, I remember nothing, except I have a vague memory of Ned and Ted carrying me up the stairs. Ned was rattling on about a certain time when he was fifteen years old and a particularly heavy fog descended on the pig farm. He went out to make sure the gate was locked and wandered too far. Ned said he was walking along with his hands out in front of him, feeling his way, and suddenly touched a length of silky hair. Apparently there was a girl down the lane he had taken a liking to. Thinking it was she, as lost as he was, he pushed aside her hair to give her a friendly kiss on the cheek. His lips met an entirely different sort of cheek, followed by a sharp shove from a hoof. Mercifully I slipped back into a state of unconsciousness before hearing more."

"When are you going to let those strong boys of yours do a little work for Bow Street?"

"When are you going to recognize that my help in this investigation can be valuable to Bow Street?"

Mr. Lavender scowled and consulted his notebook. "The watchman said it took him quite a while and a splash of cold water to get you to tell him your name and direction."

"Water? On one of my good coats?" I asked, temporarily diverted. "Good God, the garment must be ruined."

"Put thoughts of your fancy coat aside for the moment," Mr. Lavender advised.

"There is nothing 'fancy' about my coat. The cut is elegantly simple. The idea is for clothing to be so perfect that attention is not drawn to a gentleman because of it."

"Very well, if you say so," Mr. Lavender said, burring his *r*. "Who do you think did this to you?"

I leaned forward in my chair. "I do not know. But I can tell you who did *not* do this to me, and that is Lord Petersham. Even you must agree the viscount would never dream of harming me."

"People resort to desperate measures when they feel the law might take them from the comfort of their homes and place them in a cell."

I made as if to rise. "I shall not discuss the matter with you further if you cannot accept that Petersham is blameless regarding last night."

"Sit back down, laddie," Mr. Lavender said, waving the toothpick at me. I complied, but fixed a stony look on my face. He said, "Give me an alternative to Lord Petersham, then."

"Arthur Ainsley."

"He's out of Town, in the country with his family."

"He could have arranged for my 'warning' before leaving London."

"True. Someone was following you, waiting for an opportunity. Or someone who was in White's with you sent word to an accomplice. Was Lord Petersham present?"

I chose not to answer. "Arthur Ainsley is the only one of the men present at that dinner in the Pavilion who would have had a motive for harming the Prince. Here, I shall make you a diagram of the persons at the table." I pulled a piece of paper towards me and hastily sketched a drawing.

"Ainsley's motive is weak at best. No, there's more going on here than we've uncovered thus far. Mr. Townsend and I have only begun looking into the lives of the people present that night at the Pavilion. Meantime, we've got to hope no one makes another attempt to assassinate the Prince of Wales."

He accepted the drawing I passed to him, merely glancing at it before folding it and shoving it into a pocket. His manner told me he was unwilling to share what they had learned so far. Very well, from now on I would not reveal anything I found out either.

"Prinny is even more well guarded now than he was before the attempt. I feel him safe enough," I said. Then, "By the way, how is your daughter? Has Miss Lavender made any progress with the Frenchwoman?"

The Bow Street man pushed the small revolving bookcase that stood near his chair until it began to go around. Clearly, he was not happy with the change in topic. "My daughter and I have not crossed paths since yesterday. She spent the night at her shelter, and if she came home today, she would not have found me there." He turned and looked me in the eye. "She's taken too much on herself. The lass needs a husband, someone of her own station in life, to take care of her."

Like the grocer who brought a fond smile to her lips?

Though Mr. Lavender had not been responsible for the warning I had received the night before, he was most certainly giving me a warning now. There had been a slight emphasis on the words "of her own station." Yours truly does not fall into that category.

Not that I entertain any amorous thoughts of Miss Lavender. Oh, all right, I have admired her porcelain-like skin, auburn hair, and green eyes. And she does have a impudent way about her I cannot help admiring. More important, she has a kind heart and is eager to help others . . .

I looked up to find Mr. Lavender staring at me, eyes narrowed.

A knock at the door saved me from further fatherly rebuke. "Enter!"

Robinson came forward holding a folded letter on a silver salver. "A footman in the Prince of Wales's livery delivered this, sir. I thought you would want to read it straightaway."

"Thank you, Robinson," I said, accepting the folded vellum. "You may go."

The valet turned on his heel, closing the door behind him with a sharp click.

I opened the paper and scanned the lines quickly, then addressed the Bow Street man. "Prinny is asking for me. It seems he is lonely and bored confined to Carlton House."

Mr. Lavender stood and began walking toward the door. "You'll want to go then. While you're at Carlton House with your noble friends, keep an eye on the Prince of Wales. See that he is not somehow bored *to death*."

Can it be that some of my sense of humour is wearing off on the grouchy Bow Street man?

17

A bored, cranky Prince is not easy to entertain. I know because, for the following week, I danced attendance on Prinny every day at Carlton House.

There had been no further threats to his life, but I was tempted to rectify that by the fourth day of his whining, complaining, and constant airings of various theories he concocted regarding the assassination attempt.

Also frequently present was Jack Townsend. The head of Bow Street was jovial in his assurances that he had the matter well in hand. I suspected Mr. Lavender was the one doing all the work, while Mr. Townsend took advantage of the Prince's hospitality.

His Royal Crabbiness did not seem to realise an important consequence of his demands on my time. He prevented me from further investigation of the very matter he claimed had brought him to the depths of despair. Frustrated, I did what anyone else would do: I ate and drank myself to the point where it grew difficult for me to fasten the buttons at the waist of my breeches.

Chakkri had no one to converse with in my absence, so he was no happier than I with the situation. Or so I liked to think.

Robinson, however, was in good spirits. The gossip at the royal residence increased by day. The valet's sense of self-importance increased along with it as, at every opportunity, he raced to his favourite pub, The Butler's Tankard, with the latest tidbits.

I wrote to Freddie often and wondered if she would soon grow as tired of me as I was of the Prince. But her letters were full of encouragement and confidence that I would overcome my current "obstacles" to victory:

> . . . For you know, George, though I cannot think how you do it, you have a way of discerning how other people's minds work. Then you put that information together with people's behaviour to come to a concise conclusion. This ability is only one of your many fine qualities and one of the reasons I admire you as I do.
>
> Here is something I know will interest you. I have had a letter from a friend who lives in the same county as a certain Mr. A known to both of us. Mr. A arrived at his father's estate, and has been known to be in a high temper ever since. The purpose of his visit seems unclear, and my friend says she cannot say if Mr. A accomplished it, for he departed after only three days.
>
> At Oatlands, we are kept constantly busy by the antics of Minney's pups. They are at the chewing stage. I fear Ulga left the door open to one of my wardrobes, resulting in the destruction of several pairs of my dancing slippers. It cannot signify,

however, as when shall I be dancing?

This weekend is the last of the month. May I dare hope to see you at Oatlands?

> Yours, ever, and truly,
> Freddie

I made a mental note that as soon as I was freed from my royal prison, I would make a trip to Bond Street and buy Freddie a half-dozen pairs of dancing slippers. Perhaps if she continued to shy away from Town entertainments, I might be forced to dance with her myself at Oatlands. One could hope.

As for travelling there this weekend, at that moment I felt fortunate whenever I travelled to the door to Carlton House for a breath of fresh air.

At last, the day of the St. Clairs' party dawned, and claiming a prior commitment, I was finally released from Prinny's grip. Mrs. Fitzherbert's arrival from Brighton helped speed me home.

Standing on the threshold of the St. Clairs' ballroom that evening, clad in my impeccable Alexandria-blue coat over white waistcoat and formal black knee breeches, I noted this was no small gathering. A select list of those who had neither retired to their country estates for a bit of fox hunting, nor retreated to take the waters in Bath, were present.

More than two hundred finely dressed members of Society drank, danced, flirted, and exchanged gossip. In a separate room set up for cards, the ladies played as feverishly as the men. The party was sure to be deemed a "crush" and therefore could only be to Lady St. Clair's social credit.

Her husband perceived my arrival and came up to greet me. "Brummell, good of you to join us."

"A delightful entertainment, my lord," I said with a bow.

"Anything might appeal to you at this point, though, I expect. I hear you have been much at Carlton House."

"Indeed," I replied, unwilling to discuss my visit.

Lord St. Clair did not seem to mind my reluctance. "I find these sorts of festivities tedious in the extreme, but they do have benefits, I suppose." He waved a hand in the direction where his daughter, the beauteous Lady Chastity, held court amongst a crowd of admiring swains. She appeared to favour one of them, Victor Tallarico, bringing a frown to her father's face.

"No doubt Lady Chastity will have an even larger choice of suitors during the Season next spring," I ventured.

"If she is not carried away with an unsuitable match before then. I tell you, Brummell, I cannot like Lord Perry's Italian cousin. My wife invited him tonight out of politeness to the Perrys. My suspicions that he might be a spy for Napoleon grow stronger."

I raised my right eyebrow. "Oh?" I said, thinking his lordship had new information.

"The man is a subject of the French Emperor's now. England cannot be too careful of foreigners."

Was the country of Tallarico's origin the sole basis for Lord St. Clair's misgivings about the Signor? This narrow view seemed out of character for his lordship. Perhaps his disapproving ideas stemmed from a more personal source.

As we watched, Signor Tallarico—in yet another pink waistcoat—successfully extracted Lady Chastity

from her group of admirers and began a slow but in-
exorable walk to the tall windows that led to the balcony—a balcony where a few stolen kisses could be
exchanged.

"Excuse me, Brummell," Lord St. Clair said, taking
in the situation. A look of determination filled his eye.
"I must speak to my daughter."

Accepting a glass of wine from a circulating footman,
I thought of Lord St. Clair's other daughter and her oft-
time companion, Arthur Ainsley. Scanning the crowd for
him, I saw Sylvester Fairingdale and Lady Bessborough
with their heads together. Attired in a violent violet, the
fop was probably trying to glean every bit of damning
information about me that he could. He would press
Lady Bessborough into naming the exact length of time
I held the tainted snuff box before we all sat down to
dinner, concoct a motive for my perfidy, then present his
case to the Prince.

I took a large swallow of wine, then chided myself
for being silly. Fairingdale would not go so far as to
blacken my name with the Prince. Would he?

For the next part of the evening, I conversed with
various friends, frustrated that Mr. Ainsley continued to
play least in sight. I learned the Perrys had had to cancel
their acceptance to the party because Lady Perry was
once more suffering from her condition. I danced with
the playful Lady Chastity, who was all flirtatious
glances, then two other young ladies, each well enough
in her way, but neither had the sweet nature of Freddie.
Or the flash of fire in Miss Lavender's eyes. Hmmm,
where had that last thought come from?

On one side of the room, a long table had been set
up with various treats to tempt aristocratic palates. Tiny

iced cakes in different shapes, a selection of fruits, nuts, miniature rolls of wrapped beef, squares of small sand- wiches and—joyously—a plate of lobster patties were spread out along the white cloth. Had Chakkri been pres- ent, he would have devoured the latter. He shares my fondness for lobster.

About to select a plate and further jeopardize the per- fect fit of my clothing, I heard Mr. Ainsley's voice com- ing from an ante-room nearby. I could not quite make out what he was saying over the music, so I stepped closer, intent on conversing with him. He would not get away from me this time, deuce take it, and my ques- tioning would be more strenuous than ever before.

Then my plans were thwarted in the most unexpected way. The door was partially ajar, affording me an ex- cellent view of Arthur Ainsley holding Lady Prudence in a passionate embrace. I wondered her spine did not snap, so tightly was he holding her.

Quickly, I retraced my steps without being detected by either of the lovers. My mind raced. Had things be- tween Lady Prudence and Arthur Ainsley really gone so far? My own eyes told me they had. Although Mr. Ain- sley was an intense man, I found it hard to believe the mousy Lady Prudence could raise him to such heights of lust at her parents' own house. And why would he leave her in the middle of a simmering courtship to go to his family estate?

"What in heaven's name did you see in there to make you jump back like you were bitten by an adder, George?"

I turned around swiftly and beheld the sight of Lady Hester Stanhope looking like a goddess from mythology in a white silk gown with gold trim. A true friend, and an Original, as Society is apt to name anyone out of the ordinary, I hold Lady Hester in high regard. Her wit is sharp, the turn of her cheek exquisite, and her neck elegant and graceful. One night at Almack's Assembly Rooms, I had been so bold as to remove a pair of earbobs she was wearing. I told her she had no need to wear such things.

"Lady Hester!" I said, bowing over her hand. "I am your humble servant."

Her ladyship gazed at me right in the eye. She is a tall lady, near six feet in height. "Don't gammon me, George. Either tell me what you saw, else I shall see for myself."

I shrugged a shoulder, happy the gesture no longer pained me.

Lady Hester swept over to the ante-room, grinned and returned to my side. "I am not the least bit surprised."

"Really? Are you positive you are not going to faint from the sight of such a passionate display?"

She laughed heartily, then spoke for my ears alone. "Ah, but what is the true source of Mr. Ainsley's passion?"

I stared at her. "Lady Hester, come and sit with me by the window, will you not?"

She smiled, and we crossed the room to sit on a silver-and-green striped backless sofa.

"About Mr. Ainsley," I began, only to be interrupted by her ladyship.

"That tiresome man can think of only one thing," she said, then chuckled. "Well, two things, I suppose I must say after what I just saw."

I looked at her sternly. "There is something Mr. Ainsley wants even more than Lady Prudence's prim lips.

And you know about it, you impossible girl," I accused.

"I am hardly a girl at nine and twenty, George," Lady Hester protested.

"Cut line and give over, Lady Hester. What do you know about Arthur Ainsley?" Lady Hester's uncle is Prime Minister Pitt. She runs his household and is privy to all kinds of government gossip.

"A seat in the House of Lords," she whispered. "And he'll do anything to get one. Rumour has it he is more bent on it now than ever. He just had a flaming row with his brother, the heir, this past week while on a visit home, regarding his views of the government. Ainsley is livid that all his brother can think about is crop rotation."

"Let me ask you this, Lady Hester, and please know we are speaking confidentially. What do you think about the attempt on Prinny's life?"

She looked at me in dawning surprise. "You surely don't think Ainsley had anything to do with that?"

"You said he would do anything to get a seat in the House of Lords. What if he was promised a peerage, then the promise withdrawn?"

Lady Hester drew in her breath. "Oh, my."

"Indeed. And had not Sir Simon taken the snuff—"

Lady Hester rolled her eyes. "I beg you will not join the hordes of others praising that odious man to the skies."

"I thought he was a friend of the Prime Minister's," I said, hoping this would encourage her to tell me what she knew about Sir Simon.

"*Was* a friend. George, that was years ago. My uncle loathed Sir Simon for all that he made him a baronet. That was before Uncle found out that Sir Simon was heavily involved in smuggling. Did you know that aspect of the baronet's character?"

"I had heard something of the sort."

Lady Hester fanned her heated cheeks. "The man was a despicable criminal. Uncle told me that he'd been taken in by Sir Simon's story of a low birth, of a childhood of poverty."

"Mr. Pitt is too good."

"Too trusting, in this instance, George. The tale goes that as a boy, Sir Simon saw a fine gentleman alight from a carriage at an inn where the future baronet was begging for coins. The gentleman did not even notice the beggar boy, but Sir Simon never forgot him and vowed to be like him one day. He fell in with smugglers on a night raid, worked hard, and eventually got his own ship. Over the course of time, he built quite an impressive organisation that he managed to keep secret from the government."

"Including Prime Minister Pitt."

Lady Hester nodded. "Exactly. Sir Simon was generosity itself when it came to contributing to the government, and to the King's projects."

"He must have wanted a title desperately. And you know, Lady Hester, he must have wanted to become that gentleman in the inn yard that day. Did you ever observe how he clung to bygone fashions?"

She reached over and squeezed my hand. "You noticed that, George?" she asked in mock astonishment.

"Amongst other things. Would you care to dance, Lady Hester? Your attention has wandered to the dance floor."

"I see Colonel Smith is here. I wish to dance with him."

"Colonel Smith?" I asked, raising my right eyebrow. "Who was his father?"

"Piffle! Who was George Brummell's father?"

I smiled at her. "Who, indeed? And who would ever have heard of me if I were not friends with the Prince of Wales and knew to a nicety the gentle art of dressing oneself?"

Lady Hester hooted with laughter. "Come to our house tomorrow night for dinner, George. Do not say you have other plans! Break them if you must." Lady Hester rose to her feet. Before she walked away, she bent and whispered in my ear. "Your friend Ainsley will be there."

With that lure, she glided away, leaving me deep in thought. An arresting idea presented itself in my brain and would not be dislodged.

All along I had felt no one at the table that fateful night at the Pavilion had reason enough to kill his Royal Highness. Petersham certainly had no motive, and Prussic acid was not something that one inadvertently mixed with snuff. No, the poison was put into the box deliberately. Bow Street might think the viscount responsible, but the viscount never would. Neither would I.

I also did not believe Victor Tallarico was a spy. The only time that man would employ a spyglass was if he trained it on the female bathers at the Brighton beach.

The single suspect worth considering could be Arthur Ainsley. He was the sole person with any sort of motive to do away with the Prince: revenge for a reneged promise. I would attend Lady Hester's dinner party and continue my investigation of that man.

The simple conclusion was that, amongst the company present, Prinny had no other enemy than Arthur

Ainsley. If Mr. Ainsley proved innocent, then the idea niggling in my brain would not be refused closer examination any longer.

What was my idea? Why, that the poisoned snuff was meant for Sir Simon all along. If I was right, the killer had been clever, very clever, for he had succeeded in diverting all attention from the question of who would wish to kill *Sir Simon*.

However, little did I know then that Bow Street would shortly have another name to add to its list of suspects, one they believed might well have wished to see the Prince put permanently out of his way.

❧ 18 ❧

My reprieve from Carlton House did not last long. The following afternoon, directly after I had finished a sumptuous breakfast, which included bacon, eggs, André's special French-style toast, and slices of fresh pineapple, the knocker sounded.

Leaving Chakkri devouring a plate of eggs and bits of bacon—he does not care for pineapple—I descended the stairs from the dining room to encounter Robinson admitting a footman in the Prince of Wales's grey livery.

There was no letter, only the spoken command that I present myself at Carlton House immediately.

Ned and Ted carried me in my sedan-chair to the royal residence after a slight delay. Robinson had insisted on ridding my coat of cat fur. A few of the hairs proved stubborn against his special cloth. Seething, the valet had resorted to a pair of tweezers. I stood for this as long as I could—noting the tweezers were the same ones he used on my brow!—then took my leave.

Arriving at Carlton House, I opened the door to my chair and told the twins to wait for me.

"Er, sir," Ted said anxiously. "Couldn't we come in with you?"

Thinking the country boys wanted to see the inside of a royal palace, I shook my head sadly. "I am sorry." I turned to go.

"Wait!" cried Ned. "Mr. Robinson said we was to stay with you and protect you. We are strong, you know. Just look at these muscles."

Before I could utter a protest, Ned stripped off his coat, tossed it on top of the sedan-chair, then turned and posed, muscles flexing.

We were the object of everyone's gaze.

"Ned, put your coat back on, please. As much as I appreciate your sentiments, and those of Robinson, I can take care of myself. Wait for me here."

The twins obeyed reluctantly. Approaching the door to Carlton House, I saw even more guards stationed about the grounds. I spent half an hour cooling my heels while word was sent to the Prince of my arrival.

Finally, none other than Mr. Lavender came to collect me.

"Surely they have not reduced you to looking after his Royal Highness," I said good-naturedly.

But the Scotsman grunted an indistinguishable reply and remained tight-lipped throughout our progress to the Rose Drawing Room.

When the doors to that room opened, it became clear that the Prince had assembled the principals involved in the investigation: Jack Townsend, John Lavender, and myself, with the startling addition of William Pitt, Prime Minister of England, accompanied by his friend, Lord

St. Clair. Pitt nodded to me by way of greeting. I thought he looked unusually pale and drawn. With the exception of the Prince, everyone was standing.

"Brummell," his Royal Highness began. "There has been a development in the matter of the tainted snuff box."

"Oh," I responded equably, but feeling myself tense.

Jack Townsend nodded at Mr. Lavender, who produced his notebook and said, "Bow Street believes Lord Munro withheld information from us the day we questioned him at the Pavilion. Information about what he observed when Lord Petersham was mixing the snuff that killed Sir Simon."

A great feeling of foreboding washed over me.

"Mr. Lavender found out something about Petersham, Brummell," the Prince said. "Something I don't like at all."

"What could that possibly be, sir?"

Mr. Lavender looked to the Prince for permission, and at his nod, spoke. "It seems that Lord Munro saw Lord Petersham grind a white powder and mix it into the snuff."

Everyone knows snuff is brown. Panic rose in my chest, and I forced myself to maintain my composure. Otherwise, I might leave the room, find Lord Munro, and bang his head against the floor until he took back the damning words and promised to keep his mouth shut in the future.

"Mr. Lavender, did you question Lord Petersham as to what the powder might be?" I asked evenly.

"Aye. His lordship claimed it was sea salt," the Scotsman said, a strong measure of disbelief attached to his words.

"Er, sea salt," I said, my mind racing for a reason why Petersham thought sea salt would be a good addition to snuff.

Lord St. Clair pulled up a chair for Prime Minister Pitt, since Mr. Pitt had grown paler. I imagined the Prime Minister had enough on his mind with government matters. The fact that England was at war no doubt complicated his duties.

"Petersham told Lavender that he thought sea salt would help my breathing," the Prince said scornfully.

"I can't say I like that excuse," Jack Townsend said, speaking for the first time. "It's nonsensical."

"Not at all," I countered. I looked at the Prince. "Sir, you know Petersham suffers from asthma. Perhaps he found that sea salt relieves his symptoms and thought it might help you with your occasional breathing problems."

The Prince mulled this over.

Jack Townsend scoffed. "How do you know that, Mr. Brummell? Did Lord Petersham say anything to that effect before the box was passed to the Prince?"

"Well, no," I admitted. "At least, not in my hearing."

Prinny shook his head. "Not one word about anything other than snuff being present in the box was said to me. That is, not until Sir Simon died in front of my eyes! Brummell, when Townsend and Lavender brought the news of Munro's disclosure to me earlier in the day, I sent for you and Pitt. I wanted you to know before . . . before further action is taken against Petersham."

Pitt said, "I would never have thought a gentleman of Petersham's background would commit such an unspeakable act."

"Neither would I," Lord St. Clair said regretfully.

I gazed at the company in astonishment, then spoke to the Prince. "Sir, you cannot believe this, I know you cannot. Petersham is your *friend*. What could his reason be for hurting you?"

"I don't know," the Prince mumbled.

"The viscount said little to defend himself, when I asked him about the so-called sea salt," Mr. Lavender pointed out.

"I can well accept that. The viscount does not think anyone capable of believing him responsible for the poison. He trusts his friends. And most importantly, he has no motive," I said, but my words seemed to fall on deaf ears.

"You make a good case for Lord Petersham," Mr. Lavender said. "But if not the viscount, then who added the poison to the box?"

"Yes, Mr. Brummell," Jack Townsend remarked with a sharp edge to his voice. "Let's hear what you have to say."

There was only one thing to do and that was express my new theory. I disliked doing so before I had had a chance to explore the possibilities, but there was nothing for it. From the atmosphere in the room, I judged it would not be long before Petersham would be formally charged with attempted murder, an act sure to set the Nobility on its ears.

I cleared my throat and began, "Your Royal Highness, as you know, I have been investigating this problem. The only person present at your dinner table that night who had any sort of motive to wish you harm is Arthur Ainsley. I shall continue to learn what I can of him. In the meantime, another idea has occurred to me. Perhaps we are overlooking the obvious. Perhaps the poison was intended for Sir Simon all along."

"What?" the Prince of Wales exclaimed.

Mr. Pitt looked thoughtful.

Mr. Lavender eyed me as if I were a small child and he were the adult forced to listen to my ramblings.

Lord St. Clair gave me a look of pity.

Jack Townsend took a step toward me. "All right, I've listened to you, Mr. Brummell. Now let me tell you what I think. I think this case is not over."

Relief swept through me. There was hope for Petersham yet.

Mr. Townsend continued. "It's true Lord Petersham had no motive of which we are aware. But the fact remains that it was his snuff box that contained the poisoned snuff, snuff he admits to mixing. As for Arthur Ainsley, he has been out of Town, and we've not questioned him yet. I'm willing to hold off on further action in regard to Lord Petersham until Bow Street has spoken with Mr. Ainsley."

"Excellent plan, Mr. Townsend," I said approvingly.

Then his next words chilled me to the bone.

"However, what you said about Sir Simon, Mr. Brummell, seems the ravings of a desperate man. Are you a desperate man?"

"A desperate man? What do you mean by that?" I replied, sure I could not have understood him. Gone was the usually gracious Jack Townsend. In his place was an ill-mannered lout.

A tense silence enveloped the room.

Mr. Townsend likes center stage. He had it now. "You are very defensive of your friend, Lord Petersham. You would not want him to suffer the consequences of something he did not do, would you?"

"Of course not," I said, very much on my dignity.

"You are also anxious to turn Bow Street's attention elsewhere—in fact, to cast blame on Arthur Ainsley."

"I did not say that," I protested. "I have yet to prove—"

"Failing that," Mr. Townsend went on relentlessly, "you expect us to believe that the Prince of Wales was not the intended victim at all. No, you would have us believe that the baronet who served as his Royal Highness's food taster was meant to take the poison."

"I think it is an idea worthy of consideration," I said.

Mr. Townsend stepped toward me once again. "Going along with this ridiculous theory for a moment, what, if you will be so kind as to tell me, Mr. Brummell, would the killer have done if Sir Simon had not intercepted the box? Would he have let the Prince of Wales inhale the poisoned snuff? Would he consider the death of the Prince a mere inconvenience in his quest to eliminate Sir Simon?"

My heart began to pound. Not only would Townsend not consider my hypothesis, he was making a fool out of me in front of the Prince. "I have not had time to investigate my theory to find out the answers to those questions. I have been here at Carlton House this week past."

"Indeed," Mr. Townsend said. He came closer to me. "And you were at the table that night at the Pavilion, Mr. Brummell."

"Yes," I said impatiently, wondering where he was going with this line of questioning.

Mr. Townsend drew a slip of paper from his pocket. To my annoyance, I saw it was the diagram of the table I had made for Mr. Lavender. I darted a look at him, but the Scotsman refused to meet my eye.

Mr. Townsend, however, stared directly at me. "If I am interpreting this drawing correctly, you were seated *next* to the Prince, were you not, Mr. Brummell?"

I clenched my fists at my side. "What are you saying, Mr. Townsend?"

"Furthermore, if I have this right, you held the snuff box in your hand before Sir Simon took it back from you. You are adept at opening and closing snuff boxes, as everyone knows. Why, I've seen you do it myself. Quite clever you are, Mr. Brummell."

I assumed my most haughty mien. "I fail to see—"

"Furthermore, I have it from a reputable gentleman that Lady Bessborough saw you and Lord Petersham talking at the entrance to the Eating Room and that you, Mr. Brummell, were holding the snuff box in your hand for several minutes. Long enough to have added something to the contents of the box."

The Prince of Wales gasped. He looked at me, appalled.

Devil take Sylvester Fairingdale!

I returned Mr. Townsend's probing look without blinking. Ice dripped from my tongue. "Are you accusing me of trying to poison the Prince of Wales?"

"No," Mr. Townsend said mildly. "Not yet."

Anger welled in me. I had to struggle not to let it overwhelm me. "May I ask what my motive would be for such a despicable action?"

Mr. Townsend cocked his head. "You are a man of great determination and resource, Mr. Brummell. I think of your rise to the height of Polite Society and can only admire your tenacity. The gentleman I spoke with says you covet the title of First Gentleman of Europe. A silly nickname, perhaps, but he says you like to think yourself the supreme ruler over everything fashionable. He thinks you resent sharing any of your position as Arbiter of Fashion."

"How dare you, Mr. Townsend?" I said frostily.

The Prince looked at me aghast. "It's not true, is it, Brummell? Tell me you don't wish to be known as the First Gentleman of Europe," he said, his voice shaking.

Before my astounded brain could form a reply and force it past my lips, the Prince clutched his wrist. "Oh, my pulse! How it gallops! My physician! Someone send for Pitcairn!"

My own heart felt like it would burst from my chest.

Attendants rushed to fuss over the Prince.

Feeling I could control my anger no longer, I strode from the room without another word.

❧ 19 ❧

In nothing less than a towering rage, I exited Carlton House. I shouted the order for home to Ned and Ted, startling them with my tone, and settled into my sedan-chair. Once my heart resumed a beat somewhat approaching normalcy, I realised my uppermost feeling was that of betrayal.

Mr. Lavender had run to his superiour with the diagram I had given him. He had also remained silent as the head of Bow Street treated me like a chunk of bread he could toast over the fire. I thought the Scotsman and I had formed a friendship of sorts—an uneasy one, perhaps—but nonetheless a rapport.

Jack Townsend was either under too much pressure himself, or did not give a shilling for my opinions. Worse, he dared insinuate I would try to poison the Prince. What a nonsensical notion! Why would I kill the Prince? I am not so conceited as to think my reign over London Society would continue without Prinny's friendship.

That brought me to his Royal Highness. He had to be suffering a bout of mental disorder like the ones his father, the King, experiences to think me involved in a plot against his life. I would call on him when we could be private and discuss Mr. Townsend's offensive suggestions—suggestions made more offensive since there was a tiny grain of truth in them. As you know, I do long for the title of First Gentleman of Europe. But devil take it, I would not kill anyone for such a ridiculous reason.

Thank God Freddie had not witnessed the ugly scene.

Although I had agreed to meet Scrope at White's for an evening of gaming, there was no question of my keeping the engagement now. I doubt he would even notice my absence, the way that lad had been drinking and gaming lately. Instead, I would accept Lady Hester Stanhope's invitation to dinner so that I might finally be able to corner Arthur Ainsley.

With this goal in mind, I entered my house. "Robinson!"

The valet came hurrying from his rooms. "Sir, I did not expect you home. Is everything all right?"

"No, it is not. Bow Street's suspicion of Petersham grows by the minute," I said striding into the bookroom. No sense telling him the investigators also had me under their magnifying glass.

Chakkri sat tall in the exact centre of my desk. I seated myself behind the desk and nudged him out of the way. He did not want to move, though. The minute I took my attention from him to draw a sheet of paper from the drawer, he resumed his original position.

He gazed at me with his keen blue eyes. "Reow."

"Get down from here, you rogue, and let me write

this letter." I picked him up and deposited him on the floor. The cat stalked from the room, hopping over the threshold as is his odd custom. I heard a rumble of paws on the stairs and assumed he had retired to my bed-chamber.

"I need you to get this message to Scrope Davies at White's, Robinson."

"Yes, sir."

"I have to change clothes for the evening. I shall be attending a dinner party at Lady Hester Stanhope's, and she does not tolerate her guests being late. Have Ned and Ted ready outside the door with my sedan-chair."

"What time does Lady Hester expect you?"

"Eight o'clock," I said, scrawling a line of apology to Scrope and telling him I might be at the club later in the evening.

I looked up to hand the folded vellum to Robinson. The fussy valet was staring at the tall-case clock in horror.

I took a steadying breath. "I know we have but a mere hour for The Dressing Hour, but it will have to do. Ready some hot water for my shave."

"Yes, sir," Robinson replied in heavy tones.

Upstairs, I selected a Spanish-blue coat from the wardrobe. The minutes flew as Robinson shaved me, arranged my hair, and helped me into my clothes. I knew the valet burned with curiosity as to what had happened at Carlton House to put me in such a temper. His next words confirmed it.

"Sir, might I be of any assistance to you in your investigation?"

"Not unless you know anything about the smuggling business in Brighton."

"The smug—"

A loud crash from the direction of the dining room interrupted us. Grabbing my dog's head stick, I crossed the hall and hurried into the dining room, Robinson behind me.

My rosewood teapoy lay on its side on the carpet, the lid open and the contents emptied across the floor. Chakkri stood beside it, lashing his tail from side to side, not the slightest bit of remorse about his catly demeanor.

"Dear me," Robinson chirped in a voice that clearly said, *I told you so.* No doubt he was enjoying this confirmation that Chakkri should not remain in our household.

"What are you doing?" I asked the cat. "What is this fixation you have developed for tea? Get away from there."

The cat retained his air of supremacy. He walked past me, tail in the air, back into my bedchamber. When I followed him to fetch my greatcoat, I could hear a furious scratching coming from behind the lacquered screen that concealed Chakkri's sand-tray.

Robinson handed me my hat, and I made for the stairs, noting that Ned and Ted had only fifteen minutes to convey me to Lady Hester's.

"Do not wait up for me, Robinson. I may not return this evening."

"Where will you be after Lady Hester's?"

"White's."

"And after that?"

"Somewhere."

The valet looked mutinous. "Sir, you never tell me where you are going on these evenings you stay out all night. I know you say they are private, but what if I needed to reach you . . ."

"Then you would not be able to. Open the door," I said.

Robinson obeyed, his lips pursed. Then his mouth gaped in surprise.

For outside the door, one gloved hand raised ready to knock, stood Lydia Lavender. With her other hand, the Bow Street man's daughter held the hood of her cloak tightly under her chin. Cold air rushed in through the doorway.

"May I come in?" she asked me when I did not immediately invite her.

"Er, please do. Robinson, you may go," I said, seeing the disapproving expression settle over the valet's face. It is not proper for an unmarried female to call upon a gentleman at his residence. Miss Lavender, though, is not one to care for the conventions as Robinson does.

She crossed into the black-and-white tiled hallway, allowing the hood of her cloak to fall about her shoulders. Her auburn hair gleamed in the candlelight. "I wanted to speak with you about the Frenchwoman you left in my care."

"How is she?" I inquired, closing the door.

Miss Lavender looked past me toward the bookroom. "Might we discuss it in your bookroom?"

"I am sorry, but I am late for an important dinner party. May I call on you tomorrow when we can talk at length?"

"No, I need to speak with you now. And isn't it fashionable to be late to dinner parties?" Miss Lavender inquired, all innocence.

"Not at Lady Hester Stanhope's house."

"I've heard of her. She's known to be different from the useless Society women one normally hears about. Lady Hester won't mind your tardiness if you explain that you were looking after a female in difficulty."

"But—"

Miss Lavender paced the floor. "What do you know of the woman you gave over to me? Do you understand the extent of her frenzy? I can hardly get her to eat anything. I've been afraid to leave the shelter lest she do herself an injury. She doesn't cry. I sometimes wonder if it wouldn't do her good to cry, but she only continues in a dazed state that alternates with fear at the sight of men. I have been forced to draw the curtains at all times to keep her from seeing any man passing in the street."

"Hmmm. I do not know what to say. I told you all I know that day at the Perrys'. Have you not been able to learn even the Frenchwoman's name? Where she comes from? Who her family is?"

"No. Call me incompetent if you must," Miss Lavender retorted. She ceased her pacing to stand in front of me, her green eyes stormy.

"You are anything but incapable."

"My happiness at hearing you say so knows no bounds," she said sweetly, if sarcastically.

I pulled out my pocketwatch and glanced at it. Ten minutes to eight. "Look here, I shall call on you first thing in the morning—"

Miss Lavender's hands formed fists which she rested on her hips. "Meaning two in the afternoon!"

"How about one?"

She drew a deep breath—an action whose charm was not entirely lost on me. "The Frenchwoman has started talking. Just bits and pieces, but it's something about a fine house near the sea. Perhaps Hove. I think she was held captive there by a man."

"Held captive?" I asked in disbelief. "Miss Lavender, have you by chance been reading Minerva Press novels?"

Outrage spread across her face. "You think I am dramatizing events? Oh, you insufferable man! Go to your party, then!" she said, marching toward the door. "I'll take care of this on my own," she fumed. Before I could say another word, she was out of the house, the door swinging back on its hinges.

Dash it! What had put her in such a temper? I walked out the door and down the front steps. Miss Lavender was nowhere in sight.

"Uh-oh, Mr. Brummell. You're in trouble with that there female," Ted said. The twins were waiting on the pavement with my sedan-chair.

Ned said, "That reminds me of the time—"

"We must go at once," I said, cutting off another one of Ned's stories. I entered my chair and leaned my head back on the white satin lining, thinking I would have to rise and present myself at Miss Lavender's shelter at an indecently early hour. Noon, even.

Tonight I would finally have my opportunity to get to know Arthur Ainsley. And just how badly he wanted that place in the peerage.

However, when I was shown into Lady Hester's house, it was to find the company just sitting down to dinner. A lively bunch had gathered, including, to my surprise, Victor Tallarico. He and Lady Hester were engaged in a conversation about Italy, a country Lady Hester had visited on one of her many travels.

Even Mr. Ainsley seemed in high spirits, most unusual for him.

We did miss the company of one person. Mr. Pitt, Lady Hester announced, sent his apologies, but could not come down to partake of the meal, feeling too weary. No doubt with the weight of the war on his shoulders, the Prime Minister would sometimes prefer a solitary meal in his room than a table full of people eager to share their opinions.

After dinner, Lady Hester led everyone to the drawing room, forsaking the custom of separating the ladies and gentlemen for a space of time in which they might gossip with their own sex. I walked over to Mr. Ainsley, who lingered in the doorway.

Before I could speak to him, he addressed the room in general. "I should like to remain, but I must attend my *fiancée*."

A murmuring of surprise went around the room.

The embrace I had witnessed last night at the St. Clairs' flashed through my mind's eye. Of course, a gentleman did not kiss an earl's daughter that way unless he meant marriage.

Mr. Ainsley chuckled. "The announcement will be in all the papers tomorrow morning, so I can tell you. Lord St. Clair's daughter, Lady Prudence, has made me the happiest of men. I would have been able to make the disclosure weeks ago, but Lady Prudence insisted she have a betrothal ring first. You know how women are."

A smattering of laughter met this remark.

"The settlements were made by the first of the month, but there was a delay while we followed the Prince to Brighton, then I had to ride out to my family home and obtain a betrothal ring. Now that the ring is safely on her finger, I am free to speak."

Amidst congratulations, Mr. Ainsley took his leave.

"Well," Lady Hester said, appearing at my side. "Ainsley will get his Parliament seat now, George. God knows Lord St. Clair has enough influence with my uncle, and if not, I'm sure Lady Prudence comes with a large dowry. Enough money that now Ainsley could campaign to be elected to the House of Commons."

"Lady Hester, will you forgive me if I leave as well? I do not wish to be rude . . ."

Her ladyship patted my arm. "Go ahead, do. I know you are searching for clues in that ugly matter involving the Prince."

I smiled at her ruefully. "Searching, but finding things I did not quite expect."

Leaving the house, I gave orders to Ned and Ted to carry me to White's. All the while, my brain raced. Ainsley and Lady Prudence had been engaged for weeks! Ainsley knew they were getting married *before* coming to the Pavilion. This slashed any possibility of his having a motive to kill the Prince. Whom did that leave as a suspect?

No one. That the poison was intended for Sir Simon was more clear than ever.

I alighted at White's, saying to Ned and Ted, "You might step around to the nearest public house and have a drink, but then await my orders."

Delbert greeted me at the door. The cheerful deportment he normally wears was absent. "Good evening, Mr. Brummell. 'There's nothing in this world can make me joy: Life is as tedious as a twice-told tale vexing the dull ear of a drowsy man.' "

I stared at him as he accepted my coat, hat, gloves, and walking stick. "*King John.* Now, Delbert, what has brought you low?"

The footman looked at me. "May I tell you, sir?"

"Of course you may."

"Well, it's like this. I don't want to be a footman all my life. Not that I don't enjoy waiting on fine gentlemen like yourself," he added hastily.

"You have other ambitions?" I asked.

Delbert nodded. "I want to be an actor, and perform in the great Shakespearean plays. I want to speak aloud in front of an audience all the words I know by heart and love well."

"Have you been around to the theatres?"

"Yes, but no one wants to hire me. I've no experience, you see."

"And you cannot get any if they will not hire you."

Delbert looked at me sorrowfully. "That's it exactly, Mr. Brummell, sir."

"I know Sheridan and his crowd and shall mention your name to them. I make no promises, mind you," I said, seeing the glow of hope cross the footman's face. "All you can expect is a trial performance. Then the matter is in your hands."

"Thank you, sir. You've raised my spirits."

I turned to go, but Delbert called me back, "Sir, Mr. Davies has been waiting for you, but if I may be so bold to say, he is quite in his cups. There is one who needs your company more."

"Oh, who might that be?"

"Lord Petersham, sir. He's in the coffee room, and I have never seen him look this cast down." Delbert shifted uncomfortably. "I have not been impertinent in speaking, have I?"

"Indeed not," I said, dropping a few coins in his hand and making for the stairs.

Petersham sat slumped in a high-backed chair by the fire, a bottle at his elbow.

"Care to share a glass of whatever that is with a friend?" I asked, sitting in the chair next to him.

He looked up, a mournful expression on his face. "How can you be sure I won't poison you next?"

20

"*Poison me? Do* you want Robinson for your valet that badly? Before you resort to drastic measures, I must warn you he tries to play the tyrant," I said, signalling a footman to bring another glass, then changing my order. Best make that another bottle. The contents of this one were alarmingly low.

"Bow Street thinks I tried to poison Prinny," Petersham said incredulously, as if the idea were completely new.

Ah, I thought, something has finally pierced his confidence. "What happened?"

The viscount downed his drink. "That fellow from Bow Street, what's his name . . . er, Mr. Purple came to see me."

"Mr. Lavender?"

"He's the one. Pointed his finger at me. Literally," Petersham said, affronted.

I knew the finger-pointing gesture all too well. "What did he say?"

"He went on asking me questions about how I came to know the Prince, how long we had been friends, what my feelings were about his Royal Highness, all sorts of boring stuff. Then Munro came in the room."

I closed my eyes for a moment. "The white powder in the snuff?"

Petersham's jaw dropped. "How'd you know?"

"I had an audience with the Prince this afternoon, and Mr. Townsend and Mr. Lavender were present. They told me about the white powder."

"Sea salt! It was only sea salt!" Petersham exclaimed indignantly.

"Calm yourself, my friend. I believe you."

Petersham groaned. "Bow Street doesn't."

"Tell me, what made you think of adding sea salt to the snuff?"

"It's like this. I told you I found the sea air refreshing. I'm able to breathe better by the sea. Then I thought of how every once in a while Prinny has trouble breathing."

"True, but I think that is related to his ever-increasing girth rather than any problems with asthma like you have. Have not most of Prinny's episodes struck after a heavy meal?"

Petersham thought a moment. "Egad, Brummell, I think you've the right of it. And here I thought he might suffer as I do. I was only trying to help."

"You had best tell Mr. Lavender."

A stubborn expression came over the viscount's face. "I will, but Munro has done his damage."

I wondered when we would meander around to the topic of Lord Munro. "How was it Lord Munro came to tell Mr. Lavender about the sea salt?"

Petersham drummed his fingers on the table. "The

Bow Street man was questioning me when Munro arrived. Mr. Lavender asked what kinds of snuff Munro had seen me blend. That silly gudgeon told him, and added there was a white powder, as well, but he didn't know what that was." The viscount looked crestfallen. "Munro might as well have ordered a basket for my head to drop in after I'm beheaded at the Tower."

I furrowed my brow and gave a little shake of my head. "I cannot think they do that anymore. The mess of spurting blood, you know. We are so much more civilised now. They probably just feed murderers to the lions kept at the Tower menagerie."

"Joke if you will, but you know it's no laughing matter. You're the one who's been trying to warn me since Sir Simon keeled over dead that night."

"I know, but I am only trying to get you to brighten up and fight for yourself. God knows, I have had to defend you up to this point, since you refused to believe anyone would think you responsible."

Petersham managed a grin. "Like when we were back at school, eh? You always kept the bullies from me."

"Only this is not school," I reminded him. "I am relieved to see you taking the matter seriously, but troubled that it appears you have given up hope before really trying."

"What good is there? When a man is betrayed by his closest friend . . ." Petersham held out his glass, and I poured him another measure of wine. He slumped miserably in his chair.

"You and Munro had a falling out after Mr. Lavender departed," I said gently.

"Yes, and I broke one of my best snuff boxes when I flung it at him," Petersham said sulkily.

"What did Munro say was the reason why he mentioned the white powder to Mr. Lavender?"

Petersham gazed into the fire, a mulish expression on his face. "He said he was only trying to help. To give Bow Street a clue they could follow to find the real culprit. Imagine that."

"Do you believe him?"

"I never want to see him again," the viscount pronounced firmly. "Does that answer your question?"

"Hmmm. While the outcome was not what we would like, perhaps Munro did mean well," I said.

As you know, I cannot like Lord Munro, but I am aware that the relationship he has with Petersham is one the viscount values. I beg you will do me the favour of noticing how unselfish I am, defending Lord Munro. Do remember this the next time I tell you how I sometimes manoeuvre things to my own advantage.

But my tactic was not enough for my friend. All of a sudden Petersham began gasping for breath, wheezing, and struggling for air. His hand went to his cravat, and he jerked it loose.

I leaped to my feet. My first thought was to send Delbert for a physician. Then I remembered witnessing a similar incident where the viscount had been able to help himself. "Petersham, old friend, breathe. You must breathe through your nose as deeply as you can."

The viscount stared at me, still gasping, panic on his face.

"Petersham having one of his attacks?" a voice called from another table.

I held up my hand. "Yes, but I think we can handle it."

I crouched down beside the viscount. "You can do it.

Breathe through your nose, then exhale by blowing air out of your mouth. Pretend that one of your favourite snuff boxes is on this table," I urged, motioning to the small round table that stood between the two chairs. "The lid of the snuff box is open, and for a game, you are trying to blow it closed."

He did as I suggested. At first I did not think the stratagem would work. Just as I thought I must shout for Delbert after all, Petersham's breathing eased. "That is the thing, keep breathing. Steady. Good," I encouraged.

"I—I think I'm over it now," he said in a shaky voice a minute later. "Thanks for reminding me what I needed to do."

"Will a sip of this wine help?" I asked, offering him the glass.

He nodded and took a drink. "When the blasted asthma comes on, I can't help but feeling like I can't get any air. A fellow likes air, you know. In and out of his lungs."

"I advocate it myself," I concurred, pouring another glass of wine and swallowing the contents.

By gradual degrees he relaxed, at last sure that the attack would not come back on him.

We spent the next hour drinking steadily, talking of this and that, complaining about the lack of enough watchmen stationed for our protection—I related the story of the strange chairmen who took me away and beat me—and bemoaning the trials and tribulations of love.

Silently, I cursed Lord Munro for an unfeeling oaf. Obviously the quarrel between the two of them had been deeply upsetting to the viscount. Merely speaking of it might even have brought on his asthma attack.

Eventually, in the small hours of the morning, I judged Petersham too drunk to find his way home. Outside White's, I summoned Ned and Ted and charged them with the task of making certain they delivered the viscount to his house and into Diggie's care.

I hailed a hackney to take me to my destination.

No, do not quiz me about what I did for the remainder of the evening. Suffice it to say, I took my mind away from the menace of further action by Bow Street—action that might be to the detriment of the viscount or myself.

Even so, a part of my brain could not stop thinking about a slice of my conversation with Petersham. I had explained my theory that Sir Simon might have been the intended victim of the poisoning all along. Petersham made the comment that the contemptible baronet was capable of making instant enemies. This observation served to remind me of Lord Perry's challenge and subsequent threat to kill Sir Simon if he ever spoke ill of Lady Perry again. Also Victor Tallarico's display of his knife.

If I convinced Bow Street that Sir Simon was likely the object of the killer's wrath, would that place Lord Perry and Signor Tallarico in danger?

I would have slept late the next day, but Chakkri had other ideas. Around eight, he woke me by the simple act of standing on my chest. I opened my eyes and looked into his alert blue gaze.

"Reow," he said pleasantly.

"No, it is not time to get up," I mumbled, removing him from my fine lawn nightshirt.

A minute or two later, he hopped onto my chest again and began playing with my quizzing glass.

Are you surprised? I sleep with my quizzing glass. One never knows when one will need it.

I rolled over onto my stomach and tried to go back to sleep, but it was no use. My brain had already begun running over the harrowing events of the past few days: the assault on my person, the nasty interview at Carlton House where my own honour had been called into question, my belief that Sir Simon had been the intended victim of the poisoned snuff all along, and the repercussions to Lord Perry and his cousin if he was.

But before I could act on my suspicions, there was Miss Lavender. I could not overlook my responsibility to her, nor the Frenchwoman I had put in Miss Lavender's care.

If I wished to erase the black look she had given me last night when I did not have time to speak with her, I needed to impress her with an early arrival at her shelter.

Thus, I breakfasted—sharing the delights of André's cooking with Chakkri—and once properly attired, I ordered the twins to carry me to New Street.

When we stopped at the door outside Haven of Hope, I alighted from the vehicle and looked about the neighbourhood. The streets were crowded with wagons and drays. Humanity bustled in the area known as Covent Garden, outside Mayfair, with greengrocers calling their wares and people of the middle and lower classes trying to eke out an honest living. Some not so honestly.

I noted that a few doors down, at No. 3 New Street, the establishment of Lavell & Coxhead, Grocer and Tea

Dealer, stood ready to serve the public. No doubt this was where Mr. Lavell could be found, if one were inclined to see what he looked like—I mean, that is to say, if one were inclined to speak to him. Seeing the grocer's name on the store's sign, I realised that if Miss Lavender were to wed the man, she would not have to go to the trouble of changing the initials on her linen.

Telling myself it was none of my business, I raised my dog's head walking stick and rapped it on the door to Haven of Hope.

The green portal swung open, revealing the tall figure of Rebecca Ashton. Miss Ashton and I are acquainted through Freddie. "Miss Ashton, good morning."

"Mr. Brummell!" she cried. "How delightful to see you again. Please come in."

Before I could accept her offer, a girl of about sixteen years appeared beside her.

"Oh, Molly, are the candied violets ready for Mr. Lavell?" Miss Ashton inquired.

"Yes, ma'am," Molly responded, her gaze swinging to the twins. Her brown eyes widened at the sight of them. Ned and Ted bowed and grinned in her direction. Molly blushed and tossed her dark curls. I stood aside so she could pass, noting that Ned and Ted watched the girl's progress down the street.

"Is Miss Lavender here this morning, Miss Ashton?" I asked, entering the tiny, well-scrubbed hall. A set of double doors led to a large room, where a circle of wooden chairs had been set up rather like a classroom.

"I am afraid you have missed her, Mr. Brummell," Miss Ashton said. "She did not go home last night until near midnight and then returned at seven this morning." Miss Ashton lowered her voice, casting a hasty gaze

toward a closed door behind her. "Lydia and the Frenchwoman had been in the sitting room together before
Lydia left. I think Lydia is gravely concerned about her,
as we all are."

"Yes. Do you know if she learned anything new?"

Miss Ashton shook her head. "I do not think so. A
pitiful predicament we are in, not even knowing the
woman's name. I believe that is why Lydia went to
Hove."

"Went to Hove?" I queried, alarmed. I remembered
Miss Lavender trying to tell me something the night be-
fore about a house in Hove the Frenchwoman described.
Something about the woman being held captive there.

Miss Ashton picked up the hem of the apron she wore
and worried it between two fingers. "She told me she
was going to hire a coach to take her there, and if I had
not heard back from her by tomorrow morning, I was to
go to her father."

"Good God."

"My feelings precisely. The girls and I have been
making candied violets this morning, and I admit I could
not tell you if they came out nicely or not. I am very
anxious about what Lydia might find in Hove. Especially
since she would not take anyone with her."

A cold knot formed in my stomach. There could be
no question of continuing my investigation into Sir
Simon's death until I could be sure of Miss Lavender's
safety. I could only hope no one died or was arrested in
the meantime. "I shall go after her."

Miss Ashton gazed at me approvingly. "Oh, Mr.
Brummell, that is the very thing. I am ever so much
relieved. Do you know exactly where she has gone?"

"Dash it, Miss Lavender told me the Frenchwoman

described a house there, but I cannot bring to mind what she said. May I see the woman and ascertain whether she will tell me what she told Miss Lavender?"

Miss Ashton looked doubtful. "You can try, but I expect you know what condition she is in."

"I do."

"Very well. She is in the sitting room, behind this door."

"Ah, so that is why we have been speaking in lowered tones."

Miss Ashton smiled, her azure-coloured eyes sparkling. She turned and opened the door. A small room containing a cluttered desk in one corner, a row of books against one wall, and a cluster of threadworn chairs about the fireplace came into view. There were no windows. I thought of Miss Lavender's assertion that the Frenchwoman was upset by the sight of men passing by.

The woman herself sat in one of the chairs, holding an orange cat. Stroking its matted fur, the woman appeared as calm as I had ever seen her. In French, she called the cat "Marmalade" and declared him handsome. She then scratched the top of the animal's head, much to the feline's delight. I was amazed at the transformation in her features. Obviously a lover of felines, the Frenchwoman's skin did not look quite so sallow, nor the lines on her face so deeply etched, as she gazed tenderly at the cat.

All that changed when, in French, I said, "Good morning."

The Frenchwoman gasped and drew back in fear when she caught sight of me, causing the cat to jump to the floor and scamper past me out of the room. The loss

of her feline companion seemed to add to the Frenchwoman's distress.

Miss Ashton crossed to her side and tried to soothe
her, but the woman was having none of it. She began
muttering once more about "ze animals" and saying "no,
no." I felt myself grow impatient as the minutes ticked
by and the woman remained unresponsive to Miss Ashton's pleas to tell her about the house in Hove. I feared
for Miss Lavender's safety.

When Miss Ashton turned to me in defeat, I motioned
for her to come to me. She did so, closing the sitting-
room door behind her. We stood once more in the hall.

"I have an idea. Can you watch and make sure the
Frenchwoman does not run away?"

"She will not go anywhere, but I shall remain with
her."

"Good. Wait for me, then. I am going to collect a
friend and will return shortly. I think that with his help
we might find out what we need to know."

21

Outside, Ned and Ted flirted with the dark-haired girl who had returned from the grocer's. When they saw me, they scrambled to open the door of my sedan-chair for me. The girl disappeared into the shelter.

Ordering Ned and Ted to run, we quickly made our way to our destination. On the way, I considered alerting Mr. Lavender of the possibly dangerous situation his headstrong daughter had put herself in.

I quickly discarded the idea. Something told me Miss Lavender would never forgive me if I sent her father after her. No, it was up to me to see to her safety. After all, it was I who asked her to take in the Frenchwoman in the first place. If it were not for my request, Miss Lavender would be making candied violets along with her charges and delivering them herself to Mr. Lavell, the kind neighbourhood grocer.

Almost forty-five minutes later, I arrived back on the doorstep to the Haven of Hope, a lidded wicker basket in hand.

Miss Ashton opened the door and stared at me curiously.

I walked inside. "My cat, Chakkri, is in here. Are there any doors or windows open in the house? I would not want him to slip outside. He is not permitted to go outdoors."

"Everything is shut tight against the cold. Oh, Mr. Brummell, you are clever, thinking of bringing the cat. The Frenchwoman adores that stray Lydia feeds. We named him Marmalade."

"Let us hope Chakkri will calm her as Marmalade does. Perhaps when the Frenchwoman sees how my cat approves of me, she will allow me to speak with her."

"May I see him before you go in?"

I opened the lid of the basket a few inches. Miss Ashton peered inside, then drew back. "I have never seen a cat like him."

"He comes from Siam. Now, here is what I want you to do. Allow me to enter the sitting room with Chakkri. If I need you, I shall let you know."

"All right. I wish you good luck. I will just be in the kitchen if you need me."

The Frenchwoman sat forlornly in the same chair by the fire. When she saw me, her eyes widened and she yelped a cry. Before I could say a word, Chakkri let out a loud "reow" and raised his head from the basket. The Frenchwoman quieted immediately and stared at the cat. I bent and put the basket on the floor.

Picking the cat up and holding him in my arms, in French I said, "His name is Chakkri. I brought him specially to see you. What is your name?"

The woman made no response, but neither did she scream again. I held Chakkri close, stroking his incredibly soft fur. "I am going to sit in that chair near you so you can see him up close."

She sat still and made no protest to the plan. I slowly made my way to the chair and sat down. "Would you like to hold him? He will not scratch you."

The Frenchwoman remained silent. Chakkri decided the matter by hopping from my lap to hers, balancing himself across her thighs. Almost as if he knew she needed his comfort. He looked at her expectantly, and she raised one hand tentatively and petted his back. Her other hand clutched a cross.

Chakkri sat down and began to purr.

"I promise I only want to help you," I ventured in a low voice. "Will you not tell me your name?"

"Marie. My name is Marie," she whispered in French after several minutes of silence.

I drew a deep breath. "Madame Marie, I am George Brummell, a friend of Miss Lavender's. She is the lady who owns this shelter. Remember when I found you on the road outside Brighton?"

Marie's hand stilled. An expression of horror appeared on her face at the memory. I cursed myself for pressing her. But devil take it, I could not chance Miss Lavender getting herself hurt, and minutes were ticking by.

"Listen to me, Madam Marie. I know you are under some great strain, that something terrible has happened to you. You are holding a cross. Will you not pray for relief? There are others who may be in danger and need your help."

Marie began to cry. Not a wailing cry, but a silent expression of grief. I remembered Miss Lavender telling me the Frenchwoman had not cried over whatever was troubling her. Clutching the cross in one hand and resting the other on Chakkri's back, Marie wept now.

I reached into my pocket, drew out my handkerchief and passed it to her. She accepted it.

Then she spoke in an anguished voice, "My lady, she wore the cross and died anyway."

As much as I sympathised with her for her loss, whatever it had been, my anxiety over Miss Lavender's safety overcame all other thought. "I am sorry. Will you try to help me protect another lady? I need to know about the house by the sea."

She looked up then, the tears ceasing and the look of fear coming back into her eyes. Chakkri stood up and brushed the top of his head against her chin.

"Just the location—" I said hastily. "Please, if you could only tell me where the house is, or what it looks like."

"The animals are there," she hissed.

"Animals?"

"At the house of evil by the sea." She crossed herself.

A chill ran through me at her words. I wanted to shake her, force her to tell me instantly what I wanted to know. But that would never do. "Tell me what the house looks like. Please. It is important."

Her breathing reminded me of Petersham's at the beginning of one of the attacks of his asthma, fast and shallow. "It has many rooms, many corridors. Some of them stone. I could smell the sea."

"What about the outside of the house? What does it look like?"

She gazed past me as if remembering. "It was dark when they took me there. I could not see. Red, perhaps. Red brick with a dark door. Oh!"

I leaned forward. "What? What is it?"

Her face crumpled. "There was a brass knocker on the door. A big ugly thing. The head of a jackal. The animals, the animals," she sobbed, then burst into tears.

This time her crying was a loud, harsh sound. Miss Ashton came hurrying into the room.

Chakkri jumped down from Marie's lap as Miss Ashton went to hold her.

"I am sorry to be abrupt, but must take my leave. Miss Lavender needs me. I shall send word to you," I said, bundling Chakkri into the basket. Miss Ashton turned and nodded at me, then whispered reassuring words to Marie.

Outside the shelter door, I gave orders for Ned and Ted to take Chakkri home to Bruton Street, admonishing them to be certain the cat did not escape into the streets.

I hailed a hackney to take me to the nearest posting house, where the heavy purse I had collected when I went home for Chakkri enabled me to hire a private coach. After a short conversation with the driver, during which I promised him a handsome reward if he could make the seven-hour journey to the Brighton area in five, we were off.

Along the way, we stopped only to change horses. The driver pushed the beasts to their limits. At one larger posting house, I was able to visit the necessary room, then procure a bottle of wine, some cheese, and an apple. At another stop, I purchased a hot brick to put at my feet. Darkness was falling, along with the temperature. I was glad of the warmth of my black velvet greatcoat and my buckskin breeches.

There was plenty of time for me to think. And contemplate how I would wring Miss Lavender's pretty neck when I found her.

Devil take the Scottish female! How could she have been so hen-witted as to tear off for the sea coast without so much as a maid in tow? She might not be of the highest class of Society, but even a girl of the middle-classes knew better than to travel alone. I may admire her independent nature, which one could say is much like my own, but this stretched the bounds of common sense.

Mentally, I took myself to task for involving Miss Lavender in Marie's problem. But what could I have done? Left the Frenchwoman to wander the London Road alone in the state she was in? Now, Miss Lavender, obstinate like her father, was determined to find out what she could about Marie.

Just what was this "house of evil" Marie spoke of, and what the devil had happened there? I thought of the Frenchwoman's tears and her sad declaration that her lady had died. Apparently Marie was a lady's maid or companion. Had her mistress died at the "house of evil"?

I heaved a tired sigh, thinking of the way Marie had fingered the small gold cross. Perhaps her faith would—

My eyes widened as an image of the cross Marie had been holding flashed through my brain. I had seen a cross like it, only larger, just recently.

Around the neck of the girl Freddie and I had found dead on the Brighton Beach. The one Doctor Pitcairn declared had died from a blow to the head.

Yes, yes, it was the very same cross. A distinctive piece and costly. Tiny emeralds graced the ends of the design, which were shaped as a fleur-de-lys. Exactly the sort of thing a young woman might bestow upon a much-loved governess or companion.

And if Marie had seen her young lady killed, that would certainly account for her terrified state.

But what were the "animals" Marie referred to? And what had happened in this "house of evil"? Had the two ladies been lured there and then attacked, with only Marie escaping?

The house Marie described was large, no hovel a ruffian might take a victim to. And both the unfortunate girl on the beach and Marie still retained their valuable jewelry. A common thief-turned-murderer would never leave his victims in possession of something he could sell for money.

Who, then, would have committed such a heinous act and why?

I looked out into the darkness with what must have been a rueful expression on my face. My abilities in investigating murders must be judged futile. Though I had been successful in a recent case, I now had two murders to contemplate and was none the wiser about either. Perhaps Mr. Lavender had the right of it, and I should stay out of his way.

That would also please whoever had hired the two ruffians who set upon my person and bloodied my nose.

At last these self-deprecating thoughts were cut off as the driver pulled the coach to a halt in the yard of a Brighton inn. Settling my bill with him, complete with the handsome tip I had promised, I hired a horse and set out for Hove.

Once in that western part of Brighton, it did not take long for me to realise that if I wanted to find the house Marie had described, and Miss Lavender, it might be best if I stopped and asked some of the locals if the building sounded familiar.

The first two people I asked—a young lad carrying a shovel over one shoulder, and a fisherman, if the odour clinging to him was any indication of his profession— both denied knowledge of such a house. I gained the distinct impression that the fisherman was lying. He had looked to the west when he spoke, though, so with no better plan, I headed my horse in that direction.

The hour neared six o'clock and I saw no one else on the dark road. Tired and aggravated, I decided to stop at the first farmhouse I came to with a light within.

Thus, only five minutes later, I tethered my horse and knocked on the door of a one-story structure with a weedy garden.

The wooden door opened, revealing an old man dressed in a coarse linen shirt and brown homespun breeches. His gaze ran over my fine clothing. "What kin I do fer ye?"

"I am searching for a house I know only by description and hope you can help me." I jingled some coins in my pocket to encourage him.

He narrowed dark eyes under grey eyebrows. "I reckon seein' how I've lived here all me life, I could tell ye what ye want to know. Iffen ye don't mean no trouble to the people."

I returned his gaze. "Certainly, I do not."

He held out his hand expectantly. I dropped several coins into his open palm. He pocketed the money and nodded for me to continue.

"The house is red brick and quite near the sea. The front door sports a brass knocker in the shape of a jackal's head."

The farmer made to close the door.

I pressed my hand against it hard, forcing it to remain open. "Wait!"

"Ye filthy swell!" the farmer shouted.

"I beg your pardon," I said, very stiffly on my stiffs. "I am known for my cleanliness. What is more, I do not have time for you to stand here and quibble with me. A friend of mine—a lady friend—may be in trouble."

This speech was met by a snort. "Ain't no ladies at that there house. It be a house no *lady* would ever visit."

"That only makes the situation more urgent. Whom does the house belong to, and how can I find it? Please, I must know," I said in a voice as close to pleading as I would allow.

The farmer stood in the doorway and seemed to take my measure. At last he said, "It be four miles down the road to yer left," he said pointing past me. "Iffen ye go too far, ye'll be in the sea."

"Thank you," I said, passing him more coins, then turning to go. His next words stopped me.

"The owner's dead. Sir Simon was poisoned. Serves him right, too. Evil attracts evil, is what I always says."

22

"*Sir Simon owned* the house I seek?" My stunned brain could hardly assimilate the information.

"Aye," the farmer replied. He leaned out the door and spat into the bushes. "Sir Simon was a greedy cur. I reckon now he's gone, we'll have less rackety goings on. Unless ye mean to stir things up."

"No, as I told you, I am merely here to collect a friend. I know nothing of the house and only a little of Sir Simon. He made his fortune in smuggling, did he not?"

The farmer hesitated. Only after I produced a few more coins did the man nod. "A shameful fortune what brought him shameful friends. Some of 'em high born. All the money he made warn't good enough fer him. He kept on leadin' a large smugglin' operation 'til the day he died. Greedy, like I told ye."

"Is that why you call him evil? I thought townsfolk commonly turned a blind eye to smuggling, some even participating in it."

"No, warn't his dealin' with the Frenchies, was the other."

"What 'other'?" I persisted.

"Peculiar things, evil things, that's what," the farmer said, raising his voice. "Things no real gentleman would involve hisself with. Sir Simon was no gentleman. And if ye were a gentleman ye wouldn't be tryin' to find his house."

With that, the farmer shut the door in my face.

Damn and blast! I mounted my horse and set off at a near gallop down the moonlit road the farmer had indicated, cursing each new delay. The farmer had neglected to tell me the road branched into two on the way. I grant you he could not have known about the fallen tree. After I took a false turn, and a bone-rattling jump over the tree, the house finally came into view down a tree-lined lane.

I slowed my horse to a halt, taking in the lay of the land. A long, circular drive of crushed shells led to a large brick manor. The house looked respectable enough from the outside, with well-tended lawns and shrubbery. Light could be seen coming from within. The problem was where to leave my horse so I might approach the house on foot without being seen.

Glancing around, I noted a thicket of trees to the right and behind the house. Slowly, and as quietly as I could, I led the horse to this area, dismounted, and secured him to a tree.

"Don't move, I have a pistol."

I froze, my fist closing around my dog's head stick; then, recognizing the voice, I relaxed. "What you ought to have is a good pair of spectacles."

"Who is that?"

"If you would put that gun away and come closer you would see it is I, George Brummell, Miss Lavender."

She stepped out from behind a nearby tree, leaves rustling under her booted feet, and I caught my breath. Seeing a lady with her hair down, after all, is a husband's privilege. Her auburn hair streamed out from around her face in a tangled mass of curls that hung halfway down her back. The glossy strands gleamed sensuously in the moonlight.

Perceiving my scrutiny, she raised her chin. By way of explanation she said, "I had to ride on the outside of the coach that brought me to Hove. Not all of us can afford to pay the price for an inside seat."

"Your hair is—is quite lovely," I said, suppressing a sudden desire to touch those soft tresses. I cannot like the effect Miss Lavender sometimes has on my senses.

"I lost my pins in the wind, otherwise I would have attempted to constrain it. But never mind my hair. What are you doing here, Mr. Brummell? I thought you too busy with dinner parties and your social life to involve yourself in my problems."

"You wound me," I said, placing a hand over my heart. "Here I have ridden *ventre à terre* to come to your aid and . . . er, I say, could you put that gun away? Does your father know you possess such a weapon?"

"Who do you think taught me to shoot?" she replied, lowering the gun.

"Does he know you are nearsighted?"

"I am not nearsighted!"

"Yes, you are. What prevents you from wearing spectacles?"

"The fact that I don't need them," she said in a voice one might use to speak to a dim-wit.

"Perhaps you care for what is fashionable after all," I mused aloud.

And perhaps Mr. Lavell, the grocer, would not care for a wife with spectacles, I thought.

"That's not true," she said hotly. "Unlike you, I cannot waste my time trying to dress and look flawless."

"Dressing well is not a waste of time."

"Yet you suffer from boredom, don't you? Else you would not be involved in yet another murder investigation, would you now, Mr. Brummell? That's all right," she said before I could answer. "There's no need for you to admit it. You strike me as a man too intelligent to be satisfied with merely having perfected the knot in his neckcloth."

I bowed. "Your generosity when it comes to my character warms my heart. It grieves me to tell you I cannot return the compliment in the matter of your own intelligence. Or perhaps intelligence is not the proper term, for you are knowledgeable. Common sense is the commodity of which you are in short supply."

"What!"

"Do not shout. An educated female, which no doubt you are, who journeys from London to Brighton alone, without the company of even a maid, can only be thought of as hen-witted."

"How dare you? I ought to rub dirt on your neckcloth!"

"I beg you will restrain yourself. Come now, let us cry friends, and indeed, allies, since we are here for a similar purpose. How long has it been since you arrived?"

Miss Lavender's eyes smoldered, but at last she said, "Only a few minutes. I had to walk all the way out here from where the coach stopped in the town centre. I believe this to be the house the Frenchwoman described."

"Yes, Marie said it had a brass jackal's head for a door knocker, and this one does," I said. Suddenly, I remembered the animal-shaped patch Sir Simon wore near his mouth. It could very well have been the shape of a jackal. And I thought I had seen that shape on a ring, but I could not recall who had been wearing it.

"Marie? Who is Marie?"

"Oh, I have not had a chance to tell you, have I?" I said, my thoughts returning to the matter at hand. "I paid a visit to your shelter, and the Frenchwoman spoke to me. Her name is Marie."

Miss Lavender's lips parted in surprise. Diverted by the action, I had to ask her to repeat the question. She said, "How did you get her to talk?"

"Chakkri, my cat, helped. You see, Marie has a fondness for cats."

"Yes, I've noticed she spends a lot of time petting Marmalade."

"Indeed, I observed the same thing. I thought if I were to go home, collect Chakkri, and bring him along, the Frenchwoman might relax enough to speak to me. The notion proved a good one. Marie revealed not only her name, but the fact that her young lady had died. I believe Marie was a governess or companion to a French lady of genteel birth."

Miss Lavender shivered in the night air. "Goodness, that is terrible, but would the death of a young girl account for the severely shocked state Marie is in?"

"It would if the young lady was murdered," I said grimly.

Then I told Miss Lavender about the body Freddie and I had found on the Brighton beach, how the doctor had proclaimed that she had died of a blow to the head, and how the cross the unfortunate girl wore was a larger, more expensive version of the one Marie held clutched in her hand.

Miss Lavender shook her head sadly. "This is appalling. Do you think Marie witnessed the murder?"

"I do not know. She became upset again before I could question her further. There is more, though."

"Faith! What else?"

"On my way here, I stopped to ask directions of a farmer. He told me who this house belonged to. Does the name Sir Simon mean anything to you?"

"He's the hero who died testing snuff for the Prince of Wales!" she exclaimed.

"Wrong. He did die after inhaling snuff at the Prince's table. However, I cannot believe he is a hero. He was a smuggler who had used this house as a base of operation for his free-trading, and for some other nefarious doings."

"But he saved the Prince's life. Father told me so."

"I believe Sir Simon was the intended victim of the poisoning all along. A view scoffed at by Bow Street, I might add."

"Why? Why don't you believe the Prince's life was at risk?"

"Because of a simple lack of credible suspects. Ones who had the necessary motive along with the opportunity the dinner at the Pavilion presented. I have given this matter a great deal of time and thought. No one there that night disliked the Prince enough to want to kill him."

"But who might want to kill Sir Simon?"

"That is a question I have not yet had time to explore."

"Do you feel a smuggling partner who felt cheated might be responsible?"

"I cannot say, but no one of that nature was at the Prince's table the night Sir Simon died. Mayhaps the killer's reason for murder had nothing to do with the smuggling nature of his enterprise. The farmer I spoke to hinted at some other, even more unsavoury activities that Sir Simon was involved in."

"What activities?"

I took a deep breath. "I have some ugly suspicions, Miss Lavender, and for that reason, I want to escort you back to Brighton. Then, I shall come back here and see if I can gain entry to that house."

"You'll do no such thing! What do you think I'm here for?"

"I realise you came out here with the intention of helping Marie. But this is more complicated than you thought. The situation could be very dangerous. We will find a respectable inn where you might partake of a meal while I find out what is going on."

"No!" she exclaimed, a stubborn look on her face. "I'm staying with you. I shan't be tucked away like a child."

Gazing at the disheveled woman before me, I thought she hardly resembled a child. A Scottish temptress would be a more apt description.

Still, I could not allow her to place herself in any

further danger. I opened my mouth to tell her so, when the sound of a gunshot startled both of us.

"It came from the house!" Miss Lavender said. She lifted her skirts and ran out of the copse of trees we had been standing in before I could stop her.

I dashed after her, silently cursing her impetuous nature.

Approaching the house, I caught up to her, grasping her arm and spinning her around to face me. "Go back to the relative safety of those trees!"

She tugged her arm out of my grip. "No!"

"Fine, but you are putting me at the mercy of your father's wrath should anything untoward happen to you," I said. "I shall not thank you if he has me drawn and quartered. At least stay behind me." With that, I strode toward where light revealed a set of tall glass doors swinging open into the night air. Then, the sound of hoofbeats caused me to fling a protective arm in front of Miss Lavender.

We hurried along the side of the house in time to see a masked rider galloping into the night on horseback.

"He's away," Miss Lavender said.

"Yes, let us see what he left behind. Allow me to go in first," I cautioned.

Stepping through the open glass doors, I found myself behind a large desk in a study. Moaning could be heard from the other side.

I advanced into the room.

The body of a large man lay on the floor, a bright red spot growing in the centre of his chest.

23

"Heaven save us!" gasped Miss Lavender.

"Go outside," I told her, but she did not obey. Why was I not surprised?

I moved closer to the man, whom I recognized as one of Sir Simon's brutish footmen. A muscular, bald fellow, he lay bleeding. When he saw me, he tried to raise his arm.

" 'Elp me. Oi'm shot."

Crouching down next to him, I saw the ball had entered in the region of his heart. While I am no doctor, it was clear nothing could save him. Still, I reached around his neck and untied his dirty neckcloth. "Who are you?" I asked. "Who did this?"

He pressed his hand to the wound, perhaps to try to stanch the flow of blood, but it was pointless. "Wheeler. Jemmy Wheeler. Oi'm shot. 'Elp me."

"Who shot you?" I asked.

He looked at me and blinked. "Know you. That night, in the alley . . .'E ordered it done."

Good God, he was one of the men who had attacked me. "Who gave the order?" I demanded.

But the man was in shock, losing blood fast. "Oi can't believe 'e shot me. 'E never shot Sir Simon."

"Tell me who did this," I commanded again, more urgently. "Why would he shoot Sir Simon?"

"Blackmail. Sir Simon blackmailed 'im." Wheeler looked puzzled. " 'E never shot Sir Simon," he said, his breath rattling in his throat.

My voice rose along with my frustration. "What man? What man blackmailed Sir Simon?"

"The fine gentleman what killed the virgin girl," Wheeler said in a weak voice. Then his head rolled to one side, and his eyes stared sightlessly at the desk. I would get no more information from him.

"Oh, Lord," Miss Lavender moaned.

I stood and walked to her side. "There was nothing we could have done for him. And he did not do enough for us."

"Aren't you being rather callous? The man has just lost his life!" Miss Lavender's eyes were wide, and she leaned against the side of the desk. Another female might have fainted at the events unfolding.

"He and a partner beat me senseless the other night. And for all we know, he was involved in a blackmail scheme. No, I have little pity for Wheeler. I am more concerned for your well-being."

"I am fine," Miss Lavender said. Her hands clutched her cloak tightly around her chest. Noting they were steady, I looked about the room. Intent on finding out what Sir Simon had been involved in, I walked around Miss Lavender to the desk and began pulling drawers open.

"What are you doing? Shouldn't we be sending for help, the magistrate, perhaps?"

"Spoken like a true Bow Street investigator's daughter. We shall send for help, but not until I have some answers." I thrust my hand into the back of a drawer and pulled out a sheaf of papers. Scanning the lines, I determined it was a list of goods brought in on a ship from France.

The contents of the other drawers revealed nothing more than household papers, a few bills—I raised an eyebrow at one from Sir Simon's tailor, noting the man's name so I could avoid him—and a letter from a hopeful sea captain wishing to join Sir Simon's organization.

Sitting back in the leather chair behind the desk, I pondered over where Sir Simon might have kept his secret papers. Why, in a secret drawer, of course.

"What are you doing under the desk?" Miss Lavender asked a moment later.

"Searching for—ah, here it is." I released the mechanism hidden behind one of the drawers. A small compartment opened, releasing its contents to the carpet. I gathered them up, tossed them on the top of the desk, and seated myself in the chair once more.

"What is all that?" Miss Lavender asked, coming to stand beside me.

"You ask a lot of questions."

"So do you!"

"Well, let us see." The mask caught my attention first. I picked it up and examined it curiously. In the shape of a jackal's head, it was meant to wear over one's face. "This could conceal a person's identity quite nicely."

"I wonder why Sir Simon had such a thing."

"Not for attending respectable masquerades, I would wager."

I put the mask aside reluctantly and picked up a seal. "Another jackal's head. Sir Simon must have been fond of the animals," I said wryly.

"Did you hear what you just said, Mr. Brummell? You said, 'the animals.' "

I stared up at Miss Lavender, my hands stilled over the items. Mentally I could hear Marie sobbing about "ze animals." "Just so, Miss Lavender."

A folded piece of paper was the last item. The writing revealed a list of dates and times. Above the dates—one of which I noted was the day after tomorrow—was the word *Anubis*.

Miss Lavender read over my shoulder. "Anubis. That's the Egyptian deity with the body of a man and the head of a jackal."

I refolded the paper before the intrepid Miss Lavender could see the dates. "Precisely."

"What does it mean? Anubis was the guardian of souls. He conducted the dead to judgment. Was that a fitting description of Sir Simon? You say he was a smuggler, and that dead man over there said he was a blackmailer. That doesn't sound like a person I would want guarding my soul."

"No." I stood.

Miss Lavender eyed me shrewdly. "What are you thinking? I can tell you have a theory. You had best tell me."

"The theory is not one suited to a lady's ear."

Miss Lavender leaned close. I could smell the scent of autumn on her—wet earth, damp leaves, apples, and cinnamon.

She stared at me in the candlelit room with those green eyes of hers and said, "Have you forgotten? I am not a *lady*."

For some reason unknown to myself, the thought crossed my mind at that particular moment that it would be quite pleasant to kiss Miss Lavender. Hard on the heels of this ill-conceived idea came the notion that Miss Lavender might very well allow me to do so.

The point could be argued.

An equally lively debate could ensue as to whether my kissing a girl of Miss Lavender's station in life would, after all, be wise.

My hand closed over the dog's head walking stick Freddie had given me.

Miss Lavender sighed. Why she did so, I could not tell you, but the matter was pushed aside when the sound of footsteps came from the front hall.

"Doubtless that is Wheeler's partner. Since I hear he is known as Devlin the Devil, I suggest we take our leave," I said, assembling the mask, seal, and list, then thrusting them into my pocket. I grabbed Miss Lavender by the hand, and we made a swift exit into the cold night air.

We hurried to the thicket of trees where my horse was still tethered. Untying him, I glanced at Miss Lavender. "Do you not possess a proper riding dress?"

She put her hands on her hips. "Not with me. I'm sorry to incur your disapproval, but I did not expect to be travelling by horse."

"Er, well, how shall we do this, then?"

"Oh, for heaven's sake! Just give me a hand up and then get behind me."

I did as she bade, placing my arms around her, my

head next to hers, and grasped the reins. I must say that it was not at all a disagreeable posture. Though I cannot help feeling that inferiour wool is exceedingly rough underneath one's chin.

Once in Brighton, I ordered a private coach, and we began the journey back to London.

To avoid Miss Lavender's inevitable questioning, the moment we settled ourselves in the coach, I yawned. "I confess to being overcome with fatigue. You will excuse me."

"No, I won't, Mr. Brummell. I wish to discuss all that has transpired."

"Much as I regret being so disobliging, I fear I shall insult you more if I fall asleep while you are speaking."

Under her protests, I propped my head against the side of the coach and closed my eyes. She looked weary as well, so I hoped that after a short length of time, she would succumb to sleep.

Meanwhile, I considered the information I had gleaned over the evening. The pieces of the puzzle began taking form, if not quite falling into place.

Evidently, Sir Simon ruled at the head of a secret club called Anubis, whose members met at his house. Everything pointed to it: The farmer in Hove had spoken of "peculiar things" of which Sir Simon was involved. He had said the baronet was evil. Marie had called the place a "house of evil." To add to that, I recalled Lord Yarmouth telling me that fateful night at White's that there was a club on the sea coast whose activities went beyond the pale.

Then there was the jackal's head mask I found in Sir Simon's desk, along with the seal and the list of dates, which I could only assume were planned meetings.

But what went on at those meetings?

One could only speculate. Yarmouth's description was the most telling. The club's endeavours most likely went beyond high play at the gaming tables or the sampling of smuggled wine.

The key might lie in the name Sir Simon had chosen for his secret club. I suspected that the baronet would have chosen the name Anubis, not so much out of respect for any Egyptian god, but more because Anubis represented the jackal. Jackals hunt in packs, at night, and are base creatures known to be insatiable.

My sense was that this described the secret club, or at least some of its attributes. While the members might not go outside and hunt, perhaps their hunting had been done for them prior to their arrival.

The prey might very well include innocent young women. Wheeler spoke of the "fine gentleman what killed the virgin girl." A mental image of the young girl found dead on the Brighton beach appeared to haunt me once more.

Could she have been "prey" for the club members?

Revulsion welled up in me at the thought of a "fine gentleman" destroying the innocence of a young lady. How had she died? Had the man in question killed her in order to keep her quiet? Was that what Marie had seen that had frightened her so?

"The dastards." Unconsciously, I had spoken aloud. My eyes flew open. For a moment I thought Miss Lavender would discover I was only pretending to sleep. But as I looked across at her in the semi-darkness, I saw her long dark lashes laid against her porcelain-like skin. Her head rested on her folded hands against the side of the coach.

Not even when we stopped to change horses at about midnight did she awake. Climbing back into the coach as silently as I could after paying the posting house for a team of fresh horses, I gazed at her sleeping form and frowned.

The conventions state that a gentleman who has spent the better part of a night with an unmarried female alone in a coach has thoroughly compromised her. Regardless of the fact that Miss Lavender is not of my station in life, she is an educated female, not some tavern wench.

We would not return to Fetter Lane until the small hours of the morning. While I know that Miss Lavender is not a stickler for the proprieties, her father is another matter altogether.

I swallowed the cup of wine I had purchased at the posting house in one long gulp. My dog's head stick rested against the seat beside me. With a tender touch, I caressed the silver top with my gloved thumb. When I returned home, I would have to write to Freddie and tell her of my findings. Furthermore, I knew she would expect me at Oatlands this weekend. If I could untangle the muddle around Sir Simon's death, perhaps I might feel free to visit her.

Unless I was spending the weekend with my new bride.

I closed my eyes and leaned against the squabs of the coach, concentrating on Sir Simon rather than any forced nuptials.

If I needed any confirmation that the baronet had been the intended victim of the poisoned snuff all along, I had it now.

But who were the members of the secret club, Anubis?

On whose hand had I seen a jackal ring?

Which one of the members had Sir Simon been blackmailing?

How did the young girl die?

Why had Sir Simon and Prime Minister Pitt had a falling out?

The answer to the last question I would find out tomorrow, or today actually, from Lady Hester.

Or I would find out how it felt to stand in front of a vicar speaking my marriage vows.

❦ 24 ❦

As it turned out, I only narrowly escaped speaking those sacred vows.

Upon our arrival in Fetter Lane, I helped Miss Lavender out of the hired coach, hoping against hope that her father would not hear our arrival.

Luck was not on my side.

As I walked Miss Lavender around to the private entrance to her father's lodgings, the man himself swung open the door and hurtled down the steps. Clad in a plaid robe, with slippers on his feet, he still managed to look fierce.

"Where, by all that is holy, Lydia, have you been?" the Scotsman demanded. He darted a disbelieving glance at me, then spoke in an awful voice. "Lydia! Have you been with *Mr. Brummell* all evening?" The ends of his enormous mustache seemed to leap skyward in indignation.

"Father, let's go inside out of the cold and I'll explain—"

Enraged, the Bow Street man stared at me. "I never thought to have the leader of the *Beau Monde* for a son-in-law, but have you I will, Mr. Brummell."

I gripped my dog's head stick, Freddie's dear face flashing through my mind. "Miss Lavender and I did ride in a closed carriage together from Brighton, but—"

"From Brighton!" Mr. Lavender bellowed. He took a step toward me. "You'll be at the church at nine. That should give me enough time to rouse the vicar. By God, I've always wanted grandchildren, and now I'll have them. Ones who spend their days endlessly wrapping linen around their necks until the folds fall just right, rather than tramping the fields getting muddy and learning how to hunt grouse!"

"Hunting, after all, is a beastly sport," I ventured.

Mr. Lavender's hands balled into fists.

Miss Lavender put a hand on her father's arm. "There will be no wedding."

"Oh, yes, there will be, Lydia," Mr. Lavender contradicted. "You are compromised. What man will have you now?"

Miss Lavender spoke in the voice of reason. "Mr. Brummell and I merely rode in the same coach, Father. You are enacting a tragedy where there is none. Nothing happened. Come, I'll make you a cup of hot rum against the weather."

My own voice sounded calm to my ears. "Your daughter is correct, Mr. Lavender. My behaviour tonight was that of a gentleman. But since I am a gentleman, I am prepared to do the honourable thing and marry Miss Lavender if that is what she wishes."

What else, I ask you, could I do? Mr. Lavender was

correct. If word got around that Miss Lavender and I had, for all intents and purposes, spent the night together, no man would marry her. Not even her grocer.

"Aye, you'll be wed as soon as I can arrange it," he agreed.

"Father!"

"Which church do you prefer? I shall see that we have flowers. Miss Lavender deserves that at least."

"What I deserve is—"

"I'll send word to you, Mr. Brummell. Be waiting for it, and mind you don't leave your house until you have it. By the Lord, it won't be the wedding her mother— God rest her soul—always dreamed of for her daughter. But we might get dear Mrs. Lavender's wedding dress out and air it in time."

"Miss Lavender, I hope Mr. Lavell will not suffer from a fatal depression at losing you," I said sympathetically.

Finally able to express her feelings about the plans being made for her, Miss Lavender appeared distracted by my last statement. "Mr. Lavell? The grocer? He's past his sixtieth year! What would he have to say in anything?" she asked incredulously.

For some reason, a sense of relief filled me that she was not romantically involved with the kind grocer after all.

"No one will have anything to say other than me," the Bow Street man, used to being in charge, pronounced.

But Miss Lavender had had enough. "Father, you are wrong! *I* shall be the *only* one deciding my future. There is no reason why I should wed Mr. Brummell, and I tell you I *shall not* wed Mr. Brummell! You cannot force me. What's more, the very idea that a woman should marry for the sake of satisfying some ridiculous rule set forth by who knows who, is outrageous. I'll not bow down before such nonsensical thinking."

"But, Lydia—"

"No, Father," she said firmly. "Good night, Mr. Brummell. Send word to me when you have learned more about Sir Simon. I shall be at my shelter later in the morning."

So saying, the independent Miss Lavender took her father by the arm and bear-led him up the stairs. The sound of the two arguing carried over the night air.

Wearily, I was about to walk around to where the coach waited for me, when the sound of Mr. Lavender's voice reached my ears.

". . . cannot matter about Sir Simon. Bow Street is about to charge Lord Petersham . . ."

The door shut before I could hear the rest of what he said. But, then, I had heard enough. Just as I felt the weight of impending nuptials lift from my shoulders, another sort of apprehension filled me. For now I was the only thing standing between my friend Petersham and his complete disgrace.

Back in Bruton street, I fell into an uneasy sleep. My brain felt as if it continued churning along despite my slumber.

Visions of Petersham being led off to Newgate where no one would help him with his asthma attacks tormented me. Then, the image of Perry standing before a judge being accused of carrying out his threat to kill Sir

Simon sprang into focus. Lady Perry, heavy with child, was there, weeping.

Another dream brought the image of Victor Tallarico and his gleaming knife being led away by Bow Street. In a pink waistcoat, dirty and stained, the Italian paced the confines of his cell at Newgate, reliving past feminine conquests for no one's benefit but his own.

In what would be the final nightmare, I stood in front of the Prince of Wales at Carlton House. Many of my friends were present. The Duke of York sat next to his brother, with his wife, my dear Freddie, at his side. In ringing tones, Prinny told me my presence was no longer desired at Carlton House. Our friendship was at an end. So was my place in Society.

Worst of all, I saw Freddie slip her hand into her husband's. She did not look at me.

Abruptly I sat up in bed, my head pounding and my jaw tense. I glanced at the clock, noting I had been asleep only a few hours.

Nevertheless, I rang for Robinson, instructing him to bring me some tea and breakfast before my bath.

From the top of the fireplace mantel, Chakkri watched my every move. His tail lashed perilously close to one of my Sèvres pieces. The cat's mood reflected my own agitation as he jumped from one spot to another like a monkey in a cage, occasionally emitting a clipped "reow."

Clad in my Florentine dressing-gown, I breakfasted and drank my tea. The twins brought up my bath, and I ordered them to ready the sedan-chair for travel.

My thoughts centered on Sir Simon. More specifically, who had wanted to kill him. I thought I would call on Lady Hester and find out if she knew what the quarrel had been that caused the end of the baronet's relationship with Prime Minister Pitt. Lady Hester had said the friendship had cooled when Pitt found out Sir Simon was still smuggling. But I wondered if there was more to it than that, a clue that might lead me to a motivation for the murder.

Before I left the house, I wanted to write a letter to Freddie. My dream about her had disturbed me.

Once dressed and downstairs, I had Robinson bring me another cup of tea in my bookroom. He handed me the post, which included several personal letters, one from Freddie herself. I scanned the lines rapidly, reading with amusement Freddie's description of an encounter between one of her ostriches and the short-legged Humphrey. The ostrich had been the loser. Also, one of Minney's pups had found her way into the pouch of one of the kangaroos kept at Oatlands. The kangaroo had quite adopted the ball of puppy fur as her own.

Freddie could always bring a smile to my face.

Her letter ended with a plea for news, so I began to write. I told her of my visit to Marie and the resulting trip to Brighton and Sir Simon's house. I debated the wisdom of telling her about my coach ride home with Miss Lavender. Was there a chance she might hear of it? Deciding there was not, I omitted it from my account.

Stretching out my hand for my cup of tea, I was startled when Chakkri suddenly leapt onto the desk and knocked the teacup over.

"Confound it! *Will* you leave the tea things alone? What is wrong with you this morning? Robinson!"

Leaving the valet to clean up the mess, I grabbed my letters and returned to my bedchamber. My temper was short from lack of sleep, and I was in no mood to subject myself to Robinson's Martyr Act nor Chakkri's antics.

Finishing my letter to Freddie, I broke the seal on a missive from Lord Perry.

Brummell,

The Prince held a musical evening last night and I expected to see you there. I wanted to ask you what you know about the investigation. John Lavender came to my house yesterday. He questioned Victor and me about our opinions in regards to *Sir Simon*. What the devil is going on?

Perry

I frowned. No invitation to the Prince's musical evening had reached yours truly. Just as well, I supposed, as I was otherwise occupied and would have had to make my excuses to Prinny.

Did Mr. Lavender's questioning at Perry's house mean that Bow Street was taking my theory of Sir Simon being the intended victim seriously? I wished I might speak with Mr. Lavender on the topic, but did not think he would be willing to sit down and converse with me after last evening's . . . er, controversy.

Breaking the seal on the next letter, I saw it was from Petersham.

Brummell,

Where were you last night? I have no friends any longer since Munro's traitorous behaviour toward me. Yet I do have a stranger shadowing my every move. Unfortunately, he looks like one of Bow

Street's runners. Let me state now for the record that when they take me away, you may have my collection of snuff boxes. Last I checked, none contained any poisoned snuff.

Petersham

I tossed the note aside, more anxious than ever to visit Lady Hester Stanhope.

❧ 25 ❧

"*Why, George, what* brings you calling? Have you developed a fatal passion for me?" Lady Hester said as she swept into the drawing room.

Her jaunty tone belied her unusually care-worn appearance. Rather than insult her by asking what was wrong, I decided to wait for an appropriate opening in the conversation and then inquire.

I rose from where I had been waiting for her on a brocade sofa and bowed. "Developed a passion? Why Lady Hester, I have been a good deal smitten with you these three years past."

She laughed. "Only three years? You awful man. Now tell me why you have sought me out when you are obviously done up. You look exhausted."

Have you ever noticed the disparity in what a lady can say to a gentleman versus what a gentleman can say to a lady?

We sat next to one another on the sofa. "A late night and too little sleep," I told her.

"Oh, anyone I know?"

"Hardly." Miss Lavender did not run in the same circles as Lady Hester. I spared a moment to consider how
well the two would understand one another, both of
them being of independent spirit. Alas, Lady Hester
Stanhope has little patience for the members of her own
sex.

"Shall I ring for tea? Or is this an occasion for wine?"

"Neither, thank you, I shall not take up much of your
time. I would like to ask you a question about Sir
Simon."

She turned her head to one side and shot me a sly
look. "Has this to do with the investigation into the attempt on the life of that worthless individual, the Prince
of Wales?"

I smiled at her opinion of Prinny. "Yes."

"How fascinating! The tainted snuff box is the talk
of the Town. Victor and I were speaking of it at dinner
the other evening."

"Victor Tallarico?"

"Yes. A simply divine man." A faraway look came
into Lady Hester's eyes.

"Good God, not you, too," I groaned.

"Whatever can you mean?" she asked in all innocence.

"Only that every female that comes within sight of
the Italian falls at his feet."

An impish expression appeared on Lady Hester's
face. "At his *feet*, you say?"

"My lady, you shock me," I replied with prodigious
gravity.

She laughed. "I doubt that, George. But I hope Victor
has not earned your disapproval. Not that I could say

he'd care. He's grown quite popular since his arrival in England. Even my uncle approves of him."

"Signor Tallarico gets along well with Mr. Pitt?"

"To be sure. You left my dinner party the other night too early to know this, but Uncle finally did come downstairs for a while. He and Victor struck up a conversation. The two talked at length about Napoleon's rule over Italy and how England might dislodge the Corsican monster."

"Hmmm," I said, as visions of Tallarico playing the spy flashed through my mind.

I sat in thought for a few minutes, prompting Lady Hester to finally say, "What was the question you wanted to ask me, George?"

"Oh, yes. I remember you telling me that Prime Minister Pitt cut his connection with Sir Simon when he found out about the baronet's smuggling enterprise. But I wondered if it were as simple as that. I do not wish to imply that Mr. Pitt would condone smuggling, but I thought perhaps something else caused the rift between the two men. Something in particular that triggered the rupture in their relationship."

"Indeed, there was, George. You see, Sir Simon had been pestering Uncle about reinstating the tax on tea. Ever since the tea tax had been slashed oh, back in '84, I believe, Sir Simon had lost a great deal of income. Tea was no longer a commodity ripe for smuggling."

My right eyebrow rose. "Petersham mentioned to me recently that there is a possibility that the tax might be implemented again now. I admit to being surprised since Mr. Pitt was the one who cut it, was he not?"

"He was. And it will not be reinstated while Uncle has anything to say about it."

Then she suddenly looked pained by her own words.

I leaned closer. "What is it, my friend? I can tell you are distressed."

She let out a tired sigh. "I know I can trust you not to speak of this matter."

"You have my word as a gentleman."

"I'm worried about Uncle. His health is failing, and I blame his condition on his working so hard and his worries over the war. He has a continental network of spies that have been keeping him informed as to Napoleon's manoeuvering. A report arrived this week."

"Not good news?"

"Apparently not. He hasn't told me the details, but he received an urgent dispatch last night and has been ill all of today. My concern for him is growing."

I reached over and placed my hand over hers. "The Prime Minister is fortunate in having you for a niece. You will care well for him."

"I do whatever I can." She straightened and said, "Now, tell me your suspicions, George. What has the smuggling of tea to do with the attempt on the Prince's life?"

"I think the poisoned snuff was meant for Sir Simon all along. In looking for the murderer's motive, I view the baronet's smuggling activities as a possible source."

Lady Hester's eyes widened, then she smiled. "What a delicious idea! You know I could not abide the baronet. In fact, I'd wager he had plenty of enemies. How will you find out which one was responsible?"

"I have reason to believe he was a blackmailer. If I find whom he was blackmailing, I've found the murderer."

"George, what a discovery! Blackmail is a marvelous reason for killing someone."

"Yes, well, I thought that if I found out what Sir Simon did that turned Mr. Pitt against him, it might help narrow the field. But I see that it was simply a matter of personal ethics; the baronet's greediness being repugnant to the honourable Prime Minister." I thought for a moment, then said, "Lady Hester, Mr. Pitt is still strongly opposed to reinstating the heavy tax on tea, is he not? There is no chance it will happen?"

"No, I don't think so. Uncle has been quite put out by the rumours circulating around Parliament that the tax might be raised. Even Lord St. Clair had taken up the torch, but Uncle persuaded him that the idea won't wash."

"Good. Petersham would not be pleased. He mixes teas as well as snuff, you know."

"You'd better not tell Bow Street about that, George. God knows, Charles doesn't need further ammunition against him."

"Exactly."

A short time later, I took my leave of Lady Hester, feeling quite sorry that Mr. Pitt was ill and that his niece was spending her days nursing him.

I commanded Ned and Ted to stop at a flower stall. I ordered a bouquet of flowers sent to the lady with my thanks for her company. After signing the card in my best handwriting, I exited the shop.

I spent the next half hour in Bond Street, procuring five pairs of dancing slippers for Freddie. I hoped I would be able to deliver them personally to her this weekend.

As I walked back to my sedan-chair, my gaze was

caught by a stunning length of Brussels lace displayed in the window of a dressmaker's shop. Immediately, a vision of Freddie attired in a gown made up of the material burst into my brain. I could present the dress to her for Christmas.

Frequently I spend Christmas at Oatlands. The Duchess has set the custom of exchanging little gifts, ones of moderate value. Although a gown made out of costly Brussels lace would hardly fit into the category of "moderate" value, why should Freddie not have the very best?

I retraced my steps and spent over an hour giving the delighted merchant my instructions.

All in all, what remained of the day was spent with various members of the merchant class as I purchased goods.

It was when the last of the merchants expressed his gratitude for my custom that an idea regarding Sir Simon's death presented itself in my brain and would not be dislodged. The notion was incredible, unbelievable almost. Yet, it refused to leave my mind.

Feeling the need to lay before the Prince all I had learned, and wishing to mend any broken fences there might be since Jack Townsend's ugly insinuations, I instructed Ned and Ted to take me to Carlton House.

Dusk fell as the twins carried me through the streets of Mayfair. Down St. James's Street, past White's and Brooks's and Boodle's, past King Street where Almack's Assembly Rooms were the scene of fashionable gatherings during the Season, to Pall Mall we went. By the time we dodged the carriage traffic on that last busy road, twilight had surrendered to darkness.

Arriving at the royal residence, I alighted from my sedan-chair. A line of guardsmen in full military regalia stood at assigned posts protecting the imposing structure from any possible invasion. Torches burned, illuminating the area around the entrance.

I extracted one of my calling cards from a thin silver case and handed it to a footman.

Cooling my heels on the pavement, I saw, much to my chagrin, that Sylvester Fairingdale stood nearby, waiting for an audience with the Prince, as well. I gave him a chilly nod. He looked down his nose at me.

Tonight he wore yellow breeches and a red-and-white spotted waistcoat, topped by a white coat with large brass buttons. The garments were laughable. Perhaps he was here at Carlton House as the court jester.

However, laughing was the furthest thing from my mind when, a few minutes later, the footman returned to me, his expression wooden. He stretched out his hand and gave me my card. "His Royal Highness does not know a George Brummell."

I felt the blood drain from my face.

I trust I kept my expression perfectly bland.

Even when Sylvester Fairingdale was waved inside, crowing loudly with mirth.

26

I was ruined.

Fairingdale would go straight to White's after meeting with the Prince. He would recount the tale of my humiliation at the gentlemen's club. From there, I estimated it would take no more than half a day for word to spread throughout fashionable London that the Prince of Wales had refused to receive Beau Brummell.

No tailor, no less a duke, would open his door to me. In fact, tailors and other assorted tradespeople would be banging on *my* door, rescinding credit and demanding I pay my debts immediately. With the sum of cash I currently had, I could sooner envision sheep speaking—in French—than I could foresee meeting my obligations. In my mind's eye, I saw my father's frown of disapproval.

With great dignity, I returned to my sedan-chair where Ned and Ted stood open-mouthed. "Let us go home. I am weary. And there is no need to speak to Robinson of what just happened."

"Yes, sir, Mr. Brummell," Ted agreed.

"Reckon the Prince ain't here, Ted?" Ned asked, confused. "Are all these men standin' around waitin' for him?"

I entered my sedan-chair without hearing Ted's reply.

It is hard for me to tell you exactly how I felt at that moment. Riding home, my emotions ran the gamut of anger at the fickle Prince, who is known to cast aside friends as quickly as out-of-fashion coats, to determination that I must clear my name.

Rapidly.

Though not tonight.

Tonight I wanted to make plans, then seek my bed. I had spoken nothing less than the truth when I had told the twins I was fatigued. Unlike strapping young Corinthians who can ride hell for leather, box at Gentleman Jackson's, fence with Angelo, carouse all night with opera dancers, and submit to a mere four hours' sleep daily, I am a creature who requires rest. Intellectual endeavours can be equally as strenuous as physical, you know.

Thus, arriving home I told a dubious Robinson I was not hungry. "I shall retire for the evening. See that I am not disturbed."

"Very well, sir," the valet replied, eyeing me curiously. "Do you not wish me to help you undress?"

I waved a hand. "No, I am going to select a book and then hibernate in my bedchamber."

I walked into the bookroom, never once looking back. Closing the door, I strode to my desk and pulled out the items I had found in Sir Simon's study. Scanning the list of dates on the paper, I was satisfied to see I had remembered correctly. Tomorrow's date was listed.

Stuffing the paper and the seal back into a drawer, I pocketed the tawny jackal's head mask and exited the room.

Upstairs in my bedchamber, the fire had been built up. Chakkri stood next to its warmth.

"Good evening, old boy. We are in the suds now," I told him.

He watched solemnly as I undressed and donned fresh nightclothes.

"Never fear for your lobster patties, though: I have a plan." I threw back the bedcovers and climbed atop the firm mattress. The cat hopped onto the bed. Soon, I lay on my back, a position Chakkri took as an invitation to lie on top of my chest and stare at me.

I stroked his soft fur. "In the morning, I shall behave as if nothing has happened. Robinson might fuss over my rising early, but it will be nothing compared to his reaction if he finds out I have fallen from grace."

Chakkri placed a sympathetic paw on my chin.

"Please. There is no need to grow maudlin. My reverses are only temporary. For I shall hire a coach and travel once more to Sir Simon's house. I shall wear that mask and attend the meeting of the baronet's secret club. Then I shall find out what the devil they are doing."

"Reow!"

"And just who is directing Anubis now that Sir Simon is dead."

I rolled onto my stomach, dislodging the cat. What would the feline's fate be without me to care for him? Would anyone else put up with him lying down in the centre of the bed and falling asleep as he did now?

And what of Petersham? Would he be capable of defending himself against Bow Street?

What about Lady Perry? What would happen to her if her husband or his cousin were accused?

My eyes closed, but in the darkness I could envision the expression on Freddie's sweet face should she learn of my downfall. That would be my nightmare come to life. How could I bear it if I were no longer welcome at Oatlands?

Oatlands? Dash it, I would be lucky to stay out of debtors' prison once word got around that I was no longer in royal favour. No, unless I could uncover Sir Simon's murderer at the Anubis meeting tomorrow night, the only course left open to me would be to flee the country, never to see those I cared for again.

"I have business in Brighton and will not be returning home today."

"Yes, sir. Shall I have one of the twins hire a coach?"

"A comfortable coach with an amiable driver, Robinson. I have no wish to be at the mercy of an ill-sprung vehicle and an inebriated coachman."

The valet helped me into a Turkish-blue coat. "Er, does your journey relate to the unpleasantness at Brighton?"

"Yes," I said, picking up the walking stick Freddie had given me. I might need its deadly blade. Guns have no place in my household, as I cannot abide shooting birds and have yet to be challenged to a duel.

"Sir, once you were asleep last night, I went around to The Butler's Tankard."

"Oh," I said, feeling myself tense. Had Robinson heard what happened at Carlton House?

"I did not stay long, in case you needed me for any-

thing. While I was there, Rumbelow, who serves as un-
derbutler at Vayne House and cannot keep his tongue in
his head—"

"I know who he is," I said in some amusement. It
was hard to say whose tongue ran faster: Robinson's or
Rumbelow's.

"Rumbelow says Lord Petersham's father, Lord Harrington, is about to instigate a slander case against Bow
Street for maligning the viscount's name."

"I cannot say as how I blame him. Robinson, have a
care will you? One of my York tan gloves has a spot on
it." I handed him the glove, much to his consternation.

A second later he said, "I do not see anything."

I raised an eyebrow.

Robinson went down to the kitchen to clean the
glove, which I admit was not dirty. I merely wanted a
ruse to take him from the room. Once he was gone, I
took the jackal's head mask from my bedside table
drawer. Ruing the way it marred the lines of my coat, I
nevertheless folded it into my pocket. Then I slipped
downstairs into my bookroom. There, I opened a locked
drawer of my desk and extracted a substantial amount
of money.

I was waiting in the hall when Robinson came back
with my glove. "Here you are, sir."

"Excellent. Now wipe that glum look from your face,
man. All is in order. I shall return very late tonight, if
not tomorrow morning, so do not wait up for me."

"Are you sure you do not wish me to pack a bag and
accompany you? It is a long journey to make and return
in one day."

"True, but it can be done. Where is Chakkri?"

"In the kitchen watching André debone a chicken."

"Good," I said, fighting a feeling that I would not be coming back. "I bid you good day, Robinson. Thank you for . . . for cleaning the glove."

The valet gave me a puzzled look. Swiftly, I put on my hat and walked down the front steps to the waiting coach.

After giving the driver detailed instructions, I was on my way. I noted the time was just eleven o'clock. I drew the blinds over the coach windows, wishing to be private.

As we reached the edge of London, the coachman halted the vehicle and performed the errand I had commissioned. From that time on, we only stopped to change horses. Once London was far behind us, I raised the blinds and watched as we rolled by the autumn English countryside.

All the while, the idea that had first come to me outside the merchant's yesterday grew in my mind. My blood boiled with indignation. If I was correct, and the murderer was who I thought he was, the revelation would turn the aristocracy on its ear.

When at last we reached Brighton, I paid the coachman and once again hired a horse to take me to Sir Simon's house by the sea. I wound my way to the same copse of trees where Miss Lavender and I had conversed the other night.

Miss Lavender! Devil take it, I had forgotten to send word to her. Dismounting, I shrugged and sat on a fallen log, trying not to think of the effect such an action must have on my previously pristine breeches. Instead I kept watch over the house.

After a while, when darkness had fallen, I unwrapped a chunk of Stilton cheese and a piece of bread I had purchased in Town. There had been no sign of life at Sir Simon's, so I had nothing to do but wait.

Around ten o'clock my efforts were rewarded. One by one, coaches began to arrive and deposit mask-clad gentlemen. A footman came running from the front door to greet each one and take them inside.

I counted fourteen arrivals before all became quiet again. Reaching into my pocket, I pulled out two items, one of which was the purchase I had had the coachman make for me. The contents of the packet would make Robinson faint. For it was a pair of *lace* cuffs. Most unfashionable. Gentlemen like myself, concerned with a neat, masculine appearance, wear pleated cuffs. But the lace cuffs would serve as my only disguise other than the second item, the jackal's head mask. I fixed the lace around my wrists.

Then, I pulled the mask from my pocket, placed it over my face, and made my way to the front door.

The crushed shells under my feet made my approach audible to the footman on duty. He came outside. "Good evening, sir."

A nod of my head seemed all that was required of me to gain entrance to the house. I breathed a sigh of relief.

The footman conducted me toward the western part of the house, down a torch-lit stone stairway, to where another footman stood guard. "Your ring," he barked.

I held up my right hand, then looked surprised. "I had it on a moment ago," I said from behind the mask. "The damned thing must have fallen off my finger."

He eyed me skeptically for a moment, then apparently decided my language and dress suited him. He opened the door.

Another stone staircase leading downward met my gaze. I descended the stairs just as if I had done so many times before, for the benefit of the big man standing guard outside yet another door.

As I drew closer and heard the sounds of male and female laughter coming from inside, I could also ascertain the identity of the footman I approached. He was none other than Sir Simon's other pugilistic footman, Devlin the Devil. The one who, along with the late Jemmy Wheeler, had attacked me.

He glared from beady eyes set in a full face. "Password."

"What?" I said.

"Give me the password."

Blast! I feigned drunkenness. "Pashword. Uh, lemme see."

"Hey, Devlin, that fellow there wasn't wearing his ring," the first footman called down to us.

"No ring. No password." Devlin the Devil glared at me, then pulled out a gun with one hand and grabbed me by the arm with the other. He pushed open the door and marched me through it.

❦ 27 ❦

The scene before my eyes was one of shameless decadence.

Long tables were set out, laden with meats, fruits, and numerous bottles of wine. But another sort of feast was also being offered.

The females of the company were dressed—if one could call it that—in the sheerest of muslins. This material concealed little. I confess my gaze lingered on the ladies longer than what could be considered strictly necessary. One woman's gown had fallen from her shoulder. She did not seem to mind being discovered in such an immodest state, or in the position she was in with her partner, a man stripped to the waist.

As to the acts being engaged in by some of the other couples, well, a gentleman does not speak of such things. You will have to use your imagination. Lord Yarmouth had not exaggerated when he told me the club's activities were beyond the pale.

All of the men, who I assumed from their dress were

those on the fringes of Society, wore jackal's head masks, even the man playing the fiddle in one corner.

When everyone perceived my arrival, the fiddler stopped playing and there was general whispering. A tall man, evidently the leader, extracted himself from his place between two females and approached.

Devlin said, "This one says 'e can't remember the password."

"Knew it yeshterday," I bluffed.

"Doesn't have 'is ring either."

Abruptly, the tall man reached out and ripped the mask from my face.

Amidst gasps, a cultured voice said, " 'Tis the Beau!" Men scrambled back into their shirts and gathered their possessions. None of them wanted to stay to be identified under these circumstances.

"Hold the gun on him, Devlin. We shall take him upstairs to the study," the tall man said.

I recognised his voice immediately.

"Do not be concerned, gentlemen," he told the room at large. "There is no doubt in my mind that Mr. Brummell can be persuaded to remain silent about what he has seen here. Or perhaps we shall decide to admit him to our selective few."

I felt a small measure of satisfaction. He was exactly the one I suspected. The one I now remembered seeing with the jackal's head ring on his finger. The feeling of triumph was followed by one of sadness, then apprehension, as I was let back up the cold stone stairs.

We entered the study where Miss Lavender and I had found Jemmy Wheeler's body. The killer walked around the desk and seated himself, still masked, while Devlin held the gun against the back of my head, rendering me immobile just inside the door.

My only choice was to use my cool composure and humour him as long as Devlin held the gun, lest I be shot dead. I must not let on that I knew his identity.

"Well, sir," I began, "you have caught me out. I am not drunk. I admit to an overabundance of curiosity about your club."

"An admirable try, Mr. Brummell, but you and I both know better," the tall man said.

"I do not understand," I said pleasantly.

"Yes, you do. In point of fact, that is the problem. You understand far too well. Tell me, why would a man like yourself, whose company is sought after, whose taste is deemed the standard for elegance, and whose loyalty to his friends is well known, trouble himself with investigating a murder?"

"Murder? I was only seeking pleasure. Er, could you ask this man to take that gun away from my head? The sensation is most disagreeable."

"Do not play the fool, Mr. Brummell. I am very much aware of your inquiries."

I glanced around the room as if thinking of a reply. In truth, I was trying to find something I could use as a weapon. With a length of steel pressed into my carefully groomed hair, my only chance was to slump to the floor and make for cover. Surely Devlin was not an expert at shooting a moving target. Was he?

"You are correct," I said, spotting a strong leather whip tossed into a chair by the desk. I hesitated to think of its use. "I have been trying to determine who would poison the Prince. I fail to see what that has got to do with your club, sir."

"You are intelligent enough to have realised the tainted snuff was not meant for the Prince, Mr. Brummell. Somehow you have found out about Sir Simon's—now my—secret club."

"I heard rumours. Have you taken over, then, since his untimely death? Is this all some sort of rite of initiation? If so, I fear I must tell you I do not find it amusing—"

"Enough of this game! You may have found out about Sir Simon's club, but that is as far as you will get," the tall man declared, rising to his feet. "Devlin, take Mr. Brummell down to the caves where the sound of a gunshot will not be heard."

The pugilist's grip tightened painfully on my arm. There was no choice but to try to remain in the study. Here, I might have a chance. In a cave during a one-to-one fight with Devlin, I feared I would be the loser. The strength of his punches was already known to me.

I decided to gamble on the study. Keeping my tone amiable, I said, "Since you are going to kill me anyway, why not take a minute to clear up a few things first, *Lord St. Clair.*"

His lordship grew still.

My gaze locked on the eyes behind his mask.

Slowly, he turned around and moved back to the chair. He removed his mask and seated himself. His manner was nonchalant. "How did you know?"

"Through careful deduction and a bit of luck."

"Should Oi kill 'im now, milord?" Devlin asked.

Lord St. Clair held up a hand. "In a moment. Tell me how you found out I was involved. Have you told anyone else?"

I was not reckless enough to answer the second question. "I shall tell you what you what to know if you have your henchman remove that pistol from the back of my head."

At a nod from Lord St. Clair, Devlin lowered the gun from my head, but only to the small of my back.

"At the Pavilion, my initial reasoning was that Mr. Ainsley might have reason to wish the Prince harm."

"Why is that?" Lord St. Clair asked.

"It seems Mr. Ainsley and Prinny had a disagreement over a peerage that would lead to a seat in Parliament. But this never seemed a strong enough motive for the young man to have resorted to poisoning the heir to the throne. However, it was indeed a Parliamentary matter which brought about the murder of Sir Simon."

"You intrigue me," Lord St. Clair said in a flat voice.

"Sir Simon, greedy fellow that he was, wanted the high tax reinstated on tea. That way, his already profitable smuggling enterprise would become even more lucrative. But how could he persuade Prime Minister Pitt to reinstate the tax? He had no credibility with Mr. Pitt. They had quarrelled over the matter in the past. Then Sir Simon was presented with an irresistible opportunity to get his way. Through you. Everyone knows Mr. Pitt respects your opinion, my lord."

Lord St. Clair had perfect control over himself. I admired his aplomb, if nothing else. "Yes, he does. And I told that bastard baronet that I would not persuade Pitt to reinstate the tax."

"So Sir Simon resorted to blackmail, and you, having an understandable aversion to blackmail, decided to kill him."

"Naturally. A blackmailer is never satisfied. I did initially go to Pitt and speak with him about the tax. There was talk of it in Parliament. But I would not jeopardise my position with the Prime Minister by pressing the matter. That is when I decided Sir Simon had to be eliminated once and for all."

"How did you come upon the idea of the poisoned snuff?" I asked in the manner of one discussing an idea no more lethal than where to hold a picnic that afternoon.

Lord St. Clair had that smug look of someone who thinks himself clever. "I had been lingering in Brighton, waiting for an opportunity. You see, it had to be the consummate murder. I cannot have my family name tarnished."

"You sent the letters to the Prince."

"Ingenious, was it not?" Lord St. Clair said, warming even more to his topic. He was bragging a bit now. "What better way is there than to kill someone, then make it look like another was meant to die? I hoped the Prince would come running to his Pavilion to hide like the cowardly baby he is, and I got my wish. Then, Sir Simon fell right into my hands by toadying to the Prince. My first thought was to conceal myself and shoot Sir Simon while he was at the Pavilion. Everyone would think the shot was meant for the Prince."

"But the house was heavily patrolled."

"The grounds were not," he pointed out. "And the Prince is so prone to hysterics, he would immediately assume the shot was meant for him."

I could not argue with this. "Then you were at the Pavilion that night after we all returned from the Johnstones' dinner. You heard Petersham talk about how he was mixing a new blend of snuff. You heard him promise to let the Prince be the first to try it."

Lord St. Clair spread his hands. "A chance like that does not come along every day."

"What if the Prince had inhaled the poisoned snuff?"

"Do not be ridiculous. Sir Simon was playing his role of food taster for all it was worth."

"Even so—"

"I expect I would have intervened had not Sir Simon taken the box from your hands. In a manner that would reflect well on me, of course. As it turned out, there was no need. All I had to do was slip the poison into the box while everyone was moving about after dinner. A sound plan, if I say so myself."

A plan that chilled me even now. "What about the blackmail, Lord St. Clair. How did the girl die?"

For the first time, his lordship appeared to grow angry. "You found out about that, too? Really, Mr. Brummell, the world will be better off without you."

"I know of those who would agree. Still, if you would be so indulgent as to tell me what happened with the young lady . . ."

Lord St. Clair made an impatient sound. "That silly girl. Josette was her name. If she had not put up a struggle, she would still be alive."

"French, was she not?" I encouraged, though reeling in horror inside.

"Damn all those cursed Frenchies. Yes, she was an orphan raised in a convent. During the course of pirating a ship in the Channel, one of Sir Simon's men came across a vessel sailing to Calais. Josette's governess had decided the roads between Rouen and Calais were too dangerous for the young heiress to travel and had chosen the sea instead. Ironic, eh?"

"Indeed," I uttered through gritted teeth.

"Josette had been on her way to marry a widower her trustees had selected for her. Through our club, Anubis, Sir Simon was aware that I have a taste for untouched young women. He had Josette brought here and saved for me."

"Lady St. Clair—"

"Smells of the shop," Lord St. Clair sneered, referring to his wife's background in the merchant class. He shook his head with regret. "If only Josette had not struggled. The stupid chit protested so much, I had her drugged. Even that did not quell the fight in her. She fell and struck her head. What a waste."

"And you had her body thrown into the sea."

He chuckled mirthlessly. "Imagine my surprise when she came back to shore. Seemed she wanted what I had to offer, after all."

My chest burned with unleashed anger at Lord St. Clair's callous view of the young girl.

Lord St. Clair, done with relating how astute he had been, looked at me. "You will admit, Mr. Brummell, that I have delayed the time of your death long enough."

I thought quickly. I needed to catch the pugilist off guard. "Why not kill me right here in the study like you did Jemmy Wheeler?"

The strategy worked. I felt the pressure of the gun pressed to my back ease a bit. "You was the one who shot Jem? He was my friend," Devlin said in a hurt voice.

Confusion reigned in the next seconds. With all my might I drove my right elbow backward into Devlin's stomach. He grunted, then sank to the floor. I swung around and watched him, puzzled that my thrust had been that powerful.

Then my startled gaze rose to where Miss Lavender stood on the other side of him, the butt end of a pistol in her hand. I could hardly believe my eyes. "You saw today's date on the list, despite my precautions, you mad girl. Give me that gun."

But Miss Lavender had apparently been listening to Lord St. Clair's cold-hearted recital of the events leading to Josette's death. Her green eyes gleamed with fury as she stepped over the unconscious body of Devlin and came forward into the room. Her gaze never wavered from Lord St. Clair.

"Miss Lavender, give me that gun," I commanded, fearing that the intrepid female's dedication and passion for the rights of women would overcome her good sense.

Lord St. Clair rose from behind the desk and grabbed the whip from the chair. He advanced menacingly toward Miss Lavender. "Cursed females! I am surrounded by them at my home, now this!"

He raised the whip into the air, about to strike Miss Lavender.

I lunged for the gun.

Too late.

Gripped by a white-hot rage over what she had heard, Miss Lavender took aim and fired her pistol at Lord St. Clair.

He howled, clutching the inner portion of his thigh.

Rapid footsteps echoing from the hall heralded the arrival of John Lavender. "Lydia! I followed you from London to see what you and Mr. Brummell were doing. What the devil happened here? Is that Lord St. Clair on the floor?"

Miss Lavender stood breathing as if she had run a mile.

Quickly I took the gun from her shaking hand and stood at her side. "Your daughter shot Lord St. Clair while defending herself, Mr. Lavender. St. Clair is the one who put the poison in the snuff. The poison was meant for Sir Simon as I, ahem, had thought. The baronet was blackmailing his lordship."

Lord St. Clair writhed on the floor in pain, blood running down his buff-coloured breeches.

Mr. Lavender, a man apparently immune to shock after years of Bow Street work, eyed Lord St. Clair. "Is that so? Well, I'll have a doctor summoned before I arrest his lordship. Lydia, since you're safe, I'll speak with you later. And you, Mr. Brummell." He shot me a disapproving look and then went back out into the hall, shouting for a footman.

I put my arm around Miss Lavender's trembling shoulders. "I am so angry you came here, I could shake you if you were not shaking already. It is a very good thing you missed anything vital when you shot Lord St. Clair."

From the circle of my arm, Miss Lavender looked up at me. "Perhaps I do need spectacles after all. My aim was off by a good three inches."

Outrageous girl!

❧ 28 ❧

"*His Royal Highness*, the Prince of Wales, and Mr. George Brummell," the butler at Lord and Lady Perry's Town house intoned.

The company present in the drawing room bowed low.

For the Prince, of course.

Lady Perry had insisted upon giving a small party before she and her lord retired to the country for the winter. I greeted her and Perry now. "Lady Perry, how kind you are to be giving a dinner. May I hope you are feeling more the thing these days?"

She nodded. "Thank you, yes. Although I shall be happy to settle into Perry Grove until spring."

Her husband stood at her elbow. "I insisted that Cook be aided by Gunter's excellent catering so that Bernadette need not fret over the menu tonight. If I had my way, we would already be enjoying the country air."

His wife rolled her eyes heavenward at Perry's anxiety.

Victor Tallarico approached, and we exchanged greetings. "You have already been to the country at Oatlands, I hear, Mr. Brummell."

"Yes, I have. Autumn in the country is a balm to one's senses," I said, wondering how he knew of my visit to Freddie's estate.

The Italian gave a pained smile. "Sad to say, the Duchess hasn't invited me to Oatlands yet. But I plan to correspond with her regularly and have hopes for an invitation before long. Her Royal Highness is a *bello* creature, too often alone."

I fixed the Lothario with a seemingly benign look. Certainly he showed no sign of awareness that I wished to throttle him. Which I did. "You are all kindness, I am sure, but the Royal Duchess does not lack for anything. Pray do not trouble yourself with her happiness in the future."

Tallarico could not have misinterpreted my message, but he could choose to ignore it. "A lady can never be too happy, Mr. Brummell. And as to the happiness of ladies, I am particularly sad for Lady St. Clair and her daughters."

"Their circumstances cannot be comfortable," Lady Perry said.

"On the contrary, my love," Perry said, "Recall that Lady St. Clair's family is quite wealthy. They shall rise above the scandal, wait and see."

Yes, I thought, money could open many closed doors. Lady St. Clair and her daughters would retire from Society for a while. Eventually the scandal of her husband's deeds would die down. Mr. Ainsley would marry Lady Prudence in a quiet wedding. No doubt the young man would use his bride's money to pursue his ambitions. He might very well be elected to a seat in the House of Commons.

Speaking of scandal, this very evening party was designed to put a halt to any gossip Sylvester Fairingdale had initiated regarding a break between the Prince and me. Throughout the drinks and mingling that preceded dinner, everyone present could clearly see that his Royal Highness and I were on the best of terms. If they could not, then they were shortly enlightened.

After chatting with the assembled guests, the Prince turned and spoke to me for all to hear. "Brummell, I want to show my appreciation for your loyalty." He pulled a heavily jewelled snuff box from his pocket.

There was a general murmur of appreciation at the sight of such a costly item. Rubies encrusted the lid, broken only by a pattern of diamonds in the Prince of Wales's feathers. The box sparkled in the candlelight.

The Prince extended his hand, offering it to me. I hesitated, then took it. The expression on his Royal Highness's face was anything but one of generosity. Instead, he looked miserable at having to part with what had—perhaps suddenly—become his favourite snuff box.

Petersham stepped over to examine the box. "Impressive, truly impressive. Rundell and Bridge, your Royal Highness?"

"Yes. Made for me over the summer." Prinny's face was positively glum.

Lord Munro came over and raised his quizzing glass to inspect the box. "Very fine craftsmanship, but then that is to be expected from Rundell and Bridge."

Petersham deliberately ignored him, and Lord Munro

quickly walked away. Their relationship had not been restored.

The Perrys' butler returned and announced that dinner was served.

"A moment, your Royal Highness. As much as I am honoured by the generous spirit of your gift, I would be pleased if you retained the box for yourself. My allegiance to you needs no reward."

The Prince gladly accepted the trinket back from my hand. "Good of you, Brummell. I'll have another made for you. Er, not right away, though. I'm spending the winter at my Pavilion."

I bowed, thinking I would sooner see females admitted as members of White's than be gifted with another snuff box by Prinny.

"Best be careful, your Royal Highness. You remember what happened the last time Mr. Brummell passed a snuff box to you," Tallarico jested.

Everyone waited nervously for the Prince's reaction to this artless remark. But then Prinny laughed, and the company followed suit.

Lord Perry shot me a look that plainly said, *I told you my cousin was trouble.*

As we moved toward the dining room, I pondered whether between us Perry and I could contrive a way to ship the Italian back to his homeland.

The atmosphere over dinner was jovial, though. The Perrys' table abounded with delicious food. Conversation was lively.

Later, I went home in a pleasant state of mind, other than having the niggling feeling that I wished Tallarico would leave Freddie alone. She had not spoken of him during our too-short weekend together, which I took as a sign that the Italian had not yet orchestrated his way into her life. And the devil would not succeed in doing so if I had anything to say in the matter!

Dear, sweet Freddie. Her generosity and kind nature extended to Marie. The Royal Duchess had arranged passage for the troubled Frenchwoman to return to her homeland. Perhaps there Marie would eventually recover from the tragic events that had befallen her.

Climbing the steps to my bedchamber, I thought back over Freddie and our long walks together, the card games we played, and the afternoons when we enjoyed watching the puppies' antics.

Freddie had indicated a desire to learn the finer points of archery. Manfully, I had volunteered to teach her in the spring, banishing mental images of holding her so I might show her just the way to pull back the bow. She already knew how to bend the *Beau* to her will.

In my chamber, Robinson helped me undress for bed, still miffed over having to remove both Oatlands dog and Siamese cat hairs from my clothing.

After leaving me alone with a tea tray, the valet strode from the room, head held high.

"Well, Chakkri, my latest adventure is over. I daresay I am looking forward to spring and the Season. Everyone is always on their best behaviour then, eh?"

The cat stood at his favourite place by the fire. He licked a spot over his left shoulder.

I pulled my portable writing desk out, sat in the high-backed chair near the table with the tea things, and balanced the desk on my knees. The cat heard the rustling of paper and jumped to the arm of the chair to watch. I stroked his fawn-coloured body, then turned to the task at hand.

"Here, I am going to make a sketch of some spectacles for Miss Lavender. Although her father will be furious at the thought of my giving his daughter a gift."

"Reow!" the cat said.

"I daresay Miss Lavender might not feel obliged to tell him." My pencil flew over the paper, drawing a feminine and fashionable pair of spectacles.

"Mr. Lavender and the local magistrate closed down Sir Simon's house, you know. Most likely the property will revert to the Crown since the baronet died without heirs. The revenue men will be glad that one segment of the smuggling trade will cease." I reached for my teacup and took a sip of the hot brew.

Chakkri shifted his weight on the arm of the chair.

Studying the drawing in front of me, I decided it would not do. The design was too ornate for Miss Lavender. She would want something feminine, yet simple. I crumpled the paper and tossed it into the fire.

Chakkri flew after the balled paper, skirting the tea things. He stood and glared mournfully as his would-be toy was consumed by the flames.

"You want to play? I shall indulge you. I am so pleased you managed to get past my fine Sèvres teacups without mishap. I do not know what had made you so clumsy around the tea things lately."

I made the offer gladly, but the capricious ways of felines are a mystery to me.

Chakkri ignored my invitation to a game. Instead, he cast a look of catly disdain over his shoulder at me before he turned and walked from the room, favouring me with only a view of his tail end.